For Carlo, Always.

And for my amazing critique partners,

Tiffany, Elyssa and Maggie,

with my eternal gratitude.

Prologue

Maxine knelt on the torn linoleum of the dingy bathroom floor, one hand gently holding back her mother's long, unwashed hair so that it wouldn't fall in her face as she hung her head over the 70s-style powder blue toilet. The other hand clutched a faded yellow towel Max knew would be needed to wipe her mother's mouth with when she was through heaving up Max's attempt at that night's dinner—spaghetti. Yum. Not something she was going to be making again any time soon.

Max bit back a sigh of disgust as she listened to her mother's low groans. This yak-fest was fast becoming a Friday night family tradition in the Deveraux household—and a Tuesday and Thursday night tradition. Oh, and the occasional Monday night. And a standing Saturday mother-daughter date.

It had gotten so that Charlene no longer bothered to wait until after her fifteen-year-old daughter had gone off to bed before she started in with the drinking. More often than not, Max came home from school and found her already passed out, sprawled in the tattered Lay-Z Boy—that didn't laze anymore—in front of the television set that most times wasn't even turned on. Usually with a bottle of whiskey at the floor by her feet, handy for when she came to and wanted another swig.

It was the time in Max's life when she should have

been joining the cheerleading squad and talking to boys and getting ice cream at the mall with her friends. But instead, she was rushing home after school to make sure her mother hadn't drowned herself in the tub or burned the house down with a smoke left dangling carelessly between her fingers while snoring off last night's hangover.

Whoever that guy was who said the teen years were the best of your life was seriously going to get Max's foot in the ass if he ever dared darken her door, spouting that crap.

Max tenderly finger-combed her mother's hair and whispered soft words of comfort. God, were the parent/child roles reversed or what? How sad was it that the only time her mother could tolerate her own daughter's presence was when she was throwing up her dinner into the toilet?

But that wouldn't stop Max from cleaning her up and tucking her into bed after the dry heave stage had finally passed. Max would make sure she slept it off in a clean nightgown and that she had a glass of water and a bucket by the side of her bed. She would close the door very gently and refrain from making any noise that might disturb her mother's alcohol-induced stupor.

Sometimes Max thought of leaving.

Oh, not for good—although even that thought had crossed her mind a time or two.

No, when her mother was like this, Max just wanted to go somewhere to have fun for a change.

Fun? Geez, what was that?

It would be nice—except the sad truth was Max had no friends, no one to have fun with. Even if she had wanted to try out for the cheerleading squad, the other girls would laugh her right out the gymnasium door. Trailer trash like Maxine Deveraux would never be cheerleading material.

And forget going to the movies with a boy, or making

out with a boy, or even talking to a boy. Oh, she got plenty of looks from the dirty, slimy losers her mother brought home every once in a while if she was still half lucid by the end of the night. But the boys her age didn't look twice at someone like her. Max was tall and skinny and her clothes were so ratty, even the Salvation Army would have left them on the curb.

Max was nothing like the polished and pampered popular girls who came to school with their artfully applied make-up and professionally highlighted hair. Nor was she like the smart girls, the ones who dressed more conservatively, their bright clean faces glowing with the wholesome upbringing and lofty ideals their white collar parents carefully instilled in them, the ones who kept to themselves except for a select group of like-minded friends.

No, if Max was lucky, she was ignored completely by both the girls and boys alike. Case in point, pretty boy and muscle-bound jock Baron Silver—star basketball forward, star short-stop, star everything—and overall high school dream guy. They'd been one year apart in the same school for the last four years, and he didn't even know that Max existed—a fact she was totally fine with, since she didn't need him to talk to her for her fantasies to play out in her dreams. Still, a part of her sometimes wondered what it might be like—

No. It *so* wasn't worth it.

Wondering wasn't worth the pain, not when she had to face such a harsh reality every day.

Reality was the nasty whispers she couldn't help but overhear, and the uncomfortable side glances directed her way, the kind that said the other kids were embarrassed *for* her—the poor homely girl with a man's name whose mother slept around with all their daddies when she wasn't passed out drunk or high as a kite.

Reality dictated the closest she was ever going to be to the school hunk was getting stuck in study hall with his sickly younger brother Jackson Silver, because they both needed to make up time for missing too many classes. Jackson was a nice kid, but so different from his brother Baron. It was too bad he was sick so often that he'd fallen behind, because he was really smart.

Jackson surprised her tonight by coming by with the extra credit homework she forgot to pick up from Mrs. Tulecki after school. Max had been mortified when he'd shown up at the door of their rundown trailer. Charlene started in screaming at the kid to get the hell off her property. Max had wanted to explain, but then she didn't bother. There was really nothing *to* say that everyone in town didn't already know.

At least she hadn't seen pity or disgust in Jackson's eyes. Only an understanding sort of awareness and an unspoken offer of support, for which Max had been surprisingly grateful for.

Maybe she had one friend after all.

"Finally," Baron muttered under his breath as he spotted his brother plodding slowly up the walk that wound through the park and out to their street. He raced over to meet him, long muscled legs eating up the distance. "Hey—Jacky! Where have you been?" Glaring hard at the little twerp in an attempt at brotherly intimidation, Baron wasn't afraid to let his annoyance show with an exaggerated huff.

If it weren't for Jacky, Baron could have been playing ball with his buddies—all right, maybe it was getting a little late to be out at the field, but that didn't mean there weren't a thousand other things he would rather be doing than chasing after his kid brother. "You know Mom has a cow when you take off like this. You were supposed to come home right after school."

"I had something...to do." Jackson's voice was halting as he struggled to regulate his breathing. "And I didn't...take off."

"Look," Baron started. He couldn't help feeling sorry for Jackson. "I'm not saying you shouldn't be able to go out and do whatever you want. But you could have at least let me know. Mom's had me scouring the neighborhood for you since she got home—which means I haven't eaten yet because of you." Baron slugged his brother good-naturedly in the shoulder and shook his head when Jackson winced, massaging the spot. "Suck it up, bro. That didn't hurt."

Jackson eyed him, obviously wondering if he was in for another shot in the arm. "I just needed to see a friend after school." He shrugged. His face was sweaty and pale, and his bony fingers shook as he brushed a hank of lifeless blond hair from where it hung down over his forehead.

Just a year apart, the brothers were so alike, and yet so very different. Both of them had blond hair, with the same crisp blue eyes. But where Baron's blond was lit with golden highlights that glowed in the sun, Jackson's hair was washed out and lifeless, oily, and forever hanging limply in his face. And while Baron's eyes sparkled with health and an insatiable verve for life, Jackson's always looked drawn and tired.

Both boys liked baseball and hockey, and the same flavor of ice cream—rocky road—and they shared the same charismatic grin that no stranger could resist. They both had the same head tilt to the right when they were thinking really hard, and they were both left-handed and taller than average for their age. But where Baron was energetic and athletic, with a healthy tan and wiry muscles that showed all the signs of maturing into a man's strong, solid frame, Jackson was scrawny and weak, and despite his height, he still sported the delicate figure of a child. Perpetually pale, he always looked like he was recovering from the flu. In fact, Baron hardly ever got sick, but Jackson frequently missed school due to an illness of one kind or another.

"Well, where have you been hiding?" Baron asked, the exasperation in his voice growing more pronounced as the evening's shadows deepened around them. "If you get sick again because you overexerted yourself, you know I'm the one who's going to get in trouble for not keeping a closer eye on you."

At sixteen years old, Baron had long ago started to resent all the time he was forced to spend watching over his little brother—making sure Jackson didn't overdo it, keeping him company when he was home sick. Walking him home from school so he didn't get picked on, and hanging out with him because he didn't have any friends of his own. It would have been stifling for any boy Baron's age, but because his brother was so "delicate", Baron felt guilty when he lashed out at Jackson.

It wasn't the kid's fault he was so weak and Baron was so strong. Every time he told Jacky to scram and suck dirt—like his other friends did with their own brothers—he ended up cursing himself for causing that look of defeated acceptance and self-hatred in his brother's old, old eyes.

He was used to Jackson's low energy levels and poor endurance, but when he started coughing, Baron's annoyance with his brother quickly turned to worry.

"Hey, what's the matter, bro? You okay?" He leaned over and put an arm around Jackson, conscious of the hard angles and bony protrusions of the other boy's shoulders, virtually bare of any muscle.

Jackson fell to his knees, fighting to drag enough air in and out of his lungs, but each cough seemed worse than the last. Baron hated to just stand there and watch, but he didn't know what to do.

Jackson's fingers closed over his throat as his breathing turned raspy and hoarse, the hacking coughs building one on top of the other until Baron feared the fit would tear his brother's already fragile body to pieces with the force of the spasms.

"Jacky, hey. Come on man." Baron straightened, keeping his arm reassuringly around his brother as he searched the park for some help. Shit. There was no one around and it was only seven-thirty. It was October, so the sun was already hanging low in the sky and the shadows had grown tall around them, making it seem as though the two boys were completely alone in the world.

The coughing fit finally started to taper off. Jackson stood and took several deep gasping breaths.

"Holy hell, Jacky are you—? Oh *shit*." The line of blood dripping from the corner of Jackson's mouth to his chin was very, very red against his pasty white skin.

That was when Baron lifted his brother up into his arms and started to run.

Chapter One

"Hey! You going to just stand there all night, or do you think you can get your ass moving and give me a hand over here?"

Baron ducked the swipe of claw intending to cleave his head from his shoulders. The demon roared and lunged for him again, forcing him back into a defensive position.

"Actually, I *am* just going to stand here." Alric leaned one hip against the hood of his car as he calmly observed the fight to the death that was taking place before him, looking for all the world like he was taking in a UFC match...or maybe the Ice Capades. Baron could have been dancing a damned waltz with this crazed Vuxi demon for all the partnerly concern Alric showed him.

"How are you ever going to learn if not through hardcore personal experience?"

"Yeah, yeah, yeah," Baron muttered, ducking another pass of the Vuxi's razor claws. He shot back with a hard right that hopefully broke the creature's nose—or whatever that gaping maw of slime was in the middle of its face—and then followed that punch with another and another, finally turning the tables and forcing the demon on the defensive.

This penny-ante shit wasn't going to get the job done, but it felt good. There was nothing like whaling on evil monsters from hell to keep a body in prime shape.

"So, why is it that whenever your wife kicks your sorry ass out of the house, I'm the one who suffers for it?" The Vuxi lunged, and this time Baron barely managed to dodge those wicked teeth. He swung around and used his momentum to hit the demon with a hard roundhouse to the chest, knocking it to the ground.

He shot a look of disgust Alric's way when the other Immortal just laughed. "Well?"

"What do you mean? Diana hasn't kicked me out. We had a small disagreement, and she's already seen the error of her ways." Alric nodded his head in the direction of the demon, which was already back on its feet and within striking distance.

Baron snorted as he pulled a gleaming sword from the custom-made casing he wore strapped to his back. Time to take out the trash and move on. Without taking his eyes from his snarling opponent, he said, "Sure she did. So tell me again why I'm sharing my bunk with you tonight?"

"Because you think I'm hot?"

Baron spared a look back at him, sweeping a mock assessing glance up and down Alric's huge frame. "Nope. That ain't it. You're much too hairy for my tastes."

The demon surged forward, rushing Baron, but he'd had more than enough of this "training session" for the night. "I think it's more likely you—" Baron's blade flashed as he swung hard and sure, "—haven't seen the error of *your* ways yet." With one strong, clean slice he cleaved the demon's still growling head from its body. "And that's why I have to share my room with your ugly Saxon butt tonight."

He grunted as he pulled the blade back and watched in satisfaction as the Vuxi disappeared in a blinding flash of smoky green light. Taking a soft black cloth from the pocket of his long leather jacket, Baron wiped his weapon clean of the monster's corrosive green blood, then slid it over his shoulder and into the sheath on his back.

He turned to Alric, who was nodding his massive head in approval. "Good job. Although, you almost let it cut you that one time."

"It almost cut me because you just stood there flapping your mouth off when you should have been helping."

"Oh, well, there was that. Sorry. Too distracting for you?" Alric grinned unrepentantly

Baron groaned. He knew where the older Immortal was going with this conversation. "No it wasn't distracting. I don't have a problem tuning out your pointless prattling."

Alric laughed, the sound rich and full, echoing off the walls of the now deserted alleyway. When Baron considered all that the big lug had suffered in his long existence, he was amazed at how much his partner loved life. At odds with the job they took on night after night, Alric had been known to wear a smile that could rouse the sun over the edge of the horizon before its time. But that had less to do with his sunny nature and everything to do with his wife, the beautiful Diana.

"Good. I'm glad." Alric turned serious. "Because you have to learn to be able to take in everything, notice everything, deal with all comers, but not let yourself get sidetracked by it all so that you can't see where the next attack is coming from."

Baron nodded, taking the coaching tip as the helpful advice it was meant to be. It had been like this for the past year and a half, ever since he was approached by Rhys and "recruited" into their ranks. Baron had been skeptical at first—who wouldn't be when a seven-foot-tall stone cold warrior reeking of deadly purpose, walks up to you and says there are demons afoot? But he had joined their secret war, and since then he'd seen some things that would have set other men to drooling and begging to be fitted for a straight jacket. So far, Baron had been able to take it in stride.

Mostly.

And that was due in large part to his special ops military training. A career in SFOD-D—Delta Force—had prepared him for a lot. And Rhys had prepared him for the rest.

Baron approached the passenger side door of the black Hummer. "So are you going to tell me, or not?" He opened the door, but paused before leaning down to get in, looking at Alric over the hood of the car.

"Tell you what?"

"What you did to Diana to get your ass stuck with all us groin scratching, smelly guys all week."

Alric groaned. "Not your business, youngster. Don't go there." He chuckled. "And I seriously doubt Amy lets you go around scratching and belching and otherwise making a monkey out of yourself. She'd beat you black and blue before you disrespected her home—never mind that it is an old warehouse."

Now it was Baron's turn to groan. Alric was right—not that it was a chore to behave himself—but Amy sure was a stickler for the whole manners thing, and it had been a long time since he'd lived with a woman underfoot.

"Whatever." He rapped on the hood of the car. "Are you so sure I can't help you with your lovers' spat? Seems to me even though you are so much older—ancient—compared to me, I've still got to know more about women than you do, since *I* never get thrown out of the ladies' beds."

"Don't start comparing your cheap one-night stands to my meaningful and fulfilling relationship with Diana," Alric warned as he got behind the wheel.

"Meaningful and fulfilling, huh? Sounds like you memorized it. Have those words been imprinted into your little pea brain by way of selective programming?" Baron joked as he joined him and immediately reached over to turn on the stereo.

"Fuck you." Alric promptly turned it off again.

Baron gave a long, melodramatic sigh. "Come on, old man, turn the tunes back on. Music hasn't been the devil's tool since Elvis. You do know Elvis, right?"

"That hardcore rap shit you listen to is hardly Elvis, Baron. And there's more to a marriage than getting laid, which even you should appreciate. Maybe one day, if you're lucky enough to find someone who can put up with your horrible taste in music, you'll realize it's also a lot of hard work...and pain."

Baron laughed. "Lucky? To be in pain? And here I thought love was all about eternal happiness and shit."

Alric turned dead serious. "You heard me. Pain. Hard. It's a lot of work to make a relationship, Baron. And when you factor in the added baggage we're carrying around as Immortals, it's virtually impossible." He sighed, eyes remaining firmly on the road in front of him as he drove. "Haven't you ever heard the expression—love is about two percent happiness, and ninety-eight percent the most horrible pain on earth?"

Baron swallowed his laugh. "Ah, no. No, I hadn't heard that one."

"Yeah, well it's probably true." Alric turned his head and speared Baron with his gaze, those silvery eyes that were so like Baron's own, shining with a rare expression of dark, swirling emotion. Coming from Alric it was so out of character that it almost scared him. "But that two percent happiness...that is so totally worth all of the rest, you feel me?"

"Sure. Hey, I'm sorry man. I was being an ass, you know?"

Alric nodded, some of the intensity passing from his expression. "Yeah. I know. Don't worry about it."

Baron might act like an asshole ninety-nine percent of the time, yanking his friend's chain when it came to the man's marriage and pulling practical jokes on Rhys every chance he got. But it was done in fun.

Out of them all, only Alric and Rhys were involved in any kind of serious relationship—with a woman anyway. Roland's obscene obsession with his Ferrari didn't count, although it came pretty close, given the amount of time he spent washing the thing. So it followed that the two attached Immortals were going to take some good-natured male ribbing about the female influences in their lives.

All kidding and practical jokes aside, Baron recognized how fortunate his friends were to have found love. Real love, not the kind that came with twenty differently colored condoms and a long list of lies.

They were Immortals. And given the world they were forced to live in and the job they took on every day, it was good Rhys and Alric each had someone to help make it all mean something. So that the world still made sense at the end of the day. Because God knew it could be a struggle to handle all that violence day in and day out. The humans walked the streets with their heads in the clouds, unaware of the evil that stalked them. And the reality of it was, if Baron and the others were doing their jobs right, none of those humans were ever going to know enough to appreciate the sacrifices that had been made so they would live to see tomorrow. No one was going to say thank you for making sure they didn't end up demon grub. It was all very MIB. And that was just fine. That's the way it was supposed to be.

But no matter how much Baron might be happy for his colleagues that they had found love, it wasn't something he planned to gamble on for himself. There had been a time long ago when he might have entertained illusions to that effect—in a brief, weakened moment—but a lot had changed since then, not the least of which was Baron himself. He wasn't so young anymore, or optimistic...and just maybe he wasn't so selfish either.

He casually watched the streets as they drove, senses always tuned to any hint of trouble. It was like having the TV on in the background so you could keep track of the score of the hockey game while you were doing something else.

This kind of constant awareness was a habit he had honed in the military, a skill that had also proven to be of use in his new profession, especially when combined with Baron's other unique gifts.

The night air was a bit crisp for this time of year. The full moon hidden behind dark clouds ripe with moisture. "Alric, stop the car." There was something other than moisture in the air tonight.

"You see something, kid?"

Baron groaned. "Would you stop calling me that? You want me to call you grandpa?" He tilted his head to the left, and Alric pulled down a dark side street.

"Why don't you try it, and see what happens." Alric smiled and stopped the car.

Baron jumped out and started heading back the way they had come, his senses telling him the disturbance he'd felt was coming from a location about two deserted buildings back. Alric followed. "Hey, don't jump into this half-cocked all on your lonesome. Whatever you think you saw, we handle it properly. Together. Prepared. Got it?" His expression was stern and his tone brooked no argument.

Baron nodded. "Yeah. Got it." He pointed to the entrance of a rundown apartment building. It looked empty, but he knew he had seen movement, shadows. A ghastly certainty came upon him. His internal radar immediately kicking into super high gear, bringing his attention to the evil psychic taint in the air. "You wanna go in first, or shall I?"

Alric pulled a heavy duty magnum and waved Baron ahead. "Lead the way, my friend; this is your show. I'm just the backup dancer tonight."

Baron shuddered. "I'd just as soon not be forced into a visual of you in a pair of tights, if it's all the same."

They carefully approached the doorway. Baron

motioned for silence as he pressed an ear to the door. Sure enough, his better than human hearing picked up the shuffling and scratching sounds of something moving around within. It could have been nothing—a cat and mouse duking it out, or a runaway who had found a place to crash for the night—but Baron didn't think so. With a look over one shoulder to Alric, he pushed aside his leather jacket and pulled his glock from the holster clipped at his hip.

He moved into position in front of the door, knowing that once they were inside, they would have only a fraction of a second to assess the situation and determine whether or not human lives were at stake, and if those lives could be saved.

One. Two. Three.

He nodded to Alric, then kicked the door hard, knowing from experience exactly where to hit it, the sweet spot that would send it careening open. He was ready for the rebound with his shoulder when it bounced back to him off the inside wall. He'd made that mistake his first mission out. Gone in with his weapon cocked and ready, kicked the door open...and it smacked him right in the nose on its way back, teaching him an important lesson about strategy that he'd never forgotten.

Baron and Alric surprised two vampires who looked up at them from their dinner of wasted middle-aged homeless guy. Blood dribbled from their mouths down colorless faces and under their chins. Both drew their lips back in matching hisses of feral rage at being discovered and interrupted.

"Sorry to intrude," Baron drawled, the sneer in his voice making it very obvious he wasn't sorry in the least. "But is this a private party, or can anyone crash it and dust your asses?"

The two vampires rose from the dirty floor with ghastly synchronicity, the human they had been feasting on forgotten and crumpling at their feet in a heap of limbs and grimy, ragged clothing.

The male lifted its nose to the air and inhaled deeply, as if picking up the scent of their very blood. "Ah, now this is interesting," he said. "Immortals. What a treat. I thought we were going to be stuck with meat loaf tonight, but it looks like we'll be having steak for dinner, my dear."

The female smiled, her long fangs protruding from behind stretched lips. "I've never had an Immortal before, baby," she purred, her voice a lush, husky sound that hypnotized. Baron found himself having to consciously fight the draw of it. "Get it for me."

Alric stepped forward. "Look, we have no issue with vampires...generally," he said. "We couldn't care less about your sick little blood clubs or your conversion treaty, but when you start taking blood from humans who have not consented, you break your own rules and something will be done about it."

"Not by you, Immortal. We vampires have our own laws, and our own system in place to enforce those laws," the male hissed. "None of which requires your involvement."

Baron could feel the strength of the vampire's psychic power as the creature probed the barriers he had already subconsciously fortified to keep them both out of his head. The male was strong, obviously the older of the pair.

Alric's expression showed strain as he too fought an invisible battle against the vampires' combined power. "If your Enforcer isn't here to stop you, then we certainly have no problem getting involved."

At the mention of the Enforcer, the female let out a low, keening sound of distress, causing the male to growl at her sharply. She cringed and went silent, but her eyes were wide and round. The male's hands curled into fists at his side. "This does not involve you." The vampire's eyes seemed to glow with his next words and Baron felt a forceful...push in his mind. "Just turn around and forget you saw us here tonight. This is not your business."

The sneaky little bastard was trying to send them a compulsion. And he was strong, too. Alric had already partially turned to head out the door.

Baron sent power surging along the same psychic line the vampire was using against them and zapped him back with his own juice. He got a rush of psychic feedback and had to shake his head to clear away the fuzz. At least the vampire was even more unsteady.

Baron knew he had a true and clear shot and quickly pulled the trigger before the vampire could try something else, but it was fast, so fast that Baron didn't even see it move. One second the bullet was racing toward it, and the next second the vampire was behind him, leaning in close with its hands pulling on Baron's shoulders. Baron's wasted bullet smacked a hole into the wall where the vampire used to be.

The suck-head was going to bite him.

Fuck that.

Baron whipped his chin up and brought his head back, hearing as well as feeling the satisfying crunch of the vampire's nose. He swung around to double whammy the break with his fist and the vampire growled, blood pouring from him in a steady spray. With a roar, the creature sprang for Baron, a blur of teeth and claws, but he had expected the attack and stepped back, parrying the vampire's far-reaching swipe with his fists.

The female shrieked and launched herself at Baron as well, but Alric intercepted her. She fought like a banshee. Wild. Screeching and scratching at the other Immortal, her teeth flashing in the darkness.

The male vampire danced around Baron so fast, he felt like an eight year-old trapped in the hall of mirrors, turning this way and that, seeing things that were there one moment and gone the next. The thing wouldn't stay still long enough for him to get in a shot, and it was pissing him right off. His fingers tightened around the handle of his weapon, itching to pull the trigger.

At Alric's shout, Baron swung round to see the female with her teeth sunk deep in Alric's upper arm. His fist was in her hair, and he yanked her from him with a low roar, his face a mask of disgust.

Her mouth hung open, dripping his blood to the floor. She screamed, struggling with desperate urgency to get her teeth into him again, flailing and heaving against his hold. Her attack had lost all semblance of control or strategy; she was now motivated only by the blood lust.

Alric was attempting to draw his blade against her, difficult considering it took both of his arms to hold her off of him. The male vampire abandoned his attack on Baron to defend her at the same time Baron aimed his glock.

Baron shot her.

Everything moved in slow motion from that point forward. Baron cocking his gun, pulling the trigger. The bullet whizzing toward the female's chest. The male vampire's shout of furious rage. Alric's arms bringing the sword down in a wide arc that severed her head from her shoulders, sending vampire blood splattering over his forearms.

The male vampire raced to her side, but fast as he was, he couldn't save her. There was nothing left of the female but fine particles of ash that were already settling with the caked-in dirt on the old milky-looking parquet floor.

The vampire went ballistic, flying at the Immortals with a loud snarl of rage and pain. Shit, the thing had been fast before, but now the bastard was virtually invisible, a blurred tornado of flying fists and teeth and venomous purpose. It took all Baron had just to keep its deadly claws and fangs from tearing into him like the jagged teeth of a rotary mower.

With the two of them pounding on the vampire, their

odds had drastically improved, but it was quicker than they were, and strong. The damn thing was stronger than any demon Baron had fought to date.

"*Baron. Alric.*" The vampire called their names, taunting them now as it danced around them both, always one step faster. Just out of reach. "I see you. I know you. I've been in your heads already."

"Oh, good." Baron turned in a circle, trying to track the vampire's movements. "If you're reading my mind, then I won't waste my breath telling you what I'm going to do to you." Baron pulled his sword, twisting round as he waited for an opening.

It just laughed. A creepy sound like every evil laugh from every villain in every low budget movie he could remember watching. "You can't stop me. Neither of you have quite what it takes. But it was a good try, and I'll be sure to tell your wife just that Alric. Do you think she'd like to hear about how you two killed my mate? Do you think she'd enjoy learning exactly what the term *an eye for an eye* really means?"

Alric roared, rage giving him a burst of speed. His reach was still an instant too short, but Baron had remained still, watching, and he thought he could anticipate the vampire's next move.

Baron wasted no time. He plunged his sword into the bastard's chest.

The vamp came to a full stop, from superman on steroids to superman on kryptonite in a twist of the blade. Baron pushed it in deeper, until the point came out bloody on the other side.

The vampire's scream of pain and fury ricocheted like a ping pong ball in his mind—a ping pong ball covered with sharp metal spikes. The sound was piercing, sharp, and unbearable. Baron closed his eyes against it. Only for a moment, but when he opened them again, the vampire was gone.

The two Immortals looked at each other, both of them

still breathing heavily, both bloody and bruised. "What the hell was that?" Alric demanded, his expression tight, his voice ripe with disgust. "Why'd you stick him in the chest? Don't you know you have to take a vampire's head?"

Baron shoved his weapon back into its sheath with a brisk, irritated flick of his wrist. "Fuck no. How the hell was I supposed to know that?"

"Everybody knows that."

"Well, I must have missed the blood-suckers 101 class, because everything I know about vampires I got from the *Scream* channel."

"No kidding. And since when do you believe everything you see on TV, dumbass?"

"Hey, *dumbass*—you weren't exactly forthcoming with useful information." They both exchanged identical looks of frustration and then sighed heavily.

"Shit," Baron muttered.

"Yeah."

"Shouldn't we go after him?"

"No point now. The sun's almost up. He's already long gone."

"Shit."

"Yeah."

Baron walked to the door and looked up and down the quiet street, still dark and sleeping, waiting for the sun to slowly touch the sky with gold. There wasn't a sound or a shuffle of movement anywhere. Not a cat. Not a dog. No wounded evil vampires. His senses weren't picking up anything.

Damn it. It really pissed him off that the creature was going to get away—this time. But he made a vow to himself that it wouldn't get far. "Alric?" he said as the two men made their way back to the car.

"What?"

"Go home to your wife."

Alric paused and then nodded. "I got no problems

with that."

Chapter Two

"If he's alive, I'll find him for you."

Had she really promised Jackson something so foolish?

Of course she had. What else were you supposed to tell a dying man when he asks for a favor? A dying man who also happened to be your best friend in all the world?

Yep. That explained why she wasn't at home tucked nicely in her comfortable, safe bed. Although it didn't necessarily account for why she was stuck on the side of the road in the middle of nowhere at God only knows what time of the freakin' night it was, kicking the crap out of her rust bucket death trap of a VW Beetle.

Because of a promise.

Max groaned aloud and swore a blue streak into the misty night air as she struck her toe against the hard black rubber of her front tire.

She should have known the car wouldn't get her to Chandler. The ancient hunk of scrap metal hated her. It must. The thing was Christine, and it hated her. The only time it had ever run properly was on the ill-fated day she'd been duped into buying the piece of shit car from her cousin Sally's boyfriend. Since then Max had had nothing but trouble from it, everything from leaking oil and fried spark plugs, to flat tires, faulty brakes and a busted gasket. She didn't even want to know what the hell was wrong with it now, but from the thick gray smoke coming from underneath the hood...it wasn't going to be anything good.

Great. Just freaking great.

Because of a dying man and his last wish, because of her mushy soft spot for Jackson and his need to mend fences with his brother, Maxine was stranded on the outskirts of an unfamiliar town, with a cell phone that was as useless as a bathing suit to an Eskimo since it hadn't picked up a signal for the last six miles before her car uttered its last, dying sputter and stalled out on her.

With the way she was feeling right now, even if Max managed by some twisted turn of fate to find Jackson's selfish, heartless, insensitive asshole of a brother, she was seriously going to deck him for making her go through all this—before dragging him back home to Jackson like she had promised.

"Okay," she muttered to herself, needing to break the silence that hung heavy and thick in these unfamiliar surroundings, even if it meant talking to herself.

Rubbing at the goosebumps that had risen all along her bare arms, she thought it was uncharacteristically chilly for June. It was closing on midnight, and there'd been no signs of life coming from either direction in a long time. "First things first." Max had to find out just where she was, and then she would know whether she would be spending a long, cold night in the car, or if she should risk getting out to hoof it to a pay phone to call a tow truck.

A worried glance into the dark forest that loomed on either side of the road decided that particular dilemma for her. She would not be walking.

Hell, right now she didn't even care to get the car towed; the piece of crap could stay where it was until the end of time. But she'd need a taxi.

Would a cabbie even come out here at this time of night?

With one last swing of her booted foot at the tire—the only part of her car that might actually still work—Max sighed and got back in the car. Rummaging through the glove compartment, she pulled out a neatly folded map of the minor metropolis of Chandler, glad now that she had thought to pick one up at the last gas station. Before deciding to stay home and care for Jackson, she had done a lot of traveling. With her business it was virtually impossible not to, and she had quickly gotten into the habit of grabbing a map first thing upon entering any new town.

Reaching above her head, she pressed the button to turn on the car's interior light and unfolded the map over the steering wheel.

A sharp rap on her driver's side window startled her and a small squeal of fright erupted from her throat. Max couldn't help jumping in her seat, her fists crumpling the map in her lap. Her hand immediately went to her back, feeling for the heavy comfort of the SIG-Sauer she never left home without, but of course the gun was in the glove box. A glance in that direction reassured her the door to the small storage compartment was still hanging open.

She looked through the window to find a man staring in at her, smiling. Though it was pitch black outside and hard to make out the details of his face, she didn't think it was a nice smile.

It was amazing how being alone in the dark could make a person imagine ghosts and goblins under every rock and behind every blade of grass. She hadn't even heard him drive up.

"Sorry to startle you," he called through her car window. He seemed to be trying for friendly and reassuring, but Max thought she heard a trace of unhealthy excitement in his thready voice. She swallowed hard and forced herself to quit being ridiculous. "I saw your car sitting here and wondered if I could offer some assistance."

There was no moon in the cloudy sky, and so very little light filtered past his shadowed form and through the window. Max could just barely make out sharp, angled features in a pale face. He had dark hair that hung down low over his forehead.

She fervently wished she could see his eyes. She had always trusted her instincts when it came to seeing the truth in people's eyes. But even without the eyes, her instincts were telling her she needed to run.

She wanted her gun badly.

The poor guy must have sensed he was making her nervous, because he straightened and stepped back from the car, hands spread out at his sides in an effort to show her he was harmless. The shadows shifted around him, giving her a glimpse of his face, and she gasped, unable to keep it in, pressing a hand over her mouth. The left side of his face was covered in an angry red burn that was only half healed. Max couldn't imagine the pain he must have experienced. Just the sight of the horrible, puckered skin made her flinch and wish there was more between the two of them than a mere pane of thin clear glass.

She told herself she was overreacting and tried to make her mind and body relax, to let go of the insane idea that she had just met a serial axe murderer on the road to Chandler. The man had recently been in an accident, that was all, and it was nothing to be afraid of. Given the suit jacket and long trench coat the man wore, he was obviously just an average guy on his way home after working a late night in town. A banker. Maybe a lawyer or an accountant. Something boring. Something mediocre. Something ordinary and safe.

Wasn't this exactly what she had been hoping for not ten minutes ago? That someone would come along and offer to help her so she wouldn't be stranded here all night?

Yes, but that didn't mean she wasn't going to play this situation nice and safe.

Max casually slid the lock of her driver's side door before she rolled the window down a fraction of an inch, hoping he wouldn't be offended by her overabundance of caution. "Hi there. Uh, sorry for the freak-out. It's just...it's dark, and well..."

"No need to apologize miss, I understand completely." He gave her what Max supposed was meant to be a reassuring smile, but it didn't make her feel a whit more relaxed. "A woman has to be careful when she's out alone at night these days," he continued. "My name is Devon."

His voice...it was low, calm, almost hypnotic, but there was something *off* about it, almost as if the display of smooth affability was a façade and behind the scarred mask, he laughed at her.

It was totally creeping her out.

She forcibly shrugged off the strangling sense of impending doom, putting it down to an excessive amount of anxiety and imagination, both of which she could have done without at a time like this. Max generally didn't ignore her instincts. But in this case, she didn't have much of a choice if she wanted to avoid being stuck here for the rest of the night.

"Devon you said? Do you happen to have a cell phone on you?" Of course he would have a cell phone. Who didn't carry one of the digital doggy tags around with them at all times these days? "If I could borrow it to call a cab, I'd really appreciate it. Mine isn't working for some reason, and my car seems to have breathed its last."

"Yes, I do have a cell phone, but unfortunately my dear, they don't ever work in this area. Something about the old uranium mines." His smile got bigger, toothier. "I could drive you into town myself."

It came to Max again that she hadn't heard him drive up. She realized she had no idea where this guy had come from. He hadn't parked a car in front of her, and a quick glance in the rear view mirror confirmed there was nothing parked behind. Craning her neck to try to see past his imposing figure and down the dark and deserted street, she could still find no sign of a vehicle.

Her instincts were screaming at her to hurry and get far, far away. *Now*. But she had to stay calm. In control.

She was trying very hard not to show this guy any fear, because if he were some kind of psycho, fear would be the catalyst, the thing that was sure to get her killed and her body dumped somewhere in the thick foliage beyond the road.

"Uh...sorry, I don't see your car. Where exactly did you come from again?" Max swallowed, hoping he couldn't tell how badly her voice croaked, or see how her hand was clenched into a fist in her lap, crumpling the map into a pulpy mess of sweat and paper.

His expression didn't change, but all of a sudden her limbs felt heavy. Impossibly, his eyes seemed to be glowing, and she couldn't look away from them. She could hear his laughter, but oddly, the sound was only in her mind. An unnatural, hungry echo. She felt it ripping through her brain, sinking into the tissue. What the hell was going on?

Just what kind of trouble had she inadvertently gotten herself into?

The really super bad kind, that was what.

With what felt like Herculean effort, Max tore her gaze from Devon's disturbing eyes. Once that connection was broken, she was able to control her body better, but not by much. It was still like trying to swim in a pool full of gelatin. Her movements were heavy and sluggish.

She lunged for the glove compartment, fingertips outstretched as she reached desperately for her gun. Just as she felt the blessedly cool metal meet her palm, the laughter in her brain turned to an animal roar. She heard a wrenching squeal, the sound of metal screaming in protest as the driver's side door of her car was ripped from its hinges and tossed effortlessly across two lanes into the gravel ditch on the other side of the road.

Max's terrified cry was lost in the piercing clamor of Devon's inhuman howl. All of it inside her mind. If he didn't kill her, she knew she would quickly go mad from the sick, twisted echo, the feeling that he was all around her, inside her. A part of her.

Max tightened her grip on the gun but didn't get a chance to bring it around or point it at the madman before he had seized her arm, pulling her roughly from the car.

She screamed as her shoulder was ripped from its socket, and felt the sharp dig of his nails tearing into her skin and the muscles of her forearm. She cried out again when he yanked her forward, and she fell to her knees on the rough, dirty asphalt.

Her eyes widened in disbelief as she glimpsed the ruined door of her car lying in a mangled and misshapen heap on the other side of the road. Holy hell, the guy was strong. If he had just done that to her car, what did he have planned for her?

Her attacker had stepped away and was now standing motionless in front of her, watching...as if he had all the time in the world and was just going to sit back and enjoy her fear, and the other, varied emotions he was able to draw out of her. Panic, disbelief, and helplessness.

Max's jaw tightened. She wasn't going to make it so easy for him. If he wanted a reaction from her, he'd get it, but it wouldn't be what he expected. Better men than this psycho had tried to frighten her, intimidate her, make her feel weak and defenseless.

Now he was just making her angry.

She lifted her chin as she met his amused stare with a determined one of her own, but her new resolve started to waver when he grinned widely, baring impossibly long, sharp canines. The look in his glowing eyes glittered with pure unadulterated evil.

Max knew she was in serious trouble, but she wasn't without resources. She carried a weapon for a reason...and she so wasn't afraid to use it.

She quickly disengaged the safety and trained her gun on him, but she wasn't fast enough. Devon's fist smashed into her face and her head whipped to the side, her whole body slamming back against the hard metal frame of the ruined car. The air whooshed from her lungs, but still she held onto the gun, her fingers in a lockjaw grip around the handle.

Oh hell, that hurt like a bitch. The pain was a hot, jagged line into her skull. She thought he'd probably broken her jaw.

Her vision was blurry; she could barely see him standing before her. Just shadows. Dark, menacing shadows. Didn't matter. Squeezing the trigger, she fired, not knowing whether she was going to hit the bastard or not, only knowing she had to do something.

The sound of the gunshot boomed loud in her ears, finally cutting off the horrible laughter that had continued to rape her mind with its insidious whispers and malevolent laughter. With a grim satisfaction, she watched Devon double over, take a faltering step back. She had hit him. In the stomach.

Thank God.

Wait a minute. He wasn't falling. Why wasn't he falling? Why hadn't he keeled over onto his back yet, nice and dead like a good little maniac?

He was already straightening, laughing at her again, this time right out loud with his lips pulling back from those impossibly sharp teeth in a combination of animal snarl and evil grin.

On her knees, Max quickly scrambled around to the front of her car, using it as a barrier between them, a wall to which she could retreat and take aim at him again.

Leaning over the dusty hood, which still trailed a thin line of smoke from the engine underneath, Max trained her gun on Devon. Damn. He hadn't gone down. She knew her bullet had hit him, but besides that little stagger and the low moan, he hadn't fallen to the ground.

As she watched, he spread his arms wide, mocking her attempt to do him in. "Go ahead and shoot me again my dear," he dared, his voice ripe with warped amusement. "Your weapon isn't going to kill me."

"We'll see about that, you asshole."

She did shoot him again, but while she knew her aim was true, Devon moved so fast—too fast for her even to see. He was just...gone, and the bullet smashed into the trunk of a tree in the thicket across the road.

Before the loud crack of the shot had completely died out, he was standing by her side, not a foot away from her. He wrenched the gun from her hands.

Max fought. With everything she had, she fought him, but his strength...his strength was colossal...not human.

Oh my God, he's not human.

He laughed again, obviously enjoying her struggles, her fear, and Max knew she was going to die. "You're right." His voice betrayed his excitement, the sick enjoyment he was getting from this. "On all counts, I'm afraid. I'm not human, you are going to die, and yes...I am reading your mind."

His hand was tight around her throat now, squeezing, crushing her windpipe. She clawed at his wrist, his arm, trying to loosen his hold enough to pull oxygen into her burning lungs. Her vision was quickly going fuzzy and dark, black shadows like syrupy globs of ink floating in front of her eyes.

"Fuck you," she rasped on her one last puff of air, fingers still clawing at the manacle of a wrist that held her to him.

His head bent to her neck, and she felt those teeth grazing the column of her throat, felt his tongue come out and lick the sweat from her skin in one long swipe. At that moment she knew exactly what was happening, exactly what she had unwittingly come up against—

Vampire.

His claws dug into the flesh and muscle of her upper arms as he pulled her closer to him. He smelled of dirt and blood and evil—exactly what you expected the essence of insanity to smell like. She gasped as the teeth tore through her skin with brutal efficiency. She could feel her blood trickling thickly down her neck to the valley of her breasts, sticky and hot. Inside her mind Max felt his satisfaction, his eagerness. He wanted to rip her apart like an animal, but she sensed he was weak and his need for her blood was great. He couldn't afford to waste any of it with games.

The teeth that pierced her went deep, and she couldn't help the moan passing across her lips at the sharp tug of his mouth on her skin as he started to draw her blood into his mouth. The sounds were like something out of a bad movie, sucking and slurping and great hungry swallows.

Oh God, this was really happening to her. She was going to die out here at the hands of this monster...*and it's all Baron's fault.*

Devon was surprised. Very surprised. What luck he was having this night.

He let the woman's smooth, rich blood fill him, heal him. He could feel the burns on his face fading and knew the charred, ruined skin was turning pink and healthy again. His body warmed as her blood started pumping in his starved veins.

He had intended to drain the woman dry—he sorely needed her rejuvenating blood to restore him to full strength—but she had surprised him with her spirit and fire, just as she had surprised him with her thoughts.

Baron.

Oh, it was too good to be true, but the proof was right there in her mind, in the fevered whisper of the damn Immortal's name inside her head. The Immortal who had

31

dared take his mate from him. The Immortal who had been close on his heels every night since then like a bloodhound after a scent.

Devon had been forced into hiding—an animal on the run. Hunted.

A week after losing Bettina, the bastards had found and raided his lair in the city, forcing him out onto the street just moments before dawn. He'd managed to avoid the sun, but only barely. And two nights ago, they'd found him again. Only by the skin of his pointed vampire teeth, by the strength of his hatred and desire to have vengeance upon their hides, had he managed to escape the fire they'd set to trap him. Thankfully, he found his way into the subway tunnels before the sun could do more than just blister his skin.

He still suffered from the painful burns, and it didn't help that he was forced to seek shelter out here in the middle of nowhere to avoid the Immortals that continued to hunt him mercilessly. Here, where human traffic was non-existent at night, making human blood impossible to find. Injured and weak as he was, he needed a large amount of it to heal him completely and there was none to be found...until tonight. Until one lone woman's car just happened to break down on the side of the road only meters from his newly appointed home sweet home.

Devon's hatred for the Immortals thundered hotly in his veins. He hungered constantly for the revenge he had promised them. For what they had done to his beloved Bettina they both deserved to die—deserved more than death.

This surprising young woman would be his first strike against them.

Her sweet blood still flowed into his mouth, drawing a sharp moan of pleasure from his lips, and he drank until he knew she was but moments from her death.

Her heart had slowed, barely beating now, her breathing shallow. Her eyes were closed, long, soft lashes brushing the tops of her paper white cheeks, and her hand no longer clutched his wrist to pull him away, but fell limply to her side.

She really was a beautiful woman, and looking at her, Devon felt the loss of his Bettina sharply.

He pulled from her throat and scored his wrist with his teeth, pushing the bloody gash to her mouth.

"Drink."

Chapter Three

Baron lay back on the flat bench, his feet firmly planted on either side of it, and lifted the free weights straight up over his chest, then back down. Again. Again.

The workout soothed him, focused his mind.

It was late—rather, it was early morning. He and Rhys had returned home an hour ago from patrolling the city. But while Rhys had been more than willing to put the evening's dangers behind him and retreat to his room to enjoy what was left of the night with his lovely wife, Baron was still wound tighter than a two-dollar pocket watch from a street vendor at Grand Central. Unable to settle, unable to relax.

Tonight they had taken out three watchers partying it up in the downtown core, and last night Baron and the twins had ousted a nest of Vuxi demons terrorizing homeless out by the wharf. Technically, they had had a good week. No casualties, no injuries, the general human public remained blissfully ignorant of the evil lurking in their midst. But Baron couldn't shake the feeling of restless unease, an edginess that he knew very well came from the fact that he hadn't caught the vampire yet.

Devon—Alric had found out the vamp's name during the first few days of their hunt—was still out there, still eluding them. They had come close a few times since that fucked-up encounter of the first night, but it seemed this vampire had the devil's own luck when it came to his sense of self-preservation.

Every night that he continued to breathe was one more night that Alric worried the vampire would carry out his threats against Diana, and one more night that Baron promised himself he wouldn't let that bastard do anything to hurt either of his friends.

Baron slugged the free weights relentlessly, a new plan of action forming in his mind. A sharp rap on the open door startled him from his thoughts.

He looked up to find Rhys' muscular frame filling the entrance. "Baron, you had better come and see this."

Baron replaced the heavy weights. Breathing hard, he sat up and reached for his towel, swiping it across his forehead. "What is it?"

Rhys shook his head, his expression tight and unreadable. That in itself wouldn't normally alarm Baron at all, since the other Immortal wasn't known for his conversational skills at the best of times. Rhys was more a man of action than of words.

But there was something in Rhys' eyes that Baron didn't like, something that spawned a decidedly cold feeling deep in his chest. Okay, what the hell was going on here?

"All right, just a sec." He yanked on the plain white tee he'd slung across one of the machines earlier and followed Rhys down the hall to a smaller room where the warehouse's computer and security monitoring equipment was set up. Roland was there watching the screens with an equally inscrutable look on his face.

"So, what is it you guys?" he asked. "Why the grim faces? Somebody put a scratch on your car Roland?" Roland didn't blink, didn't rise to the bait at all, which meant this must be serious.

"There." Rhys pointed to one screen, displaying a view of the front loading docks. "Apparently, this is meant for you."

"This what?" There was something out there. What it was, Baron couldn't quite make out. He glanced from Rhys to Roland. Something was very wrong here. "Okay, let me see." He moved behind Roland's chair to get a better look at the image on the monitor.

Arms. Legs. Clothing.

A body.

"Shit. Who is that?" he asked.

Rhys continued to give him that look, the one that was really starting to piss him off. "What? What is this all about? Who's out there?"

"Devon left her out there."

"Devon...the vampire? It's a woman out there?" He stepped forward, bending closer to the screen. "Oh man...where's Alric? Is it—?" Shit. *Don't let that body outside be Diana.*

"No," Rhys said. "It isn't Diana, thank God."

Baron's patience had been sheared paper thin, and it showed in the acid tone of his voice. "Spit it out guys. Who is that, and why are you both just standing here staring at me like a matching pair of rainmen?"

Baron turned to leave, intending to get to the bottom of this once and for all. He would go outside and see for himself who this woman was that had been dumped on their doorstep like so much baggage.

Rhys grabbed his arm, stopping him just outside the door. "Baron, wait. Just...watch the tape before you go out there." Rhys nodded to Roland, who pressed a button to play the roll of security tape that they had obviously already watched.

With an impatient sigh, Baron stepped back inside the room and turned his attention to the other screen, but he couldn't help it when his gaze flickered back to the real-time image of the woman lying motionless outside. Why hadn't anyone gone outside to help her? Was she already dead then?

If Devon was involved in this crappy little stunt...then

probably.

Poor thing.

The tape showed the same image of the loading docks, and the time read 2:46 a.m.—about ten minutes ago.

Baron watched Devon saunter right up to the doors as if he were there to deliver the mail. He dropped the woman's body to the ground like a sack of potatoes. Baron winced as her limbs flopped lifelessly to the pavement. There was something about her. Something in the curve of her cheek before her hair fell lifelessly over her face, the shape of the body curled in on itself...

Baron's attention shifted. Devon stared directly into the camera. He was grinning, a huge toothy grin designed to show off the pointed fangs and inhuman glint in his eyes. His face was covered in blood—the woman's blood? Baron felt a chill go up his spine.

"Baron," Devon called to him, his voice easy, as if he were on the phone, leaving a message for a friend. "I have a present for you."

The vampire spared a glance down at the woman's body and when he turned back, his eyes were glowing red, and he ran his tongue out over his lips and chin like a wolf licking his chops clean after devouring the hare.

"Mm. She tasted so good, Baron. I almost didn't want to stop." His laughter was high and foul, making the hairs on Baron's forearms and across the back of his neck stand up. Baron almost forgot that the vampire was already gone, that this was just a recording. It took all he had to stop from rushing out of the room to go after the bastard.

The next moment, the frame was empty. But for the "gift" that Devon left, the vampire himself had vanished.

"What does that mean?" He turned to the others. "Did he drink her, is that what he's saying? She's dead?"

"Do you know her?" Rhys asked.

"Why should I know her? I mean...I guess I could, but I...I just don't know." He gazed at the figure on the screen again. It was possible. "I can't see clearly enough from the position of the camera. Does it matter? Shouldn't we go out there and see if she's still alive?"

Rhys sighed. "Baron, this was meant for you. Which means it's very likely that the woman outside is someone you know...and not just casually."

"Can't be. You know I don't get close to *any* women other than 'casually'." A niggling uncertainty flared, regardless of his words. There was *one* woman. But Baron hadn't seen her in years, and made a point of never thinking of her. She was a long way from here in any case.

"If the vampire went to the trouble of bringing her here for you, then you can bet your ass he was in your head and found something that told him this particular woman meant something to you. Think about it."

"Shit, I'm thinking already, but honestly, what difference does it make? We still have to go out there."

Rhys sighed, his eyes sharp, the silver points glinting in the dim light. "Fine, but be prepared."

"What the hell does that mean? What am I missing here, and why won't you just fucking tell me already?"

"She's been turned, Baron."

"Turned?" Did that mean what he thought it meant? Of course it did. What else would it mean? "All right. I understand."

"Do you?" Rhys put his hand on his shoulder. "What we should do is leave that creature outside until the sun comes up. If he's turned her this night, then she probably won't even regain consciousness before the light takes her. Her death will be swift and painless."

"But..." Baron looked again at the screen. Took a long, hard look. It made sense that Devon wouldn't have gone to the trouble of finding, terrorizing, and turning someone and then bringing her here to taunt him with the fact unless...

That *was* someone he knew. Had to be.

The certainty made him go cold, fear and guilt closing his throat. If it were true, and he no longer had any doubt that it was, it meant whatever had happened to this woman was his fault. He was to blame.

There was something about her...

No.

Please no.

There was only one woman in all the world Baron had ever cared about. It couldn't be her. He had those memories buried so deep nothing short of a crowbar to his skull would have been able to pull them from him. Had Devon been that far inside his head? What if—

"I have to go out there," he told Rhys, turning to sprint down the hall.

At the large rolling door, he stopped and took a deep breath before lifting the hatch and pulling it open.

The early morning was still dark as pitch, but the outside security lights were bright overhead, giving the gruesome scene a severe hit of reality that it had lacked when viewed through the computer monitors.

Baron noticed the blood first. It stained the woman's long hair dark, but he knew the color was naturally a beautiful blonde with shining gold highlights. Her mouth was drawn and pale, but he had felt the heat of her kiss and seen the beauty of her rare smile. Though her eyes were closed, he remembered how they shone so clear and blue with a spirit that had never been broken, despite everything she'd already been through in her difficult life.

Oh, God.

Maxine.

He felt the tears coming. They burned his eyes and blurred his vision. He fell to his knees and pulled her into his arms, unconsciously rocking her back and forth. He pushed the dirty, bloody mass of hair from her forehead with a trembling hand, and brushed at the smudges on her cheeks and nose.

"Oh, no. Oh, baby, no. What did he do to you?" He

wanted to scream. He wanted to roar. This was his fault. His failure to destroy the vampire had put Maxine in danger, had led the vampire to her.

Her head nodded lifelessly into the cradle of his arm, and he moaned at the sight of the jagged, torn flesh of her neck.

"I'm sorry. So sorry." She was so pale. White and cold as death. Not dead though. He could feel her heart beating. It was faint and slow—so slow—but it was there. He had to get her inside as soon as possible.

Rising with her slight body in his arms, Baron carried her to the door. Rhys stopped him just inside. "I'm sorry Baron, but I can't let you bring her in here."

"I have to Rhys. I know her. She's...special to me. How Devon knew...I don't know. But I can't leave her for the sun. Even if she's been...turned. There has to be a way. I'll find another way."

"I understand. I really do." Rhys' voice was thick with regret as he dragged a hand through his thick mane of hair, a telling habit that came out at times when he was forced to assume a leadership role with the Immortals. "But have you thought about what will happen when she awakens?"

Baron's arms tightened around Maxine, and he gazed down at her. Despite the drying blood and dirt, the deathly pallor in her face, she looked peaceful, calm.

She was Maxine. He hadn't seen in her over two years, but she hadn't changed much. She was still too beautiful for words. And it still caused an awful pain in his chest to look at her.

"I don't know, but I'll have to deal with it." He clenched his teeth and faced his mentor, his fearless leader, his friend. "She can't die, Rhys. She's too important. Not only to me, but—" *Shit.* "I know it's a lot to ask, and I wouldn't do anything to put Amy and Diana in any danger, but I need to have somewhere safe to take her and see her through this. Just while the sun is up.

Tonight I'll take her out of here and stay away until we get through this."

Rhys closed his eyes, obviously struggling with his decision. He shook his head. "There's more to it than just getting her through the turn, Baron. When she wakes up, she won't be the woman you knew. She'll be hungry. Hungry for blood. And she won't have any control over the need—no better than an animal. It's too dangerous." Rhys looked torn. "Amy's pregnant. And with that kind of dynamic in play...I just can't risk it."

Pregnant? "Oh, wow. I...I didn't know. I didn't think that you could, I mean... Anyway, I understand."

Baron's focus turned back to the woman in his arms. How much time before the sun came up? It couldn't be more than minutes now. What was he going to do? Where could he go to keep her safe? He still kept an apartment, but that was a twenty minute drive through town, and he hadn't been there in months.

Rhys cleared his throat. "Look, this might be a good time for Amy and me to head out. She's been wanting to go to L.A. After what happened with Gideon, he hasn't been the same and she's worried about him."

Baron knew what Gideon had been through, and he could seriously relate, but now he was just glad for any excuse to get Amy out of here.

Holy shit, if she was really pregnant...the big man was right, they couldn't afford for her to be put in any danger. The last thing they needed was for Amy to show as a blip on Devon's radar, another target in his sadistic game of revenge. Whatever was destined to go down with this vampire situation, he didn't want to be responsible for anyone else being hurt.

"I understand man," Baron assured Rhys. "You guys need to go."

Rhys paused, looking as if he wanted to say something but it was getting stuck in his craw. "Yeah, we're going to go." He cleared his throat. "You have my permission to bring your woman inside and do what you need to do, but I have to take Amy out of here. She's my priority."

Baron knew it went against the grain for Rhys to take off when a fight was brewing, for him to leave others to put their lives on the line. "Rhys, thanks. Don't sweat it. Take care of your wife."

Rhys nodded. "I'll talk to Alric and the twins. And while I'm gone, you keep them in the loop. You do not play it solo, you understand? I trust you to stay and deal with this situation. I trust you to take care of the vampire while I'm gone. I trust you, Baron, so *don't fuck it up.*"

Baron let out an audible sigh of relief. "Rhys. I...thanks."

Rhys glanced down at Maxine, who was still and pale as death. "The vampire population has always kept a low profile, and I've rarely had to deal with them—especially rogues like this Devon asshole—because they tend to take care of their own problems. I admit that I don't know a lot about them." He met Baron's eyes. "But I've heard that when a newly turned vampire first awakens, the hunger is immense, and that the first drink says a lot in determining the course of the vampire's future." He stopped, his gaze penetrating, serious. "Look, I don't know how you want to handle this thing. But it might just be that her only chance of coming through this is..."

"What? Come on Rhys, I'm flying blind here. If you know something that will help me save her, you've got to tell me."

"Your blood. She'll need it from you. Given freely. Hopefully, your Immortal blood and honorable spirit will give her the strength she needs to fight the tainted blood of the vampire."

Baron nodded, fear spiking in his veins. His "spirit" was far from honorable. It was very likely just as tainted and black as the vampire's.

"Thanks," he muttered.

"Like I said, I'm trusting you with this, Baron. Take care of the vampire," Rhys ordered. "And do it fast, because the last thing you're going to want if the situation goes any further down the toilet is the Enforcer to get his ass involved."

"Enforcer?" Baron asked. Had he heard that term somewhere before? "You mean like the vampire police?"

"Yeah, something like that. There used to be more of them, but from what I understand now there's only the one. And he's a big, mean motherfucker."

Baron barked out a short laugh. "Ah, so he's just like you. Glad I know what to look out for."

"Laugh it up, but vampires really don't like rogues in their midst messing with the rules, and this guy takes care of them in a big way. So just keep your eyes open and get the job done."

The Immortal started to go, but he turned back once more and stared Baron down with his icy silver gaze. "Be very careful, Baron. When I get back, you had better still be in one piece." The gruff show of concern was uncharacteristic of the big man, who was still uncomfortable in his role as mentor and leader. It was rare for him to show any emotion except to his mate. When it came to Amy, Rhys was a total sap, but he was a sap who loved his woman and had gained a little peace and humanity through that love, something Baron could totally respect. He instinctively held Max just a little tighter.

"Amy and I will be out of here in an hour." Rhys glanced once more at the bundle in Baron's arms and nodded before making his way down the hall.

"Rhys," Baron called after him.

"Yeah?" He turned back.

"Will she be okay?"

Rhys paused, his expression guarded. "I honestly don't know. But with you to help her through it...maybe she has a chance."

Chapter Four

Baron brought Max to his rooms and right through to the connecting bathroom, where he laid her down on the floor so that he could strip her clothes from her chilled body.

Her shirt was torn, ragged and so badly destroyed, it disintegrated in his fingers as it fell from her, revealing the pale curve of shoulder and the delicate black strap of her skimpy lace bra, a useless contraption that did nothing to disguise the rosy nipples that puckered beneath the fabric.

He wrenched his gaze from her chest, staring hard at the uninteresting geometric pattern in the ceramic floor tiles. Hell, he wasn't made of stone—or maybe he was, since that's exactly what he felt like.

Baron continued to undress her, moving to the stiff button and zipper of her heavy denim jeans. He paused at the chore when the tips of his tingling fingers brushed across Max's smooth white belly. God, he was such a sick bastard. The touch of her cold, clammy skin should not be making him hard right now.

He muttered his grievances to the floor, forcing himself to focus as he tugged the blood-spattered denim down her legs. The garments would have to be burned later, but for now, he dumped the jeans and her shirt in the corner of the room.

That was it. He knew his limits and dared not remove her bra and panties, even though the thin, gauzy scraps of lace kept drawing his eyes to the very places he was trying to avoid.

She was so still, but her chest rose and fell with short, slightly uneven breaths. He couldn't bear to look at the dark, maroon colored blood that had dried to a hard crust on the skin of her neck and breasts, and in her hair. He fought an insane urge to scrub her skin raw until it was gone, but he had a heavy feeling that no matter how much he washed her, he would still see blood staining her skin in his dreams for many a night.

Standing, he turned on the tap to fill the tub with hot water—the hotter the better to bring color back to her skin—and then carefully, so carefully, he lifted her into it.

She was thinner than he remembered, way too thin. Since when had she gotten so skinny? And why?

Max had been thin like this when he first met her, back when they were teenagers. But as she started hanging out with Baron's brother, who noticed everything—including the fact that his newest friend never seemed to have enough to eat—Jackson had contrived devious schemes to make sure Max ended up staying for dinner at least once or twice a week, and it wasn't long before she'd started to fill out nicely. Too nicely, it seemed. Baron remembered the first time he had really noticed just how much. She had been sweet sixteen and he a randy seventeen, so smug and caught up in his badass senior self, he hadn't paid much attention to the unfashionable waif his brother had befriended. He was just relieved Jackson finally *had* a friend, since it took some of the responsibilities off his shoulders.

Baron had gone upstairs to tell Jackson about his football game. When he opened the door to his brother's room, Max was sprawled on her back across Jackson's bed, her head tilted over the edge as she watched him at his desk, pounding away at the desktop computer. They were laughing about something, and Baron had been transfixed by the way Max's pert teenage breasts pressed against the soft cotton of her well worn, tight shirt, fascinated by the way it had ridden up to show the smooth curve of her belly.

His mouth had gone bone dry, and so he'd cleared his throat, which had gotten their attention. Max caught the look in his eyes and glared back at him, so he made some vague, lame excuses and left them alone, but that moment had been the beginning of the end for him.

Now, as Baron drew a wet, soapy cloth over Max's bruised and battered body, he tried very hard not to think of the past, but couldn't help wondering what she had been doing with her life since he left. Jackson used to send him e-mails—once a month or so—before Baron effectively disappeared, but he had rarely mentioned Maxine. Not, Baron suspected, out of any consideration for his feelings, probably more out of respect for Max's wishes, since she had always been very clear about how she felt about him. Baron was certain that *hate* would have been a kind word to use for what Max felt when it came to him.

Baron kept one arm firmly around Max's upper back as she lay in the steaming water so that her head wouldn't slip under the surface. Washing her face, he noticed the dark circles under her eyes. Lines of strain creased her brow, hinting at pain being felt even though she was unconscious. He could feel a monster sized goose egg pushing on the back of her skull, and a large purple bruise was rising rapidly along the smooth line of her fragile jaw. His hand reflexively clenched into a tight, angry fist around the wet cloth at the visible signs of how she had suffered—because of him.

Tenderly, he bathed her, taking care to make sure there was no trace of dirt or blood left on her anywhere. When he had her dry and warm and wrapped up in a thick terrycloth towel, he carried her back into his bedroom and sat with her cradled in his arms on the bed, his back propped up against the headboard.

He breathed in the clean, fresh smell of his own spicy scented soap and noted that her breathing seemed a little easier.

For a long time he sat there, memories he had easily repressed for years now battering against the wall he long ago built around them, slipping through cracks that hadn't been there even an hour ago, but were getting wider and longer by the moment.

Their first meeting. Their first fight—both had occurred that same day.

And their first kiss.

The one time they had made love.

God, what a disaster that had been.

Despite his every effort to stop them, all the memories rushed forward. A tidal wave crashing into the dusty, deserted corners of his mind, stirring up emotions he didn't want, stirring up regrets he couldn't afford, desires he didn't deserve to have.

Unable to stand it anymore, he gently unwrapped himself from Maxine and tucked her beneath the covers. He paced the floor. Back and forth. Shooting worried glances at her still form on every pass.

She still hadn't moved.

He should have asked Rhys a lot more questions before the Immortal left the compound with Amy, but at the time, he hadn't been thinking of anything except getting Max inside to safety.

Picking up the telephone handset from the bedside table, he dialed Alric's cell number. He didn't know whether or not Rhys would have had time to call, and Baron should at least warn his friend about Devon's attack.

Alric picked up quickly, as if he had been expecting Baron's call. "Yeah."

"Alric, where are you?"

"Hey, man, I'm about ready to head over there with Diana right now." The line was quiet, and Baron could picture the huge warrior struggling for words. "I'm so sorry Baron..."

"Hey, don't. It...I'm just glad that Devon didn't get to Diana, too. You probably shouldn't bring her here right now." Baron took a deep breath. "I don't know what's going to happen when Max wakes up."

"Max?"

"Yeah. Um, short for Maxine. She's someone from my past." The past. *Dammit*. In this case, the past should not have been able to come back to haunt him. No one should have been able to get far enough into his head that they would find any trace of Maxine there.

He hadn't even dared look back since the day he left that town and that life for good.

Alric sighed. "I understand, my man, but the compound is the safest place for both Diana and your girl. We'll all be doubly careful, but you're going to need some help dealing with this, and we've already decided. We're your friends and we're in this together."

"But—"

"Case closed. We're on our way."

Baron groaned. He knew Alric wouldn't take no for an answer—both he and Diana were too brave and too honorable—and he couldn't very well barricade the doors, since the warrior had all of the security codes and the keys. "Fine," he bit out. "I appreciate the help. Speaking of which, do we have any info on vampires? I need to know everything there is to know about what we're in for—before Max wakes up."

"I know that Roland scanned all our ancient texts a while back. It took him something like five years to do, and he's been adding to it ever since. Just tap into the online archive system and type in 'vampire'. It should contain whatever information we have on them since the dawn of time or somewhere thereabouts."

"Thanks."

"No problem. When Diana and I get there, we'll give you a hand. Talk to you later."

"Oh, hey, wait," Baron hoped that Alric hadn't already signed off.

"Yeah, I'm still here."

"Really." Baron paused. "Thanks."

There was an instant of dead air, sympathetic in its silence. "Hey, pal, don't worry. We've all got your back. Especially Rhys, even though he has to put Amy and the baby as his first priority. You know that right?"

"Of course.."

Baron put the phone down, his eyes on Maxine. How had this happened? How was he going to get her through it? And how the fuck had Devon known to use her against him?

Baron and Alric had last sent Devon fleeing like the blood-sucking coward he was two nights ago. He had been injured from the fire they set to burn him out of his latest hidey-hole down by the docks. It should have been impossible for him to go all the way to Rockford in that condition, come back dragging Maxine in tow, and still have enough time to do...what he did to her, before dumping her on his doorstep.

But that meant... Could Max have already been in Chandler?

Baron hadn't told Jackson or Max where he was. Had tried to make damn sure they didn't know, but he somehow doubted this was a happy coincidence. If Max somehow found out he was in Chandler, then she couldn't have come here for any good reason. Baron sighed as he realized that he was going to have to call his brother.

Shit. That was a swimming pool full of snakes he really wasn't ready to dive into.

First things first—he had to find every scrap of information he could about vampires.

Chapter Five

"Is he all right?"

Alric shook his head as he turned to his wife and took her into his arms. "I'm not sure, princess," he admitted, resting his chin on top of her head. "He's taking this very seriously, and he's determined to save the woman. Honestly, this is a Baron that I don't know anything about."

For the moment, they were still in bed, having been awakened a little while ago by Rhys' phone call. "What do you mean?" Diana curled her body into his and wrapped her arms around his waist.

"I've never seen him like this. Since Baron's been with us, he hasn't ever mentioned his past. Where he came from, what he did. If Rhys hadn't done a background check back when the kid went through the change, we wouldn't even know that he was special ops for the government—although seeing his expertise with a rifle probably would have tipped us off." Alric's fingers played with the ends of Diana's short, baby-soft, blond hair, and he breathed in the fresh scent of her subtle, floral-scented shampoo.

"But I would think that's pretty normal, isn't it? I can't see any of you guys wanting to get all touchy feely, talking about the lives you left behind. But that doesn't mean Baron's got some deep, dark, secret past that tortures him."

Pulling back, he met Diana's knowing green eyes, heard what she had left unsaid. He drank in the love and understanding reflected there and sighed. "Yeah, maybe. But beneath all of his practical jokes, grandstanding and whorin'—uh, playing the field with the women—"

Diana chuckled and shook her head. "What? You think I don't know your friend is a disgusting man-whore?"

Alric groaned. "Yeah. But besides that, he's a good man. And underneath the façade of casual indifference, he's haunted by his ghosts just as much as we all are." Taking Diana's hand, Alric squeezed it and thanked God for her. "And given what I heard in his voice tonight, one of those ghosts is a girl named Max."

The darkness had her.

She couldn't escape. And there was a monster in here with her.

It was strong, and she was tired. So tired. Weak. Something had happened to her, something terrible...but the memory of it eluded her, which was probably for the best. She didn't need to know how the monster got inside. It was here. And it was desperate to take her, to transform her. It wanted to destroy her...and it was winning.

She fought, but even though her mind was strong, the evil was stronger. Ruthlessly, it probed and ripped through all the layers of her subconscious, leaving nothing intact, raping her psyche until she was forced to retreat down into the deepest cavity of her mind. The darkest corner of herself where she lost all sense of time or place, reality and nightmares. There she had no name, no past, no future. It was just her and the monster. *Maxine* was gone.

Lost.

The woman left behind was ruled by pain, ruled by

fear. She *was* fear.

And the monster roared with triumph.

The beast wanted more, and she feared she would be trapped inside her own mind for the rest of eternity with it.

The constant torture overwhelmed her, weakened her. And then even that was dwarfed by the onset of hunger. Unimaginable hunger that built and built, stronger and stronger, demanding. It wouldn't let her succumb to peaceful oblivion, wouldn't let her retreat from herself.

The hunger drove her consciousness back out of her mind and into her body, a body shivering from cold, from the chill of death itself. A body that nevertheless burned with fever and was wracked with tremors. Every limb aching and every muscle shrieking.

She twisted and writhed in a desperate attempt to escape her own body, but the pain and hunger were everywhere. She tried to scream, but couldn't get a whisper of sound through the swollen passage of her throat, or past her dry and cracked lips. Her screams were but a wheezing rush of air, the echo sounding only in the blackness of her mind where the monster laughed.

She didn't know how long it went on, time was something that had ceased to exist for her. She gradually became aware that someone held her as she thrashed about, held her down with a grip like twin vices pinning each of her shoulders. She scratched and kicked and bucked against the restraint, but it did her no good.

Weak. God, she hated to be so weak.

Her head tossed from side to side as bile rose in her throat, tainting her mouth with a sour metallic taste. Her stomach contracted with sharp pangs. The hunger was going to consume her, might even do her in before the monster had a chance to break down the last of her walls. She felt it crawling beneath her skin, just as she felt her incisors lengthening, the sharp points digging into her lip.

A voice in her ear, whispering. Words of love and

encouragement, expressing faith in her strength and belief in her ability to endure.

She heard but rebelled against the false promises, wary of the monster in her mind that would trick her if it could.

She didn't have a chance, she was certain of it. But still she continued to fight. For control. For her life. If only she could reclaim her mind and sate the hunger...but it was so hard. She wanted to give in, to make it easy on herself and just give the monster what it wanted. Maybe if she relinquished her body and her mind, then it might let her sleep, let her leave the pain behind and escape into merciful, silent nothingness.

But that other voice continued to whisper. Urgent. Telling her she was stronger than this. Telling her she couldn't give up. Telling her to come back to him.

Him?

Did she believe? It seemed so hard. It was all so much effort, and for what? What did she have to live for anyway?

Baron.

The name shot into her brain, spearing through the pain and fear. A sizzling bolt of lightning over a churning black sea. *Him.* The image rose in her mind's eye, of a golden-haired boy with clear blue eyes and a brilliant smile.

She felt the surge of an unexpected reserve of strength, and the part of her that was still Maxine started to claw her way back out of the deep dark pit inside of herself.

She left the monster in that pit, left it howling with rage as she fought for focus and strength. Using the image glowing brightly in her mind as a lifeline, a rope with which she was able to pull herself out. She used it as a shield against the hunger and the pain. She used it as a sword against the beast battering away at her sanity.

And all of a sudden, she had hope again, hope that the

monster would not win.

When Maxine opened her eyes and couldn't see, she started to panic, thinking that the monster still played tricks with her mind.

Her breathing started coming in harsh, raspy moans of anguish until she realized with a blurting, heavy sigh of relief that she *could* see something—indistinct, bulky shapes in the shadows, familiar furniture sized shapes. Thank God. This was not the madness of her mind playing with her, but simply a darkened bedroom with a dresser along one wall, a wardrobe against another. Just darkness, your average garden-variety shadows. Just a room.

Albeit an unfamiliar room.

She was assimilating that fact when she detected the steady breathing of another person. It wasn't her breathing, hers was still shaky and raspy from fear. She wasn't alone in this strange room.

The scent grabbed her attention next—a musky, natural perfume that filled all of her senses, acting on her system like a drug as it called to her, bringing the hunger from her nightmare rushing back with a vengeance. She couldn't stop herself from breathing deeply, eager to take it into herself.

"Max."

Baron.

Was she surprised?

No.

Oddly enough, Max had somehow known it was him. She couldn't quite remember the reason why he was here, or how, but she knew it had been Baron who held her together during the worst of it. That it was Baron who had held her sanity in his hands as she struggled with her demons.

But had she won or lost? Should she thank him for his

efforts or curse him?

If the way she felt right now was any indication...

She sighed, running her tongue out along dry, parched lips. Her memories of the previous night were cloaked in murky shadows, suggestions of pain and darkness that she couldn't bear to dig into. Not yet.

The last clear memory she had was of getting stuck on the side of the road and being attacked. Beyond that, she couldn't be sure of anything. The rest was all blood and pain and evil laughter ringing cruelly and endlessly in her head.

Max remembered being hurt. Badly. She carefully rotated her shoulder—still firmly located within the confines of its socket—it moved smoothly and without pain. Then she flexed her jaw, and while it felt tender and a little sore, it was by no means broken.

Oh, God. Had any of that been real? Or had she already been run over by the tractor trailer of insanity, here on the road to the psych ward?

If it was true, then by all rights she should probably be dead. That she seemed perfectly healthy—physically, at least—she couldn't believe was the result of some opportune act of divine intervention, but something else entirely. She just couldn't remember...

Where am I?

"Max." He called her name again. Baron. She could smell him. Just when had he started smelling so good? Like spices and chocolate and mint. He definitely hadn't smelled like that before. Then again, two years had passed since she'd seen him last, and obviously, those years had brought with them a few changes—like that deep, rumbling voice that set the hairs on her forearms and the back of her neck to dancing.

Ah, he was close. She only now realized that he was *right* here. Right beside her...*lying* beside her. In a bed. Oh wow, it had been a long, long time since she had shared this kind of proximity with a man. She must still

55

be unconscious, because Baron sharing mattress space with her—that was a reality that existed only in her most desperate fantasies, despite their one night together years ago.

Max gasped at the rolling spasm low in her belly, a wrenching pain that got stronger as she breathed in Baron's delicious scent.

Somehow it was him. He was making her feel this way. It was his closeness that intensified the...*hunger*. The pain that gnawed frantically at her gut.

He murmured to her some more, words she didn't quite catch. She turned her head blindly toward the sound of his voice. Forcing her eyes to focus was harder than it should have been. Her vision swam, making her dizzy and nauseous. If she had been standing, she would have keeled right over.

Baron moved closer, taking her into his arms, cradling her head so that she was surrounded with warmth. His warmth. It would have been nice, but her skin was so sensitive that even this light touch felt abrasive, like fifty grit sandpaper being scraped over her arm.

She squirmed uncomfortably, and at once, his arms relaxed around her. She blinked, waiting for her eyes to focus, and when she opened them again, Baron's silhouette was less of a shadow and more substantial. More flesh...more blood.

Ah...the blood. It was his *blood* singing to her, calling out to her. To the hunger that raged now.

Oh, God. This couldn't be happening. It had to be part of the nightmare. Or maybe she was feverish and sick, imagining things. Had to be. Just a horrible nightmare, a crazed delusion.

The alternative was not possible.

But the monster inside her started clawing out of the pit she had left it in, laughing again, telling her she couldn't escape the truth, that this *was* possible, that this was no nightmare. That it was real.

No. She couldn't accept that. How could anyone accept such a thing?

The sound of Baron's steady, strong pulse was pounding in her ears now, the scent of his blood overwhelming her. His *blood*. *Oh, please, no*. Is this what she was now?

A *vampire*?

She needed to get away from him.

Her feet sliding in the bed sheets, Max wrenched herself from Baron's embrace and scrambled back as fast as she could, desperate to get some distance between them before she could no longer control the maddening cravings and insidious whispers inside her head. Reaching her arm behind her, she felt only air and tumbled from the bed onto the floor. She didn't care, the fall at least put more space between them.

"Get away from me," she said, her voice scratchy and hoarse.

"Max—" He followed her, still on the bed, but leaning over the side, his hand reaching for her.

"No," she begged, warding him off with a shake of her head. "You have to get away from me, Baron. Get out of here. Hurry."

"Baby, it's okay. It will be okay." He continued to come for her, sitting up and swinging his legs over the side of the bed now. He was dressed in long workout pants and a short-sleeved tee that was molded to his upper body.

"It isn't," she insisted, shaking her head. This would never be okay. An image of the vampire rose in her mind, his cruel grin and long teeth, eyes glittering with evil malice. She shivered. That was her. She was that monster now. "It's not okay. You don't understand."

She had to warn him. "Baron, please. You have to go. I...something happened to me last night—at least, I think it was last night. God, how long have I been out?" She shook her head. Her head was ringing and his scent was strong in her nostrils, his heartbeat pounding so loud she could hear it clearly in the space that separated them.

"I was attacked. On the road. I think by a...a *vampire*. I know it sounds..." Hell, it sounded ridiculous to her own ears, and she knew Baron wouldn't believe her—how could he?—but she needed him to. If he believed, then he would run. He would run and not come back and then she couldn't hurt him.

Her taste buds screamed, wanting something her brain couldn't bear to acknowledge.

It was getting harder and harder to resist the impulse to pounce on him. Her mouth was watering in anticipation of how he would taste. She closed her eyes tightly, willing her body under control. The feelings and urges waging war against her were so intense and overpowering that she practically drooled as she devoured the sight of him, while her stomach churned and her brain told her she was disgusting, sick.

God, if only it were a sickness.

"Max," he called. She noticed she'd been staring at his throat, watching the pulse point beating under his skin without even realizing it. "Max, it's okay. I know what happened to you. I understand what you're going through right now."

She groaned, shaking her head. He couldn't possibly know. If he knew, he would be revolted by her.

"Baron, don't try to be understanding. You can't possibly understand. Just go," she whispered, her voice catching on an involuntary sob of hopelessness as she raised her knees to her chin and wrapped her arms tightly around her legs. "Please go. I can't control it for much longer." Max clenched a fist over her stomach, pressing hard, willing the hunger to abate. But it wasn't working. The room was so saturated with his scent she couldn't escape it. Even the clothes she was wearing smelled like him. She groaned, realizing belatedly that it was because they were *his* clothes.

"Max, look at me." His voice was hard and forceful. Demanding. Surprising.

Max had once taken great care to arrange all of her memories of Baron into a neat, inflexible package—a little box with a picture on the front of a gorgeous, but useless pretty boy that she very neatly stuck up on a high, dusty shelf in her mind. When he had entered military service, that picture had remained static, unchanged. She hadn't wanted to think of him in any other way.

She hadn't wanted to think of him in *any* way at all.

For a while, that worked. He had only returned home on a very irregular basis, and they managed to avoid each other for the most part. They had come together only once, two years ago. But that encounter had been such a complete disaster, it hadn't changed her opinion of him for the better, had in fact only made it worse.

After he disappeared for good, keeping those images available whenever his name came up in conversation was one of the ways Max used to convince herself she was better off without him.

As Baron spoke, his voice reassuring and calm, the picture in her mind slowly started to shift.

Max remembered all of the times Baron had tried to tell her what to do, and how she had always laughed at him, but she couldn't imagine doing that to this man. This powerful, sure man who seemed so capable and so much in control—or was it just her imagination because she was falling apart so completely?

Max looked into his eyes and opened her mouth. She meant to plead with him again to get out of here. Instead, she groaned through another massive stomach cramp.

It was too much.

Too much.

Chapter Six

Max's teeth felt like daggers in her mouth, long and sharp. Baron's heartbeat roared in her ears like the unrelenting pattern of a tribal drum. She couldn't help it, couldn't hold back any longer. She launched herself at Baron, and in one surprisingly agile leap found herself on top of him, forcing him back on the bed.

Baron's hands gripped her forearms, holding her above him. He was strong, very strong, but whether it was the hunger driving her, or some other physical consequence of her transformation into a monster, Max's own strength seemed to have multiplied a thousand times.

"Max." His voice was so calm. Even with her body holding him down and her mouth poised inches from his throat, he was unflappable, his tone and manner radiating complete control. "Max, don't. Not like this. Don't let it consume you. You can control it."

"What?" She couldn't concentrate. Couldn't focus on anything but the pulse point throbbing steadily in Baron's neck. The blood that was so close now, she could already taste it. Coppery, thick, she could imagine it flowing into her mouth and sliding down her throat.

Her mouth watered, but at the same time her gag reflex was working overtime.

She couldn't decide whether to throw up or lick her lips.

Jesus, how could one part of her want something so badly, when every other part rebelled against it?

With a groan of disgust, she acknowledged this wasn't even the first time she had experienced the sensation of being pulled in opposite directions by her own body when it came to Baron.

"Baby, I can give you what you need, but you have to stay in control. If you don't, you're going to hurt me or hurt yourself, and neither of us wants that. You're strong and I trust you. You can do it." His voice was soothing, slow, coaching her. "Go ahead, sweetheart. Drink." His deep, sure voice was so familiar, it penetrated to the part of her that was maybe still human. The part that would rather die than do this to another person, especially to him. To Baron.

Drink.

She looked down at herself in horror, at her hands closed tightly over his shoulders, holding him down.

She abruptly sat up and back, horror at what she was about to do bringing tears to her eyes. "Oh, no. Baron, I'm so sorry."

"No, it's fine. I know you need this." He reached for her, brushing some of her hair back from her face. She had to fight not to flinch away from him.

"I can't do it. I can't drink blood. Not yours or anyone else's." Shaking her head, she put a hand to her mouth. "I should be dead. Oh, God, why didn't he just kill me?" Her mind was fracturing again, she could feel the two sides of herself—monster and human—battling it out. Who was going to win was still up in the air. "I don't know how to make it all stop. Please, Baron. You have to get out of here. Why aren't you running far away from me?"

Baron sat up and wrapped his arms around her, pulling her onto his lap and guiding her face into the crook of his neck. She struggled, trying to push him away, but he held fast. "Max, baby, it's okay," he crooned to her in a soft voice, like he would speak to a small frightened child. His hand stroked a path over her hair and down her back in an attempt to soothe her trembling body. "I know what you need, and I want you to drink from me. Take my blood with the full knowledge that I'm offering it to you of my own free will."

How could he know? How was that possible?

How could it be that his words seemed to free her? Where before it was all she could do to fight the hunger, the pain and the need, with those simple words, her body—her entire being—sighed in relief. The hunger was still there, still making her teeth throb and her bones ache, but some of the urgency abated.

Who was this man?

Where was the Baron who had slept with her and then left her on the day of his own mother's funeral, the man who deserted his brother when Jackson had desperately needed him, the man who hadn't sent a word to either Max or Jackson in over two years and had been distant even before then?

That Baron had had no problem letting them believe he might even be dead, but the man sitting with her here and now—holding her gently and stroking her back, offering her comfort—wasn't the same person. This Baron could not have been so callous and self-centered.

Unless she just wasn't giving him enough credit for his improved acting skills.

Max lifted her head and sought his gaze. Who was this man whose eyes glittered with tears, as if he shared her pain? It was true. He did. Somehow, she knew he was hurting just as much as she was. He was feeling a boatload of guilt and shame. She didn't know how she knew that, and she couldn't understand why. Yes, there were things he should feel guilt over, but this situation, at least, wasn't his fault, just a drastic result of her own stupidity.

Max felt off balance. Something wasn't right.

She realized part of that feeling came from the look in his eyes. Even filled with sympathetic understanding, they seemed like twin gems, not warm like sapphires, but cold, liquid crystal. Odd. She could have sworn Baron's eyes were the same color as Jackson's, a bright sky blue. How, after so many years, had she never known they were really this clear silvery color?

It didn't help, was just one more thing to throw her further off balance.

Who was this man who held her in his arms and calmly offered to feed her with his own blood to quench her hunger? Why hadn't he run from her in terror, or showed any surprise at her crazed, incoherent claims?

And just what exactly had he been doing with his life since he'd been gone from hers, that none of this seemed to faze him?

Baron leaned in close and brushed his lips against her mouth. Not even a real kiss; it was light and sweet, so completely not what she would have expected from him. Actually, she hadn't thought to feel his mouth on hers ever again, and if asked, Max would have said that she didn't want it.

"Do it, Max," he urged. Turning his face to the side, he bared his neck to her in blatant invitation.

How could she do this?

How could she not?

She didn't have the strength to withstand the insistent demand of the hunger. The cravings were impossible to resist any longer.

With a low moan her mouth descended to his neck.

Still trying to fight the hunger, to delay what seemed to be the inevitable, at first she simply ran her tongue over his skin. She savored the salty male taste of him, felt the steady pounding of his pulse under her mouth. But then he groaned and tightened his arms around her, forcing a more intimate embrace, forcing Max to recognize just how much the old Baron had really changed.

His body was rock solid against hers, from the awesomely defined biceps twitching under her fingertips, the muscled thighs that acted not so much as a cushion for her thighs, but a concrete slab, to the hard length that stretched his loose-fitting workout pants and pressed into her belly.

She moved closer, pressing her aching breasts against the hard wall of his chest. Her nipples tightened and a little shock of pleasure shot through her to the wet core between her thighs.

Oh.

Oh, no.

She couldn't want that, not with him. It was too embarrassing. But her traitorous body didn't seem to care. It wanted. It desired. It hungered.

The intensity of her reactions threw her off balance, and she couldn't deny the persistent demands of her body any longer.

She struck hard. It was instinctive, primal, and Baron jerked beneath her.

Now it was *she* who held *him*. She was in control. Powerful. Strong. Not a victim. Never again.

Max's palm cradled his head to her as her mouth opened over his throat and her teeth punctured his vein.

The first drop of his blood on her tongue shattered her, and she groaned as the pleasure flooded all of her senses. Taste. Smell. Touch—All overwhelmed by sensation.

She started to draw on his vein, taking his life's blood into her mouth, into her body, and the both of them moaned together in matching expressions of pleasure. The sane part of her was disgusted with herself, but another part of her—a primitive, dangerous part—felt natural, excited, uninhibited...and totally turned on.

Max was mortified by the strong sexual reaction she was having to Baron's closeness, and blamed it on the intimacy of their position and the uniqueness of the situation. Any other explanation simply wasn't acceptable, and God willing, she would never have to examine her reactions to this moment in time, to this situation, to this man.

Baron hadn't known that it would feel like this.

Nothing he had read suggested that there would be a sexual component of any kind to the act of giving and taking blood—and you'd think someone would have found that part interesting enough to mention. All the cheap B-movies he'd watched as a teenager had liked to connect vampires with sex, but Baron never once considered that Hollywood might actually be using the *truth* to sell films. Go figure.

He'd gone from worry and fear when Max remained unconscious for so long, to wanting to reassure her and comfort her as one might a frightened child when she had finally awakened, to being desperate to have her beneath him and bury himself inside of her as soon as he'd heard the husky sound of her voice.

Now, with her body pressed close and her teeth sunk into his neck, pulling on his vein, his cock surged to throbbing, aching life, demanding similar attention.

Slowly and carefully, so as not to startle her, Baron leaned back, pulling her with him so he lay full length on the bed with her body blanketing him. She moaned against his throat, her breasts, hips and thighs snug against him. He ran his hands up and down her arms, needing to touch her while her mouth pulled on his neck. The sensation of having her feed from him, of the sexy, soft sounds of her sucking, was an erotic feeling like nothing he'd ever experienced before. Intimate. Sexy.

But then, Max had always been sexy. Too sexy for his peace of mind.

He'd had to give her up.

Maybe that's why he went through women like

single-ply bathroom tissue. Because he knew that he could have had it all, but let it slip from his fingers. All the other women were simply not worth the effort. He didn't want to get to know them, so he didn't. He didn't care about any of them, so it made no difference which one he used to slake his lust.

But now, for the first time in years, Baron felt alive again, more than alive—filled with energy, with focus. He had a purpose, something that only he could do.

As an Immortal, he was a good fighter, but he was new to the game and there were others whose skill far surpassed his own. It was a simple fact. If he were gone, no one would really miss him. There would be another to fill his place before his corpse had even cooled.

As a human, he had been a good soldier, but even that was lost to him now.

He definitely hadn't been a good brother, as Jackson would no doubt attest to if he ever saw Baron again.

But right at this moment he was the only man for this job, there was nowhere else he could be but here with Maxine. There was nothing else he could do. He could give her what she needed like no other.

His hands continued to wander. He wanted to know her, to rediscover all of the dips and curves that his body had missed since they had been apart. What had changed. What had remained the same. It was a bad idea, but with her mouth on him and his lifeblood pouring into her, he just couldn't find the strength to heed any of the old arguments.

She was his.

Even if they never saw each other again after this moment, Max would be a part of him forever. If he were honest, she had been even before this earth-shattering event brought them back together after the years spent apart.

How long it had been since she started to drink? Moments only, though it seemed like eons of blissful union between them, and he hadn't even gotten her naked, hadn't yet slid his fingers inside of her like he wanted to do.

Shit, he had to stop thinking like that.

This wasn't about sex. He refused to jump all over the first excuse to jump on *her*. Max already hated him enough, and when this was over, she would leave. She *should* leave.

She *wasn't* his, could never be, and Baron wasn't going to be getting her naked, except maybe in his dreams. There were reasons why it was so, why it had to be that way, and those reasons hadn't changed, even though so many other things *had*.

Still, for just this moment...he raised a knee so that her pelvis was cradled between his thighs, curled his fingers into the supple flesh of her ass. When she whimpered and rolled her hips in closer, his cock surged against his thin cotton pants, and he dropped his head back against the headboard with a low groan, the action improving her access to his vein.

In this moment Baron would simply let himself feel, and deal with the consequences later.

Max gasped against his neck and Baron felt the gentle tugging on his throat ease. She pushed her hands against his chest to move off of him. He tightened his hold on her, wanting to keep her close, beg her to take more, but knew it was a bad idea. He wasn't dizzy or weak from the lost blood and thought she probably could have used more, but he wanted her to feel like she was the one with the control. He wanted her to know that the hunger didn't control her, and that even he didn't control her. So he let her pull away.

He watched her lick her bottom lip of the light sheen of blood that coated them. "Feel better?" he asked. "Do you still have any pain?"

She shook her head, two fingers touching her mouth. "Oh, no. Baron, I'm so sorry. I can't believe I—"

"Don't be sorry." He smiled, reaching for her hand and pulling it to his lips, placing small kisses on the pads of her fingers. "None of this was your fault."

"I can't believe that I did that...I mean that you let me..." She struggled to get the words out as she pulled her hand back and made a self-conscious fist at her side. "Why?"

Baron shrugged. He didn't want to examine the reasons why any more than he wanted to think about the consequences of his actions. "I couldn't let you die, Max."

Dammit. He hadn't meant to say that.

She was watching him now, looking for something in his expression, but Baron turned away, moving off of the bed to put some distance between them before he faced her again. "Are you sure you feel okay?"

He watched her. She seemed to be cataloguing all of her various body parts and functions. He felt a surge of fierce pride in her. Pragmatic as always, Max looked tense but showed no fear, even though he knew she must be very frightened and confused. When she returned his look, she seemed relieved, more relaxed. "Yeah. I guess. I feel...good. Different, though."

"That's okay." He nodded and took her hand, squeezing her fingers in an attempt at reassurance. "Good. I'm glad."

Max looked around the room, probably noticing her surroundings for the first time. She had always been very observant. He wondered what she would make of all this—the compound, the security, his friends. How much did he tell her?

"Where is this place?" she asked. "I don't understand how I got here. How did *you* get here? I mean, how did you know that I was in Chandler looking for you?"

"So you were already in Chandler?" Damn, he hadn't known that. If he had, maybe all of this could have been prevented. He sighed. Did he even want to know why?

There was only one thing that would have brought Max to Chandler looking for him, and it wasn't anything good. "How did you even know where to find me?"

She snorted. "I'm a PI, Baron. Finding people is what I do for a living, especially when they don't want to be found."

Max was a private investigator? Great. Trouble with a license to carry.

She eyed him, a dangerous look in her sparkling eyes. "Aren't you even going to ask about your brother?"

His own expression hardened. "I hadn't planned to, no." He could tell from the tightening of her jaw that she was not impressed with his answer.

She pulled her hand out of his grasp. "Well, there you are. And just as I was wondering where the old Baron had gotten to. At least now I know the world hasn't flipped axes on me. You're still an asshole after all." With that she stood and headed into the connecting bathroom, slamming the door closed behind her.

Chapter Seven

Max emerged from a long, hot shower feeling clean if not exactly back to normal. Wrapping a huge towel around her body, she reached for a second one to dry her hair with. When that was done, she hesitated, not sure whether she could face herself in the mirror. But of all the epithets which had been used in the past to describe Maxine Deveraux, coward was never one of them.

Turning to the mirror and wiping away the misty layer of condensation, Max let out a little sigh, relieved to see that she didn't *look* like a monster. There were no lingering bruises or scrapes to give evidence to her ordeal. She felt whole. She even felt human. Though she had a deathly suspicion that she actually wasn't.

Small telltale signs were there, though. Signs that would no doubt be overlooked by most, but to Max they were glaringly obvious.

There were the teeth, for one. She smiled. Lifted her lips back, poked and prodded at her incisors. They were definitely sharper and pointier than she remembered them being, but otherwise they looked normal, not like she expected a blood-crazed vampire's teeth should look. Remembering how impossibly long they had felt in her mouth when the hunger was at its strongest, Max decided they must extend out and retract back into her gums, although she couldn't figure out how.

Her attention shifted to examine the rest of her body, and she confirmed her earlier impression that vampirism had given her a great deal more strength than she'd had as a human. She could feel it coursing through her like she'd been shot with a few thousand volts. Power.

It was in her eyes, too, the knowledge of what she was, of the strength it gave her. And behind all of that, the fear of what that power would do to her, of the monster she sensed still lingering within...waiting. The eyes of a stranger looked out at her from within—someone she wasn't sure that she could trust.

She dropped her head down, breaking the connection between her and the demon that gazed back through the mirror.

She took several deep breaths. She would have to deal with this eventually, and now seemed as good a time as any. With stubborn determination, she glared at her reflection, unwilling to allow the demon to intimidate her. She may not be able to vanquish it entirely, but she *would* control it.

She blinked, feeling some of the tension falling away as the shadows in her eyes dissipated. At least the color hadn't changed. Her eyes were still blue, and they weren't glowing red like Devon's had been. Hopefully, no one would know. Hopefully, only Max herself would be able to see through them to the insanity and evil that threatened her soul.

She sighed. On the whole, her body felt healthy and her mind felt her own—at least for now. She didn't know what was going to happen next, didn't want to think about the next time she would have to...drink.

Running her hands through her long, towel-dried hair, Max pulled it back from her face, noting the rosy glow in her cheeks that didn't fit with her Hollywood-made image of vampires as pale, white-skinned creatures that hissed with pain when touched by the light. Oh, God, was the flush that stained her skin a result of Baron's blood flowing in her veins? *Don't think about it*. There were just some things it was better not to contemplate.

This whole situation was intolerable. There must be something that she could do to go back, to reverse whatever it was that had been done to her. Or maybe she should just go home and crawl under her covers for the next hundred years or so. That thought raised the question of whether or not the vampire stories were true when it came to the living forever thing. And what about the sunshine and garlic thing? Myth or reality?

Answers were in short supply at the moment, and Max refused to torture herself with what-if scenarios. Putting the thoughts from her mind, she straightened in front of the sink and pulled open a drawer, looking for toothpaste. It galled her to have to use anything of Baron's—even the soap in the shower—but some things couldn't be helped. She seriously needed to scrub her teeth clean.

Some paste on her finger did the job well enough, and then Max cautiously opened the bathroom door, still wrapped in the towel. Since she had awakened wearing what she assumed were Baron's boxers and one of his t-shirts—a condition that brought an embarrassed heat to her cheeks to think of it now that her mind and body weren't so distracted—Max surmised that her overnight bag hadn't been retrieved from her poor, destroyed car. Which meant she would probably have to borrow more of Baron's clothes until she could get out of here and hit a mall.

Leaving the still steamy bathroom behind her, she entered the bedroom, thankful that Baron was gone. She noticed there was a fresh set of joggers and a shirt on the bed, which had ostensibly been left for her to wear.

Pulling on the clothes, Max was made very much aware of the fact that she was without any underwear whatsoever and that, again, these were Baron's clothes covering her nakedness. And *that* reminded her quite brutally that only a very short time ago she had been writhing shamelessly on his lap, wanting to be naked with him, needing to be naked with him.

She tried to push the images from her mind and fight her body's automatic response, but it was a losing battle. Each of her senses was heightened to such a degree that even though the garments she laid over her skin had obviously been freshly laundered, Max breathed in a musky male scent from deep within the fibers of the well-worn cotton shirt, a scent she could only associate with Baron. As the soft fabric swept across her nipples, they tightened to painful little buds, sending bursts of electricity to her already swollen center, where she could feel the moisture seeping from her core to dampen the thin nylon of the borrowed joggers.

The combination of Baron's scent mingling with her own intensified the rush of need in her belly, stirring the brutal hunger again. A gasp of dismay escaped her lips, and the flush of desire was abruptly washed away like she'd been hit with a blast of cold water.

Was her need to feed connected so closely to sexual attraction then? Would she want to suck on someone's artery every time she sucked face?

God, she hoped not. She really, really hoped not. Baron may have offered his vein to her this one time, and in her desperation and weakness she had taken it, but she'd be damned if she let herself get that close to him again...especially if her body was going to turn traitor on her.

She could control it; the monster would not control her.

Forcing her mind to focus, Max wondered what time it was, what day it was. And she wondered again just *where* she was. Baron hadn't answered her when she'd asked him earlier.

Was it safe to leave the room, she wondered, or was she going to run into someone? A girlfriend maybe?

Jesus, she hoped not.

No, even Baron had enough decency that he wouldn't do that to her...right?

Opening the door, Max stepped out into a long, brightly lit hallway. She looked up and down the corridor, *eeny-meeny-miney-mo* ringing in her head, then decided to go left.

Turned out she made a good choice. At the end of the hall, she was met with a set of double doors. She shrugged her shoulders. If Baron didn't want her to snoop, he should have locked her in his room, not that it would have stopped her. She did a security gig once for a client and learned a lot about computerized systems like the one this place looked to be rigged with. She'd already seen the sensors mounted on the walls of the corridors.

She walked into a large living area filled with several cozy-looking chairs and small side tables. A large flat-screen TV hung on one wall, and at the other end of the room, was a sweet looking pool table with a bar-style, antique-glass lampshade positioned directly above it.

What was this place?

After the death of his mother two years ago, Baron cut all contact with Jackson and effectively disappeared. This was where he'd gone?

Max would have been content to never see him again, but at Jackson's behest, she spent some time trying to track Baron down. To her surprise she discovered that he had been discharged from service. Of course, he hadn't bothered to let anyone know. Max had to hear it from his former CO, who finally agreed to give her only that one minor detail when she confessed that his brother was dying. And only after handing her the hour-long, official run-around about privacy issues and national security.

But if Baron wasn't in the service anymore, why was he living in this place? It looked like some kind of barracks or military base. The communal living area was a dead giveaway to the fact that it wasn't your average apartment building.

Maybe this was a new concept for an open-style singles building. That would suit the carefree, playboy Baron that Max remembered.

She crossed the room to another set of doors, and pushing through them, she was greeted with the bright lights and clean surfaces of a huge kitchen, but like no kitchen that Max had ever had the pleasure of cooking out of. Not that she cooked.

There were several large stainless steel appliances, and a double range. A walk-in freezer was built into one wall. Everything was of restaurant quality, top of the line, and from the looks of it, fairly new.

Her private investigator's brain churned with speculation. Someone here definitely had money.

Max thought about the large denominations that had started appearing in Jackson's bank account every first Monday of the month since his mother died.

They had known right away the money was coming from Baron...somehow. Jackson had wanted to give it back, but neither of them had any clue where to send it. At first, they actually feared it might be some kind of death benefit being paid by the government to Baron's next of kin, and that was when Max discovered Baron had left the military.

Two months ago, Jackson's health had gone south again. After a long remission, the leukemia was back, and he went into the hospital. He asked Max to look into it again, to find Baron and bring him home.

She had argued against it. Vehemently. Despite her own reasons for not wanting to have Baron anywhere near her, she didn't believe it was good for Jackson's health to get him wound up with expectations and hopes that were just going to collapse on top of him like a deflating hot air balloon when Baron refused to show.

Max hadn't doubted her *ability* to find Baron—she was a hell of a good private investigator after all. On the other hand, the chances that she would be able to convince him he needed to come back with her and see his younger brother before it was too late...a different story entirely. If the bastard hadn't bothered to visit or call or write in two years, then he wasn't just going to raise his hand when she came into town and go, "Here I am, lead the way back home."

And after his earlier comment, Max was more convinced than ever that trying to bring Baron back home was going to be a mistake—didn't mean she wasn't going to do it, though.

She had made a promise.

With an inaudible sigh, Max approached. Baron was standing behind the kitchen counter making what looked like enough sandwiches for an army. He had changed into a clean pair of jeans and a fresh white tee, and the sight of his still-damp hair told her that he had also found some place to shower. Even to her prejudiced eye, he looked way too good. The shirt hugged his chest and torso, sleeves stretching tight over bulging biceps, jeans hanging low on narrow hips.

The look was classic Baron—simple but effective.

Max could admit that he had always been a hunk, one she could never completely resist. But had he really looked this good before? This ripped with muscle? She didn't think so.

His eyes hadn't had the same irresistibly sexy glint, nor had his bearing held the same aura of danger or the unwavering control that she sensed in him now. Was it a result of his years spent in the special forces? Something else?

Well, whatever he was doing these days definitely did a body good. Too good. He must be drinking gallons of milk.

Whatever rotten luck had brought her to Baron's doorstep—just one of many questions she still had no answers for—the fact was she had indeed found him, and now she had a chance to plead with him to come home with her...for Jackson. That was the only reason she would ever bother. She had promised Jackson she would bring Baron home, and she wasn't going to let her friend down without trying her very best.

And in the process, she planned to put her sleuthing skills to work to find out exactly what this new Baron's deal was.

"How much food do you think I'm going to eat?" she joked as he looked up and saw her standing there. "Oh wait, that's probably all for you. You always were a pig."

He laughed, his eyes bright with appreciation for her sarcastic sense of humor, and she unexpectedly felt like crying, memories of times just like this assailing her with their childhood poignancy.

Ever since Max and Jackson became friends, she and Baron had butted heads, trading insults and random, acerbic barbs whenever they came within ten feet of each other—mostly because Max had been a defensive, angry, cynical girl, and Baron had been an egotistical, self-centered jock with a hard-on for anything in a skirt...just like any boy his age.

Ah, but it didn't take a genius to see behind the faux animosity. Even Max had known they were really only dancing around something heavier, more potent.

Those encounters had been energizing.

Max would never have admitted it, but she looked forward to pitting her wits against Baron and feeling the rush of adrenaline that only he could make her feel. And back then, underneath all of the good-natured bickering, Max had honestly believed the two of them were united when it came to the one thing that really mattered...Jackson. She had been absolutely certain it would always be Jackson and Max and Baron, together against the world.

And then one day...

One stupid incident...

And all that had changed forever.

Ah, hell. Why did she let herself think about shit like that?

The lingering traces of humor faded from her lips, and she frowned. She turned her attention back to the food and looked at it with wary consideration. "Can I even eat, do you think?"

Baron smiled reassuringly at her, then put the finishing touches on a ham and cheese with lettuce, tomato, and lots of bright yellow mustard.

For her.

He remembered her favorite sandwich. Damn. That was playing dirty.

"From what I've read," he said, licking a drop of mustard from the pad of his thumb, "you can definitely eat. You actually need to eat. Unfortunately, the blood is necessary, but your body still requires the nutrients in food to stay strong and healthy."

"From what you've read?"

"Uh, yeah. After I saw what Devon did to you, I—"

Max shook her head. "Devon? How did you know the vampire's name was Devon? I don't remember telling you that." Then again, she had been pretty out of it for a long while, she could easily have...but she didn't think so.

Something about this whole situation was weird...*weirder*, anyway. And it set alarm bells tripping off in her brain. Max thought again about how neatly he had managed to not answer any of her questions up to this point, including the one about how she had ended up here, how she ended up with him.

"Wait just a damn minute," she demanded. "You want to tell me what the hell is going on? You admitted you didn't know I had come to Chandler. So how is it you still managed to find me and whisk me off to your strange apartment just in time to save me from becoming vampire kibble? And can you try explaining why none of this has you running me over to the town asylum, why you've taken it all in stride as if the term vampire is something from your everyday vocabulary?"

Baron's trap stayed firmly shut, and Max let out a frustrated snarl, but even that didn't get a response out of him. He simply picked up a long wooden-handled bread knife and cut her sandwich in half, his gaze on his task.

She could only hope that one of the perks of vampirism was the ability to shoot real daggers from your eyes when faced with someone so infuriating, but the longer Baron continued to stand there calmly before her without a long length of steel spearing into his forehead, the more she had to accept that whatever new abilities she had didn't include that nifty little trick.

Too bad.

"Come on, Baron. Spill your guts. I've had enough of this. How did you find me? What is this place? If it isn't some kind of military outfit, just what the hell have you been up to?"

She was on a roll now, eager to let it all out of her system. "For two goddamned years your brother—your good, kind, sick brother who needs your support and misses you desperately—has been even sicker with worrying where the hell you've been. You sent not one word, not even a 'hey bro, I'm still alive, and by the way, the military dumped my ass back into the civilian world'. Why Baron? Your life was in the service, Jackson told me how much you loved it. So what happened there?"

He opened his mouth as if he were going to actually tell her, but then shut it again and shook his head. *Damn!* Granted, the old Baron might have shut her out like he was doing now, but he would not have deserted his brother so completely in the first place—at least Max wouldn't have thought so...and yet it had happened.

That was a lesson she thought she had learned a long time ago, one she should never have forgotten.

Everybody leaves.

It was true, but...this felt different.

Baron had been overseas a lot after enlisting, but at least he had made an effort back then, he had tried to keep in touch with Jackson when he could, and came home when he could. Something must have happened to change that.

And she was going to find out what it was.

Chapter Eight

"What the hell is going on with you?"

He looked up and met her eyes, but his expression had shut down tighter than a bank vault in the Caymans, and she couldn't read anything from him, which made her even angrier. She wanted to scream and pound her fists against his chest when he just shook his head at her again.

"You assho—"

The sound of a strange male voice clearing his throat behind her startled Max, and she swung around.

"Uh, hey Baron. Are we interrupting you two? Do you want us to go?" Max turned back to Baron and raised her eyebrows in silent inquiry. Was this the reason he wasn't talking?

Baron turned his attention to the couple standing at the kitchen doors, gesturing for them to enter. "No, of course not. Come on in; I just finished making some lunch," he said.

Max sighed, knowing she would have to let this go...for the moment. She wasn't quite willing to make their personal history a public free for all—but if she didn't get some answers soon, then it might come to that.

Baron introduced her to the man and woman. She tried not to gape at Alric, but he was so huge it was hard not to. Minus the green skin, shaggy dark hair, and thick, dimwitted quality that Lou Ferrigno had been able to do so well, the guy could have been the Incredible Hulk. His hair was blond, and he spoke with a low, thick Northern European accent that rumbled out of his chest.

There was something about him that gave Max the impression he had seen his fair share of violence. A hard, implacable look that glittered in his eyes, even as he smiled at her warmly and extended his humungous hand to shake hers.

She realized it was the same sort of look that shadowed Baron's eyes—the two men even shared the same silvery eye color. Was it some kind of special contact lens? Because if that was the case someone should have told them it didn't look all that natural. It was a little disconcerting actually, and she wondered why either of them would prefer the odd color to their own.

Alric's wife Diana was equally striking in an exactly opposite sort of way. With a tiny frame and slender, fragile looking limbs, she looked uber-feminine, especially with her light hair cut in a short pixie style that brought out the startling green of her eyes and accentuated the high cheekbones of her dainty, doll-like face. Her expression was completely open, and she seemed the type of woman who made friends easily because she was always willing to listen.

"Alric. Diana. Let me introduce Maxine. Maxine is a...friend of mine."

So she had been relegated to "friend" status had she? It wasn't the term she would have used, but "bitter enemies" probably would have come out sounding awkward. *Fine, if that's the way you want to play it.* Max turned and glared at him, and Baron's apologetic look said he at least knew he was an asshole. But then, that had never been his problem. No, Baron was smart enough to know when he was being a jerk, he just didn't care.

"Hi, Maxine." Diana came forward to take her hand in a warm and friendly handshake, and Max suddenly felt dizzy and off balance, unable to understand the sudden surge of sympathy and concern that flowed through her.

Those weren't her feelings. They were coming from the other woman, from Diana. But how was that possible?

She shook her head to try and clear it, and noticed that both Alric and Baron were watching her very carefully. Pressing her fingers to her temple, she rubbed the throbbing pulse point. What? Had she grown two heads in the last thirty seconds?

All of a sudden the deluge of images and emotions seemed to clear from her mind and she felt almost normal again. Wow, that was strange. She looked down, realizing that Baron had taken her hand.

Because she liked it, she made herself draw her arm back and stuffed both her hands in the pockets of her jeans instead.

"I'm so sorry about what happened to you," Diana was saying, "Alric and I are here to help you get through this in any way that we can, okay?"

"Uh," Max wasn't sure what was going on. She turned her head back and forth from Alric to Diana, to Baron. "Sorry, what was that? You guys...know?"

Alric's brow arched high on his forehead as he shot a questioning glance at Baron.

Baron responded with an almost imperceptible nod, and Max was both intrigued and annoyed. He obviously knew these people well enough that they were able to share in a form of silent communication. Had Baron and Alric maybe been in the same spec ops unit together? It would explain at least a few things.

Diana sure knew her way around the massive kitchen. Did they all live here together? Was this some kind of communal set-up? Diana had sidled around the island and was pulling plates and glassware from the overhead cabinets and handing them over the counter to Alric, who took the load from her and set them all out on the long breakfast bar.

Max sighed and took a seat at one of the high stools,

resigned to at least a half an hour of polite conversation before she could get her claws into Baron once more.

She found herself covertly watching Alric and Diana interact, noticing the soft looks and little touches that they shared with each other. There was a visible glow surrounding them that no one could mistake for anything except complete and utter happiness and love.

Max slid a glance over to Baron, and to her utter embarrassment, she found him watching her, his expression serious and his eyes penetrating, seeing too much.

She dropped her gaze and picked up her sandwich, forcing a bite. Her throat felt thick as she tried to pretend she felt normal when inside she was crying.

You're being ridiculous.

Max had banished Baron from her memories long ago, all thoughts, all images. She had gone on with her life like Baron Silver had never existed, and if it wasn't for Jackson, she would have continued to do just that. But now this situation...the proximity was driving her crazy.

She had to get out of here.

All she wanted right now was to get her questions answered and get far away from Baron for good. She decided she would tell him about his brother and leave it up to him whether he was going to come home or not.

Diana called her name, and Max was embarrassed to realize that it hadn't been the first time. "I'm sorry. I've been wool gathering, I guess," she apologized.

"I understand, believe me," Diana replied, compassion obvious in her voice. "You've just come out of a pretty difficult night."

Had she come out of it?

She might have survived the physical transformation, but inside her a monster still seethed, she could feel it with her every breath. What was she going to do? What kind of life was she stuck with now? Max didn't know anything about vampires, not real ones anyway. How close was the myth to reality? How often would she need blood to survive? Was she going to be able to go out in the sun? Eat garlic? Could she still enter a church, or was she damned to hell forever because someone else had stolen her future, taken her life into his foul hands and changed the course of it forever?

Did she even have a soul any more?

Damn. She wasn't going to be able to eat any of this sandwich. Not with the emotional turmoil of everything that had happened churning her stomach.

Max got up to take her plate to the sink and caught Baron throwing Alric one of those talking looks again. A minute later he and Diana had picked up the remains of their lunch and politely excused themselves from the room.

An unbearable thought leaped into her head. "I hope they didn't feel uncomfortable because of me. Because of what I...am now," she said, horrified.

Baron laughed, a surprising reaction to a very reasonable worry. "Don't worry. They aren't afraid of you, if that's what you mean."

And why not? she wondered. She was afraid of herself. Why the hell weren't Baron or his friends?

With every minute, more and more about this situation felt wrong. Too many things about this new Baron were odd.

Hah! The newly-turned blood-sucking fiend should not be calling the kettle black.

She would have laughed at her own private joke, but was afraid of it coming out sounding a might hysterical, and she didn't want Baron to start worrying about her mental state on top of everything else.

Whether Max was soon to be shacking up in crazytown or not, she knew one thing was true— something was very different about Baron, and it was more than the case of a boy maturing into a man or a boat-load of military training and discipline. It was

85

something in the way he held himself, something in the eyes.

He had devoured his sandwich in record time and was now reaching for her practically untouched one, which didn't surprise her in the least. Baron had always been able to pack it away like no tomorrow, and the worst part of it was that he never gained a lick of weight.

The way he approached her now put her in mind of a great golden lion, stalking her. His movements were slow, careful. His eyes glowing. He stood close, both of them leaning against the counter by the sink, side by side. It was a familiar position, she remembered. Baron never could sit still long enough to eat a meal like a normal person. Pretty much any time she had walked into the Silvers' bright, homey kitchen, she would find him there in the process of stuffing his face with something or other as his feet kept on moving back out the door to a basketball or football game, or a date with another one of his cheerleaders.

When he was finished with her lunch, Baron turned toward her and reached slowly around her waist to drop the empty dish into the sink. He lingered, and Max dared to meet his eyes for the first time since he'd caught her staring at his friends.

What was she looking for there? Regret? Desire? Did he see the same in her eyes?

He moved in closer, crowding her, his arms braced on the counter, on either side of her. "What are you doing?" she asked. Wary. Uncertain.

He leaned in, his breathing steady on the side of her neck, tickling the little hairs and making them stand on end. "You smell good," he whispered, inhaling deeply. "Underneath the scent of my soap on your skin I can smell the essence of *you*. It never changes. I sometimes wake up in the night with that smell in my nostrils. That's how I know I've been dreaming about you."

She didn't want to hear that he dreamed about her.

Especially when she knew it for a lie—although that didn't stop her from imagining what they would be doing in those dreams. And unfortunately, she had a really good source upon which to base those imaginings.

Max closed her eyes tightly against the images that popped into her head like a home movie porn flick with naked Baron in the leading role.

No, not just images. Memories.

A few years ago, Baron had returned home—for what turned out to be the last time—to attend his mother's funeral. Lorraine Silver had passed away in her sleep from a massive stroke. It had been so sudden and so undeserved, Max had broken down and cried in public for the first time since she'd been a child. Lorraine was one of those people who, if you could choose your family, Max would have chosen her for a mother—then maybe she would have had someone to walk her to the bus on her first day of school, or show up at her graduation... someone to maybe give a damn about whether she lived or died.

Jackson had been so wrecked about his mother's death that it put his health right into a tailspin that sent him back into the cancer ward. Thankfully, his remission had held, but he'd needed a session of transfusions to get his energy and platelet levels back up.

That was when Baron had walked back into town.

It was the day before the funeral. Max had long ago assumed the position. Camped out in the chair beside Jackson's hospital bed. And then she had promptly fallen asleep. When she woke, it was to find Baron standing by the door, his unreadable eyes watching her intently.

She remembered wanting to be harsh and cold to him, but the emotions bubbling up from within had been too much, and she'd run to him instead.

He had taken her back to the Silver house, fed her and forced her into bed. But for some reason he hadn't left her then, and Max hadn't asked him to. The pain in his eyes was so starkly obvious, she had given in to the urge to offer him comfort. After all, this was Baron's family, not hers, and if she was devastated, he must be even more so.

It wasn't what she had planned, but one moment they were hugging and the next they were kissing. Desperate kisses. Fevered touches. They came together in a wild explosion of passion too long repressed, of elemental need seeking to be satisfied. There was no working up to it, no gentle exploration. Their first kiss was fierce, hot, urgent. He demanded and she yielded. She took and he gave. In minutes they were both naked, sweaty and panting. He took her hard and fast that first time, and Max screamed her release with her legs wrapped tightly around his waist and her fingers digging deep crescent shapes into his shoulders.

If only they had stopped there, perhaps Max could have shrugged the whole thing off as a poor reaction to grief and stress...but they hadn't stopped. Not even close. Baron had brought her to climax over and over through the course of that one night, and each time she had begged him for more.

Ah, the memories.

Max inwardly shook herself. She didn't want to be the one he practiced his slick prince charming routine on tonight, to be the one who got picked to scratch his itch. She didn't want to go to that place with him at all, but especially not today.

She needed time to rebuild her walls, practice her indifference...remember the reasons why he was so toxic to her, and tomorrow she would be strong again. But not now, not when she was emotionally drained, weak, and the thought of letting him ply her with soft words and teasing touches was oh so tempting to her already hypersensitive awareness of him.

When Max opened her eyes, he was watching her, his look intense...and focused on her mouth. Without thinking, she pulled the edge of her top lip between her teeth and watched the flare of heat in his eyes.

Oh, disaster. She was courting disaster.

She put a hand to his chest in a lame effort to push him back and put distance between them, which he wholly ignored, stepping even closer into her personal space. Baron had always been a very physical person. He had played sports constantly, his body always in motion—almost as if he'd been given an extra dose of energy to make up for what his brother lacked.

Now all of that physical presence was concentrated on her, transformed into blistering, crackling, hot sexual energy. Her fingers curled around the soft cotton of his shirt. "Baron—"

"Max—" he mimicked, his voice deep and husky and so damn sexy.

He was close. So close.

She was going to push him away now. Wasn't she?

Apparently not soon enough to avoid being kissed. Her body tensed with the initial contact of his mouth against hers. It was a sizzling, wet kiss that ignited a fever in her blood, but he was gentle, almost careful with her as if he half expected to get kneed in the groin.

Which was exactly what she should do.

When it came to this man, though, Max had never operated on "should". Baron had always been her one and worst weakness, the addiction she may never kick no matter how long and hard she tried.

Her lips were opening of their own accord under his gentle but insistent pressure. Damn, this was dangerous.

So freaking dangerous.

Max groaned out loud at the first delicious slide of his tongue against hers, and tightened the grip she had on his shirt, pulling him full against her. Her nipples tightened against the hard wall of his chest, aching with the awful need to be touched, teased, licked, sucked.

She couldn't help but kiss him back, thinking that it would feel familiar, bring back memories of the last time he had kissed her and all the reasons why she hated him for it. Then she could put it behind her again and push him away.

But it didn't feel the same. She didn't know why— maybe because so much had changed for each of them— but being kissed by Baron right in this moment was just like a *first* kiss.

Nervous and shivery, Max's belly tumbled end over end in anticipation of his taking the kiss further, deeper— and he didn't disappoint. His big hand rose to her hair and wrapped around the long strands in a gentle tug, angling her head to the side in just the way he wanted, forcing her to give him better, deeper access to her mouth.

Baron hadn't changed in this at least. The last time Max had been foolish enough to fall into his arms, she had discovered just how prone the man was to dominating behavior. And damn it, she mustn't have changed that much either, because it still made her wet.

His tongue thrust in and out in an intoxicating rhythm, no longer gentle, but demanding, fueling her own growing sense of urgency. Max's hands trembled as she ran them over his muscled biceps, loving that obvious testament to his strength. She was a sucker for a big, strong, capable man who would take charge in the bedroom. Trouble was, she needed a certain level of trust between her and the man she was with before she could feel comfortable and let her guard down enough to enjoy it, and that kind of trust just wasn't there with Baron. Max was turned on, there was no doubt about that, but she was even now drawing back, refusing to let herself go any further, allow him any closer.

Because she didn't trust him.

That didn't mean it wasn't damn hard to pull away. But she did, her breathing heavy, her core pulsing and hot with desire.

Baron didn't push, or yank her back to him. He just watched her, awareness and regret obvious in his hot gaze.

She cleared her throat and waited a moment for her heart to settle back down to a normal rhythm. "Talk. Ah...we need to. Talk," she mumbled. "Are you going to tell me what's going on?"

Baron ran a hand absently through his hair. His jaw clenched, and his mouth was set in a firm, stubborn line that belied the softness with which he had just kissed her. She returned his guarded expression and waited. "What do you mean?" he asked.

She was angry and hurt. Just like she'd been angry and hurt for years, though she tried to pretend she wasn't. "Don't," she said, the emotion coming through in her voice. "Don't give me any more lies. Don't brush me off. I think I deserve better than that from you."

"No, you're absolutely right." He sighed. "Come with me."

Chapter Nine

He took her hand. She wanted to resist and started to tug it back, but he pulled her along with him anyway, leading her out of the kitchen and down the hall.

"This had better be good, Baron," she sighed, letting him drag her into his bedroom. It had better be real good, she thought, since his room was not a place she was eager to spend more time in.

Once there, he sat on the edge of the bed and pulled her down beside him. "Ask me anything," he said. "I'll tell you whatever you want to know. But be warned, you may not like it and you probably won't believe me. It's going to sound pretty out there." He was avoiding looking right at her. Wow, was he actually nervous?

She laughed. "Out there? You think anything you have to tell me is more 'out there' than what I've been through in the last twenty-four hours?"

"You might be surprised."

She crossed her arms in front of her chest and scooched backward so they faced each other from what she considered a safe distance—at least as safe as she could get without leaving the room entirely. It might have seemed cowardly, but it was more a matter of self-preservation. If they were going to have this conversation, then she wanted some distance between them so she could see in his eyes whether he told the truth.

"All right. First tell me what's up with you—with this set up you've got here. What's the deal?"

"The deal?"

She barked out a laugh ripe with cynicism and shook her head. "It's like that already, is it? And here I thought you were going to be straight with me for once."

"I am—I will." Baron groaned, rubbing his eyes brusquely with the pads of his fingers. "But it's not so easy, Max. These are things I didn't think I would ever be telling you."

Of course not, because he never planned to see me again.

Why did that have to hurt so damn much? Why did he have that power over her still?

Hell.

"I'm very sure of *that*," she replied, her tone biting and dry with mockery—for herself. "That's fine. You know, we really don't have to do this at all. I don't need to know the sordid details of your life." Max swiveled her legs to the floor and pushed her hands hard against her thighs as she rose from the bed. "You just show me the door to this hellhole, and I'll be on my way home now. Thanks for everything and all that, but if it's just the same to both of you Silver brothers, I'm done being put between you." Barely controlled rage clouded her vision. "Call your brother, Baron. Preferably before he's fucking *dead*, and leave me the hell out of it from now on."

As she turned her back to him so she could make her spectacular exit—which, in typical Maxine-style, would have had her heading right for the bathroom door—Baron grabbed both of her arms and turned her back around, adding a sharp shake for good measure.

"That's it." His voice was low, but Max wasn't deceived into thinking he was unaffected. Far from it. A low growl of what could only be murderous frustration rumbled from between his clenched teeth. His odd silver eyes were glowing with a fire that threatened to unleash a blaze of such intense emotion, she was forced to draw back from it or come away burned.

But Baron was having none of that. His hands on her remained firm and unyielding, though he wasn't hurting her. "Don't. Push. Me." The words came out in a harsh, guttural rumble that sounded less like human and more like bear.

This is the point where, if she were a smart little vampire, Max would shut up and politely sit back down on the nice cushy bed to hear him out.

"Fuck you," she spat instead, wrenching her arms from his grasp and stumbling back, her heart racing with adrenaline and anger. "You don't get a break. You don't deserve anything but contempt for the way you've treated Jackson."

Baron's bark of laughter was cutting and spiteful. "You mean for the way I've treated *you*, don't you, Max? Isn't that what this is really about?"

Oh shit. He hadn't really said that to her, had he?

Oh yes, he sure had.

And he hadn't even meant it. Baron knew how much Max loved his brother, that any anger she felt toward him was a direct result of his desertion of Jackson and was nothing personal. Hadn't she always made it crystal clear that Jackson was the only reason she bothered to remember Baron's name?

"Look, I didn't mean it—" he started, but the words fell away from his lips as he met her eyes, eyes glowed darkly, her pupils cloudy with a swirl of angry red.

Max had been doing so well. She had been so strong and steady in the face of such horror that, up to this moment, Baron had almost been able to forget what she was—even the whole teeth sinking into his jugular thing hadn't pounded that reality home to him as succinctly as the look in her eyes right now.

Vampire.

Her incisor teeth had grown long again, the tips protruding slightly from the edges of her mouth. She curled her lip upward in a low growl, revealing the fangs to him in all their razor-sharp, I'm-so-going-to-enjoy-killing-you-with-these glory. As he watched, Max's normally short, clipped fingernails grew to long talons, feral looking and deadly. She clenched her fists together, pressing those points deep into the fleshy pads of her palms, drawing her own blood in an obvious effort to keep from flaying him alive.

"You bastard," she snarled, just before she lunged across the room at him. The sight of Maxine—his Maxine—in the grip of such an unnatural, killing fury was his worst fear come to life.

She struck with a hard swipe of her claws across his face. He was able to lean back, but not fast enough to avoid the hit entirely, and he hissed with pain as she sliced his left cheek open.

Baron had obviously hurt and angered her with his thoughtless remark, and a good hard slap across the face would have been normal and just what he deserved for being so crass and insensitive. This reaction was about twenty leagues past normal.

He dodged Max's next pass. Although he probably could have just barreled through her attack and taken her down, he didn't want to hurt her, so he waited. Her breathing was fast and heavy, and her eyes a deep blood red. He had to finish this before she ended up doing something she would later regret. Before Baron was forced to do something *he* would regret.

She was quick and strong, and her first shot at him had definitely taken him off guard, but Baron's experience and training kicked in and he was easily able to avoid getting cut again by those deadly-looking claws. Getting close enough to her to subdue her attack without hurting her in the process was another story, but when she next swung at him, Baron was ready. He grabbed Max's wrist, pulling her past him, sending her off balance, and then he twisted his body behind her. Trapping her arms in an X across her chest, he held her firmly against him— needing to use his whole body to keep her immobile as she squirmed and bucked, trying to break free of his grasp.

As an Immortal, Baron's talents included the ability to sense and manipulate the psychic energy of others. Right now, he felt a psychic presence surrounding Max— a hostile, inhuman presence that was all too familiar.

He had noticed the same pattern in his dealings with Devon, and again when Max had lain unconscious last night during the turn. Then, Baron's powers had allowed him to meld his mind with hers and lend her his strength. He had helped her fight the vampire's invasion so that it couldn't pollute her soul with its sick, tainted blood even though it transformed her body.

Baron had drawn on his powers to help her hold back the thick miasma of telepathic sludge that threatened to drown her—and he thought he had succeeded, but now he saw just how desperately she still fought the demon.

"Max, stop," he ordered, his mouth close to her ear. With every strained, frantic breath, her breasts rose to press against the arm he had wrapped around her chest. "Stop it. Come back to me." *Please*.

He didn't think that she heard. Her struggle was inward now, and he ached for what she was going through, wishing that he could fight the battle for her.

But Max had to get through this on her own. He knew it, even though it was so hard to step back. No matter how much he wanted to banish the monster for her, to take it out with a flick of his wrist and slice of his blade, it was not so easy this time—and this particular battle was not his to fight.

"You can do it, baby." He kept talking to her, telling

her that he believed in her strength.

She growled and hissed like a feral animal trapped in a cage, thrashing violently against him, but Baron's Immortal strength was greater than hers and he held her easily in his arms, taking care to make sure she couldn't hurt herself.

There was nothing more that he could do, save wait to see whether she could reign in the demon, or whether it would take control and destroy her completely—leaving Baron to deal with a vampire gone rogue.

After long, tense moments of strained bodies and whispered words, furious struggle and ragged breathing, Max's body suddenly stilled, all of her muscles rock solid as they bunched and seized. With her back to him, he couldn't see her face, but he thought her eyes were closed tightly.

Finally, the hostile psychic energy that he had sensed surrounding her was starting to fade. She sagged in his arms and would have fallen in a heap to the floor, but he tightened his hold around her waist to keep her upright.

"Baron," she whispered, her hand clutching at his arm. He was relieved to feel only smooth fingertips gripping him, and not the spear-like claws that she had sported only moments ago.

"Shh." His head fell to the curve of her neck and he dropped a kiss onto her skin, noting how cool it was to the touch of his mouth.

He needed to just hold her close. To breathe her in and hold her without restraining her, without fear clogging his pores.

He tried, but the fear was still there, a palpable, sour taste in his mouth. He swallowed convulsively and sighed, forcing his arms to loose their hold.

That was bad.

And way too fucking close.

Max turned in his arms and buried her face into his chest, her fists clutching handfuls of his shirt to her cheeks. Her sobs came hard and fast. Dry sobs, violent, heaving breaths that tore at the walls of his heart. He waited for the tears, but they didn't fall. Of course, Max never cried. He almost wished she would this time. She could cry on him until they both drowned in a lake of tears if it meant he could keep holding her and that she was whole and safe—and still his Maxine.

They remained like that for a long, long time. When Max ultimately released her hold on his shirt and pulled back, her face was splotchy and red, but at least her eyes were a clear deep blue once more.

He raised his hand and swiped his thumb over her trembling lips. She in turn touched his still bleeding cheek and looked into his eyes with an expression of horror. "Oh God, I could have *killed* you."

Baron turned his face from the exquisite torture of her gentle touch. She wouldn't be so concerned if she knew the truth about him. "I doubt it," he muttered.

She was looking down at her splayed hands. "Look at them," she whispered. She curled her hands into tight fists to stop them from shaking. "How normal they seem, don't they? Soft, but capable. Just as they have always been." Her voice broke on the last word, and Baron curled his own fingers around hers in a lame-ass attempt at comfort. "On the outside, anyway. You'd never know by looking that just under the surface..."

"Don't, Max. Don't do this to yourself," he urged, bringing her fists to his mouth. She tugged her hands back, shaking her head as she met his gaze. Her eyes were dark and flat.

"Don't do what, Baron? Don't admit the truth? It's not something I can really avoid, is it? Don't be afraid? Like I can help that, either." Her bark of laughter was strained and without an iota of humor. "*I almost killed you*. How do I live with that?"

"You didn't almost kill me. Not even close," Baron insisted. "Trust me, I can take care of myself."

Chapter Ten

Max forced her still wobbly legs to take several steps backward, putting a few feet between her and Baron. She didn't trust herself to stay within striking distance. She still felt wired and edgy...and angry as hell. She wrapped her arms around her body, feeling chilled. "Don't go all macho soldier boy on me, Baron. You have no idea—the strength, the power. I can feel it in me still. So much that it's hard to control...almost impossible." It scared her.

He gave her an odd look, and sighed. "I haven't told you yet why I was discharged from the service, have I?"

Now? He wanted to sit down like she hadn't just tried to rip his throat out and have this conversation now?

What the hell. It had to be better than trying to decide what to do about her own impossible situation.

"No." She felt crabby and irritated as the adrenaline started to wear off. "I'm pretty certain we didn't get that far."

"My fault, I'm sorry. I want you to know I didn't mean it. What I said before." He threw her a wry, very Baron-esque kind of smile that reminded Max of the boy he had been. "You always did bring out the worst in me, you know."

"I don't see how I could have." Even standing apart as they were, she felt him as if their bodies were still pressed together. She was very aware of the small room and the low lighting. The air didn't separate them, it connected them. Charged with electricity, the space between them was a conduit that fed her senses. She met his glittery eyes so full of secrets and promises, breathed deeply of his spicy vanilla scent. Her very blood flowed in time with his, her heart matching the rhythm of his, pounding in a steady, heavy beat.

Ignore it. Focus, Max. Focus.

"Ah..." *What was I saying?* "Even when you were still at home, you avoided me as if I was going to give you rabies or something." She intentionally said nothing about the one time he *hadn't* ignored her. Instead, she reclaimed her spot on the edge of the bed.

"Max, did you really have no idea?"

"No idea about what?" What was he talking about?

Baron shook his head. "Never mind." With a sigh he joined her on the bed, but there was a distinct gap between them this time that she didn't have to insist on.

She should be relieved that he was finally showing a healthy sense of caution around her, but instead, his reservation in the face of her horrifying attack made Max feel more hopeless. Where before she had dared to wonder if there was some way to overcome her circumstances and find a way to lead a normal life, now Max was pretty certain her fate had been sealed.

Thou shalt not suffer a witch to live. Wasn't that the saying? She decided it was probably just as appropriate an expression to use in the case of vampires.

Thankfully, she was pulled from that deadly train of thought as Baron continued. "I had returned home from a particularly difficult mission and was cooling my heels before being called in to debrief the higher-ups. And ah, I...I got sick."

"Sick? How? When was this?"

"It was just a few weeks before mom died. I ended up in the hospital overnight. None of the doctors knew what was wrong, and everyone agreed that I was good only for worm food. I was pretty sure of it myself, too, for a while."

"Oh my God." Her eyes moved over his body, checking for some sign, but he looked healthy. Perfect. Glowing with strength and life and vitality, just as he always had. "If that's true, then why didn't anybody call us—I mean, your mom and Jackson? Why didn't anyone let them know? We would have been there for you in a heartbeat. You know that."

"I know, but I was brought to a military hospital," he explained. "And I was totally out of it. Incoherent. I don't remember much of it at all. There was a lot of pain, and I doubt I could have put enough words together to make any sense, much less to ask that they call my family— which they wouldn't have done in any case."

"Why not? If you were sick and dying, you should have had them with you." She tried to imagine what it would be like lying alone and near death in a hospital bed by yourself. Max's own mother had wanted someone with her at the end, even if it was the daughter she'd barely acknowledged in life.

Her heart started to ache and tears welled up in her eyes. That's exactly where Jackson was right now. Alone. God, she needed to get back to him.

But how could she do that in the condition she was in right now? Amazingly, Baron had been treating this whole situation as if it was something he dealt with every day. But Max was afraid to leave this room and venture into the real world, where she would be a monster. It was too hard to control the changes that were still taking place inside of her, to deny the hunger that had only been barely satisfied with Baron's blood. How could she go to Jackson when she couldn't guarantee his safety?

Max blinked back her tears and focused on Baron's words. She would find a way back—tomorrow—she made that promise to herself. Whether Baron decided to be a man and join her, or not. Max was going.

"The sickness came on so strong and so suddenly that the doctors were worried I might have been infected with something on purpose. So from that point, everything about my treatment was considered classified." Baron reached for her hand, and Max let him take it. Why, she didn't know, except that finding out he had been so close to death was a shock, and maybe she wasn't thinking straight.

"Well, obviously you didn't die. I mean here you are, perfectly healthy and just as much of a jerk as ever."

He laughed, but Max knew there were still more secrets between them. There was something else he wasn't telling her, she could feel it.

"No, but a few times, I honestly wished I had died."

"What is it Baron? There's more right? What does this have to do with your career? How did you get yourself thrown out of the military?"

"First of all, I didn't get thrown out. I was given a medical discharge."

"Why? Obviously, the doctors found a cure. I mean, you're so disgustingly healthy..."

"No, actually they didn't find a cure. None of them could ever figure out what had caused my symptoms, so the doctors refused to sign me off on a clean bill of health, which meant the government was suspicious, hemming and hawing about whether or not to let me go back to active service."

"Suspicious? Of you?"

"No, not like that. It's not that *I* was being investigated, not really. But without any clear evidence to prove I was free of the infection, since they couldn't figure out where it came from to begin with, the doctors refused to give me the green light to return to my unit."

"Still—" Max was confused. If what he said was true, this illness had come on him just before Baron suddenly and completely cut all ties with everyone at home. But why would a person do that, especially if he was fine? Baron had obviously recovered and lived to see another day—many other days, in fact—so why the act of familial desertion? And what was he doing now that he could afford to send Jackson so much money every month?

"Max." Baron was looking at her, a rueful expression on his face that didn't make her feel any better. There was definitely more to this story than he was letting on.

"Come on, what is it? This still doesn't make any sense. If you were sick, you should have called your family. When you got better, why didn't you come home?"

"I've been home. I haven't been hiding or anything."

"Hah!" Max leapt to her feet and started pacing back and forth in front of him, gearing up. She could feel the anger starting to roll around inside of her again, but this time she recognized the sharp twist in her belly, and her control over it was ironclad. Nothing was going to distract her from this conversation. It had been a long, long time coming.

"Showing up out of the blue for a day or two once a year is not called 'coming home'. Nor is leaving town the day of your mother's funeral before the dirt is even thrown over her casket. It's called being a selfish asshole."

She ignored the flare in his eyes and the warning look. "Jackson loves you," she continued. "You are more than his brother, you were one of his only friends. And since your mom died, you are his only family left in this world. I don't understand why you can't see how much it hurts him. Or maybe you do see, but you just don't care. Is that it?"

"No. That's not it." Baron said. He got to his feet and stalked forward to where she stood with her hands settled on her hips. It was a defensive gesture Max used when she wanted to appear tough. In reality, all she wanted to do right now was cry. But while crying might make her feel better if she'd been alone, there was no way in hell Baron was going to see her tears.

"Well, it sure as hell looks like it!"

Baron's expression turned stormy, his eyes glittering with some unnamed emotion that Max couldn't quite figure out. What did he have to be angry or upset about? He's the one who left—Jackson. That is.

Damn it.

She couldn't help it. Max knew she had no right to think this way, but the truth was...she felt like Baron had left *her*.

True, Max had always been *Jackson's* friend. First and foremost. There was never any doubt about it.

But in her last year of high school, Jackson was too sick to go out at all, and Max found herself at the Silvers' house so often she could have started paying rent. It had felt like the two of them—Max and Baron—started to get past the sarcasm and not-so-thinly-veiled insults they had been throwing back and forth the last three years.

She had started to see past the golden-haired, popular jock with a sharp tongue, to the other Baron—the one who would snap a photo of Mrs. Felker's Chihuahua wearing a tiny top hat and tails just because Jackson would have found it hilarious. The Baron who would sit for hours by his brother's bedside and regale him with his sports exploits because Jackson hadn't been able to be there and hated to feel left out.

The Baron who sometimes looked at her as if she *wasn't* a sticky, dirty wad of gum on the bottom of his shoe that came from the wrong side of the tracks.

Oh, they had still traded creative invectives about one another's anatomy and barnyard origins...but they had also *talked*. More and more often, she would find herself hanging out with Baron, even after Jackson had fallen asleep and she should have gone home. Max had told him things about her mother that she hadn't felt comfortable telling anyone else, not even Jackson, who had enough problems and didn't need her unloading that kind of crap onto his frail shoulders.

He had told her things, too. Things she could have sworn were from his heart. About wanting to do something important with his life, about wanting to make a difference in the world. Childish dreams really, but honorable and sweet.

And Max—who had promised herself long before ever meeting either of the Silver brothers that she would never fall for any man and end up like her mother—living alone in a trailer park, sucking a whiskey bottle every night—Max found herself falling in love.

But then Baron left, proving that her instincts in love were just as rotten as her mother's had been.

"*Fuck*," she muttered. Damn him. Damn him for mattering to her, even after all this time. Damn him for everything.

"Why, Baron? What the hell was so goddamned important, you just had to do it without me? Had to cut me out of your life so completely after making me think you actually cared?" Max realized she had stopped talking for Jackson. *Ah hell*. The last thing she wanted was to reveal her true feelings to Baron—or to reveal that she even *had* feelings for him.

She spun around and bolted for the door, hoping he wouldn't follow.

No such luck. Baron caught her by both arms and turned her back to him. "Max, look at me." He forced her head up, forced her eyes to meet his. She was having a hard time breathing. Her chest was too tight. She closed her eyes.

"No. Max, *look at me*," he repeated. Waiting. Damn, knowing Baron, he would wait forever until she did what he wanted her to.

She looked.

What she saw in his strange, beautiful eyes was raw, intense...passion. Desire. Heavy and hot and *honest*. Real.

For her.

Max not only saw it in his eyes, but all of a sudden she could feel it. She gasped, the force of his feelings causing a matching thrum in her. The heat radiated off of him like he was purposely projecting it outward, and in a wave of intensity, it crashed into her.

How she was sensing this, she didn't know, but Max recognized the ability as coming from that new, *other* part of her, and wondered briefly why she wasn't able to read Baron so easily all of the time. But such thoughts were fleeting in the face of all that heat.

"Max, I did care. I *do* care." Baron's hands were still heavy on her shoulders, holding her still. He was probably afraid she would run from him—which she desperately wanted to do. Staying here and having this conversation after blurting out how she'd felt for him all this time was torture. She'd almost rather be facing off against Devon again.

"I care too much. I always did. Couldn't you see that?"

"No." She shook her head. No. She hadn't seen that. Hadn't known that.

But that wasn't entirely true, was it? She remembered the night Baron had taken her to the spring formal.

She had told Jackson she wasn't going to go since he was too sick to go, too, but her friend was having none of it, and kept insisting she needed to be there. He said he didn't want her to turn around one day and regret missing out on the important moments of her youth because she had hung out with him in a sick room day and night—Jackson had always been deep and sensitive like that, even at his young age.

Max tried to tell him it didn't matter to her, but he could be stubborn when he wanted to be—he and his brother were a lot alike in that respect. Anyways, she said, she didn't even have a dress. But Jackson surprised her, saying that "they" had gotten one for her, "they" had known she would use such a lame excuse. She had known then that the "they" included Baron, especially when he walked in and said he would be pleased to be her escort.

Max refused of course. She was convinced that Jackson had begged Baron to do it, to take her on as a charity case, and movie clips from Stephen King's *Carrie* started rolling in her head.

Neither of them had given up, though. They had everything figured out, and after an hour of fighting them, in the end, she'd reluctantly agreed.

That night Baron had been attentive and courteous. There were no snide little digs between them...and no Jackson. All of his attention had been focused on her, and hers on him. And at times, she thought she had seen something in his expression, an almost longing—which she had dismissed without a second thought so that she could enjoy a carefree night the likes of which didn't come around very often for someone like her.

They danced together, ate too much from the buffet table, and drank cup after cup of the sweet, fruity punch, and when the party was over, Max hadn't wanted the night to end. She told Baron not to bring her home right away. The reality that awaited her at home felt like a violation of the memory she wanted to have of the glorious night.

Baron seemed to understand, and he drove the car around town until they found themselves passing a dark, quiet park. He had stopped there and turned the radio down low. They talked for a while...and then he'd kissed her. Almost as if he hadn't meant to, but couldn't help himself. It had started out sweet and soft, but Max was soon eager for more and things had gotten carried away before Baron himself had stopped them from going too far.

She saw the memory of that kiss in his eyes now.

She saw other things, too—like the way he had looked at her sometimes when he didn't think she noticed, and how he never seemed to judge her for the weaknesses of her mother, the absence of her father, but had subtly challenged her to be better and do more.

"Why?"

Baron sighed, and dropped his hands from her arms. "Why? God, Max. I may be an asshole, but I had *some* honor—at least back then I thought I did."

"Honor?" She shook her head. "What has that got to do with anything? After the night of the spring formal, you had to know how I felt about you. And you just left. If you cared for me, too..."

"I had no right. You're not mine to care for."

"*Not yours*? You're acting like I already belonged—"

"To Jackson. To my *brother*."

Somehow, she had known he was going to say that.

"Jackson and I are *friends* Baron. If you wanted to think up an excuse, you could have come up with a better one than—"

"You may see him only as a friend, Max. But I always knew the truth."

"Oh, yeah?"

"Are you really going to tell me you don't know how he feels about you?" Baron asked. "Are you going to stand there and pretend that he doesn't worship the ground you walk on, that Jackson hasn't been head over heels in love with you since the day you first walked through our front door?"

No, that was something Max couldn't say. She knew. She'd always known.

"What kind of man hits on his sick brother's only friend in the world, Max?" He frowned. "What kind of man falls in love with his brother's girl?"

How could he tell her this now? How could he expect her to believe that he loved her yet had turned and walked away because of her friendship with Jackson? Didn't he know that made everything worse? When she thought of what they could have had together, all that wasted

108

time...and now it was too late.

She shook her head. "*Love*? You're going to call that love? Nuh uh, Baron. You didn't even give love a chance." Max let out a heavy sigh of exasperation. "Did Jackson know how you felt?" Suddenly she knew. "He did, didn't he? And he tried to tell you it was all right. Why else would he have asked you to take me to that dance?"

Baron shook his head. "No, he didn't—"

Max laughed. "Of course he did. Your brother might be sick, but he is far from stupid or blind." *Unlike me, obviously.*

"*Shit.*"

"So that's it, huh? Nobody thought to ask what I might want?" She saw her answer in his expression and looked away, her eyes burning. When she could turn back, she said, "You know, Jackson and I had a conversation about six months before you left town. He told me he was in love with me, and I told him that I loved him, too."

Baron looked surprised. "You—you did? You do? I mean, you told him that?"

"Yes. I said that he was the closest thing I had to a real family, and that I loved him like a brother. We both agreed that there were more important things than sex between us, and we would never let something like that ruin our friendship. Life's too short..." Max couldn't go on.

God, Jackson was dying. Her best friend was *dying*.

"I've had enough of this, Baron." Fighting back the tears, she shook her head. "He needs me, and you...don't." Even though her heart was so far up her throat she might choke on it, she forced the quiver out of her voice. "You don't deserve my time when his is so short."

"I know."

"So say what you want to say, or don't. I don't care

anymore. I have to get out of here." Max didn't dare meet his eyes, for fear he would see the guilt that would betray her for the horrible friend she really was—because a part of her *did* still care. A part of her didn't want to leave.

"Look, I want to tell you, and you deserve to know," he said. "I wasn't actually sick. When the doctors couldn't figure out what was wrong with me...it wasn't an illness, not really."

She met his gaze, confused. "What do you mean? But you just said—"

"You were never supposed to know. Any of it, but—"

"God Baron, just spit it out already." Max was going to punch him if he kept this up. She hated it. All these crazy ups and downs were draining her to the point of an emotional breakdown.

"I'm not human anymore."

Chapter Eleven

Diana watched her husband sleep.

In sleep, at least, he could put no barriers between them. The hard, protective man that he was could relax his ironclad vigilance for just a little while.

How she loved him.

But he was seriously driving her crazy.

Since this problem with the vampire had come up, Alric had gotten severely protective in a severely big way. She hadn't said anything, and she wasn't going to, because she understood what it was like to worry about someone. She knew what it was like to lose something precious, and if she were in his place, she would be reacting ten times worse than he was now.

Understanding a thing didn't make it any easier to deal with, though. God's teeth, she was well aware of that.

With a sigh, she traced a finger along the stubbly line of his strong jaw, watching as his lips pursed and then relaxed. They had been through so much, she and her warrior. Individually—and together. When she thought of what it must have been like for him all those years, trapped and alone.

Diana shivered, though the bedroom was warm. The memories from the day she had found him in that underground prison were vivid in her mind as she watched Alric's chest rise and fall in a steady rhythm.

The memory of seeing him there, trapped in the tunnel—his arms and legs manacled to the walls, his eyes so full of pain and madness—never failed to bring tears to her eyes. Sometimes she had dreams about it, but in her dreams, she was always too late to save him. His body was nothing but a skeleton, eye sockets empty and dead.

To think that he had survived in that dark, rat infested hellhole for almost a hundred years.

It had taken so much strength and courage—from both of them—before Alric had been able to embrace his humanity again. But he had. He had managed to hold onto enough of his sanity to return from the very edge, and he had showed her he was capable of such great tenderness and love.

Not human anymore?

Max was going to kill Baron. How dare he play with her like this, treating her situation like a big fucking joke? "Baron—" her voice came out choked, rage preventing her from controlling it any longer. "That's not funny. Don't you dare use what happened to me to make sick jokes like that."

"Oh, baby, trust me," he sounded almost sad. Tired and sad. "I would never do that. This is so far from funny."

"No kidding. Then what the hell is going on? What did you mean by that?"

"I meant what I said." He took a deep breath. "It's hard to explain, but it's true. Essentially, when I ended up in the hospital, I was going through the transition."

"Transition? What kind of transition?"

"Honestly, it's a lot like what you went through when the vampire turned you, but without the vicious attack and blood loss."

"I still don't follow, Baron. Which is understandable because you aren't making any sense. What are you talking about?"

"I didn't learn any of the details until after everything was already said and done—when I met Rhys and the others and they brought me here." Now Baron was the one sitting on the edge of the bed. He put his head in his hands.

"There's a group. Of men. Who've been around a long time." He choked out a strangled sounding laugh. "A *long* time. They're called Immortals, and there's a reason for that."

"Immortals." Was she supposed to believe this?

"Yeah. I guess back in the beginning—like the beginning of time—the earth was overrun by...demons."

"Demons." Had she really heard that right? "Like hellfire and horns and shit? Are you kidding me?"

"I wish I were. Really." He sounded so solemn, so un-Baron-like serious that Max bit back her snort of disbelief and urged him to continue.

"Okay, I'll bite. Go on."

"A handful of men were chosen by the powers that be to round the demons up and send them back to hell where they escaped from." An elbow propped on each knee, he sat with his thighs spread open and his hands hanging between his legs, looking way too sexy in the casual, thoughtful pose...but she digressed.

"These demons are...ah, pretty sick, and really brutal. There are different breeds, but most of them share the same disgusting green blood, snarly teeth, red eyes. Many of them can masquerade as men and women, and like to do nasty things to humans."

The look in his eyes was devastating. Cold. "You're telling me the truth, aren't you?"

"After what you've seen and experienced in the last day, do you even doubt it?"

She paused for a moment. "Ah, no. I guess I have to

admit it's within the realm of possibility—my altered reality being what it is just now." Shaking her head, she went to him, sat beside him. He looked up at her in surprise, as if he expected her to run from him in terror instead, wondered why she would even still be here in the same room with him after what he had disclosed to her. "What does this have to do with you, Baron?"

He let out a short, strained laugh. "I won destiny's lottery. Apparently the night that the sickness came upon me, an Immortal had been killed fighting one of these demons. When that happens, another man must take his place, become Immortal. I was that lucky fool."

"So someone just came along and asked you if you wanted to be Immortal, and you said 'sure, sounds like a good deal'?"

"No, baby. It doesn't quite work like that." He chuckled, this time with some honest humor. She should protest the way he kept calling her baby, but right now it seemed a petty thing to complain about. And if she was honest with herself, she'd admit she kind of liked it.

"An Immortal's destiny is decided for him before his birth. He is born human, but with a latent gene that will allow the change to take place if another Immortal dies. They call this human a 'Potential'. If no other Immortal dies before the Potential reaches a certain age, then he will never be called upon, and will live out his human life, never knowing what could have been."

"So you have this gene?"

"Apparently so."

"And you were...called upon?"

He snorted. "If you can call debilitating pain, tormenting psychic visions and near death being 'called upon'—yeah, pretty much."

Max was silent for a moment, trying to come to terms with what he was telling her. "How did you find all of this out, and how did you come to be here?"

"Rhys came to find me. He's kind of our fearless

leader. One of the oldest Immortals."

"Just how old does that make him?"

"Oh, I don't know. I think he's something like nine hundred years old. Give or take."

Max's mouth dropped in shock. Nine hundred years? That was taking retro to a whole new level. "Oh my God," she whispered. "So does that mean you're going to live forever?"

He sighed and shook his head. "Unfortunately, the odds are against that. Chances are, I'll get knocked off by a demon one of these days. But until then, I won't age anymore, I heal super fast, and I won't get sick." He paused and Max caught the look of pain in his eyes that he tried to hide. "And apparently, I can't...have children."

She ached.

Oh hell, she ached so much. It was crazy, but true.

There had been a time—a brief, insane, weakened moment in time—when Max had imagined having children...Baron's children. They would have been beautiful, golden-haired, rambunctious, smiling children. She had imagined a bright little girl with his stubborn ways, and a sharp little boy with all of the sweetness and noble ambition of his youth.

For some reason, she felt the loss of those children as if they had already been born of her body. Max hadn't realized until now just how much she had still been holding onto the dream of a future with him—crazy though it seemed, since she wouldn't ever have admitted it even to herself if this day had never come.

"You can't have children?"

He shook his head. "It's kind of complicated. There are a couple of scientists among us—other Immortals— who have been studying the problem for something like two hundred years, but so far the consensus is that an Immortal's physiology changes too much in the transition to be compatible with a human woman for the purposes of procreation."

115

"But what about Immortal women? I mean...not that you...personally...but couldn't an Immortal man and an Immortal woman...?"

"Um, no actually. There aren't any Immortal women—well, that's not quite true. Rhys' wife Amy is an Immortal. But she's a special exception to the rule, as far as we know, the only woman to ever go through the transition."

"So, no women?"

"Uh, not Immortal ones, no."

Though she wanted to hold onto it, some of Max's anger and hurt melted away. She knew Baron had always wanted children. As teens, during some of their short-lived ceasefire moments, the two of them had talked about things like that. Hopes and dreams for their future. His had always involved a decorated military career and a big, healthy family.

She pulled him into her arms, the need to comfort overriding her desire for self-preservation. "Baron, I'm so sorry." She tucked her head into his shoulder. Her voice was heavy with tears she promised herself she would not shed. Not now.

"Max," he whispered, raising her face to his with a finger pressed lightly under her chin. "Max, whenever I let myself dream of what might have been—if I hadn't been such an asshole to you, and if Jackson wasn't my brother, and if maybe I had handled things differently that night we spent together—" She opened her mouth to interrupt, but he shushed her with his finger over her lips. "Useless words you don't deserve, I know. But let me finish."

He removed his hand, and she nodded, remaining silent. "If ever I could have had children," he continued. "I would have wanted them with you. Our children would have been so beautiful and brilliant and strong, just like you. You would be a fabulous mo—"

"Oh God, Baron don't do this to me now. Please

116

don't," her voice broke, but the tears still did not fall.

Max put her hand over his mouth and shook her head, returning his look of sorrow with her own. She was completely naked and vulnerable to him now, but told herself that they deserved to have the truth between them—just this once.

Even if it was too late for anything else.

"The ironic thing," she whispered on a sigh, "is that I probably can't have children now anyway, not like this. And even if I could...what kind of mother drinks blood and can't even see her children off to school in the morning without slapping on the SPF 200 first?" She felt a stab of pain in her chest as the images of smiling children who would never be born started to fade from her mind's eye. "I guess we were just never destined to have that life."

Baron lifted her face with both palms cupping her cheeks and tenderly kissed her brow, running his thumbs along the high planes of her cheekbones and over her lips. "I would give anything to be able to go back and have that life with you. I want you to know that."

Max refused to say the same, refused to let those words mean anything to her.

She clenched her teeth tightly together, twisting her head away. "Don't."

He looked at her for a moment in silence, then dropped his hands to his sides. She caught a flash of something in his face before it was masked behind stony indifference. Regret? Hurt?

It didn't matter, she told herself. Baron had no right to hurt. He had made his choices.

So why did she feel the loss of his touch so keenly?

Part of her wanted to lean back into him and let him keep touching her. Ah, but she didn't. She caught the impulse and forced herself to focus on what really mattered. It was important that they get to the bottom of this conversation once and for all.

"I still don't understand why you never came back home. If only for your brother. Why desert Jackson the way you did?" she asked. "No visits, no more letters or emails, or phone calls. All of this sounds really crazy and you would have had a hard time convincing me two years ago—heck, two days ago—that you had somehow become this Immortal demon hunter guy...but Jackson would have believed anything of you, if you'd only given him the chance. Jackson and I *both* would have tried to understand and to support you."

God, was that even true? Would she, could she, have understood? Or would her bitterness over their past have made her biased as soon as he opened his mouth?

"You could have come home," Max said again. Oh, how she hated this perpetual state of confusion. She had been on the verge of drowning in a sea of deception and half-truths since waking up from her living death to find Baron at her side.

"No."

"That's it? That's your big explanation? *No?*"

"Look, I send him money every month," he answered with a groan. They both knew full well that it wasn't nearly enough, wasn't even close to what Jackson really needed from his big brother, and Max let him know with a loud snort what she thought about that lame-ass comment.

Baron moved from the bed to go back to pacing the floor. "Do you think it was easy for me to walk away?" he asked, turning back to her, letting her see his tortured face, stripped of the walls and barriers, his pain naked and bared for her to see. "You don't understand what it's like. What it's been like my whole life. It was bad enough when I was a kid. Every time I left the house when he had to stay home stuck in that bed, every time I went on a date, or played a ball game I felt like such a shit just for being healthy. And now? How was I supposed to go to him and say 'Hey, man, I know you're dying from

118

leukemia and all, but look at me—I'm young and healthy and strong, and oh, by the way, I'm immortal now, too. Never gonna die.'?"

She wanted to weep for him, for them both. The two brothers.

Instead, she crossed the room to Baron and squared her shoulders. "Gee, Baron, embellish much?" Her voice was heavy with sarcasm as she punched him in the ribs. Granted, she understood this situation wasn't entirely his own fault, but Baron was doing too fine a job playing the victim, and she'd had about enough of it.

"You're pretty good at making excuses, you know that? To me. To Jackson." She looked down her nose at him and sneered. "Man, what a disappointment you are."

"What the hell is that supposed to mean?" he demanded, his voice rising. Well, at least she had him angry, his mind dragged out of the pity party he would have her buy into right along with him.

"It means the man that I knew—the man that I respected even though he drove me crazy—wouldn't have let any of this bullshit keep him from doing what was right." She poked him in the chest, hard. "And from taking what he wanted." Another poke, harder. "And from damning to hell anyone who couldn't deal with it."

Baron grabbed her wrist so she couldn't poke him anymore, and they glared at each other hotly, her heavy breaths mingling with his steady, controlled ones in the air that roiled between them.

"Don't come crying to me now about poor Baron. You have everything, a brother who loves you and wants you to be by his side even after all of the crap you put him through, even after you let us think you were fucking dead. You bastard." She yanked her hand back and sneered at him. "You...you didn't give anyone a chance to believe in you, to trust in you. Not me, not Jackson. You just ran. You ran like all men do."

"All men, Max?" Baron's voice held a thinly veiled

thread of anger that betrayed his rising temper. "Don't make this be about you and your father."

She shoved him. Hard. Anger pulsing through her at a steady drum once again.

"*Goddamn you to hell.*" This whole day had been one big emotional rollercoaster after another, starting with confusion and pain, then leading to a kind of dizzy joy at finding Baron at her side. She'd quickly moved on to disgust and revulsion after learning what she had become. Then angry, sexually aroused. Now, all of those difficult emotions were fused into one massive lump in her throat that threatened to choke her.

"Right back at ya, babe." He growled, grabbing her arms, pinning them to her sides in an attempt to keep her from inflicting any more damage to his person. She was twisting and writhing, needing an outlet, something to hit, a release of her pent-up fear, anger, and regret.

"Hey," he said again, shaking her. "You're right about one thing."

"Yeah," she spat, "what's that? That you're a coward? A lying, irresponsible, hateful coward?"

He leaned in close, his glittering silver eyes flashing with white hot fire. Her breaths grew shorter, quicker, and she could feel her chest rising and falling fast and heavy against his as he held her tightly to him. Her nipples tingled, growing into hard little buds, sensitive and achy.

Damn him.

"You're right that the old Baron would have just taken what he wanted and to hell with the rest."

She knew it was coming.

And, God, she wanted it. She met it head on and welcomed it with everything she was.

When Baron smashed his lips to hers, it was brutal and hard, making her moan. She reveled in the freedom of her response.

This wasn't about love. It wasn't about trust. It wasn't about the future.

This was about the here and now. It was about anger and desperation. It was about an affirmation of life, a confirmation of humanity, and the simplicity of release.

She could deal with that.

All the rest would have to wait.

Chapter Twelve

Max pulled frantically at Baron's shirt, wanting his bare skin under her fingertips. He groaned, quick to prove just how eager he was to accommodate her. Reaching up, he pulled the shirt over his head and tossed it aside without a thought, his mouth leaving hers for less than a fraction of a second before coming back, hard and insistent, tongue probing against her lips for entrance. She sucked him into her mouth in one great breath, loving his growl of pleasure, impatient for more.

"Max," he grumbled between hot, wet kisses, "take off your shirt."

She must not have responded soon enough for him, because in one smooth, practiced move, he had gripped the neck of the thin cotton t-shirt and tore it in half right down the middle, pulling the shredded sides apart to bare her braless breasts. Her nipples were already pebbled and tight.

With a glance down, she gave him a negligent shake of her head and a little smile. "It's your shirt. I guess if you want to destroy it, I've got no problem with that." She chuckled and shrugged her shoulders. "I wasn't planning on using it for a while anyway."

He took a half step back, staring down at her. "God, you are still the most beautiful woman I've ever known," he growled out before pulling her close again as if he couldn't bear to not be touching her.

"Baron," she pleaded, knowing exactly what she wanted. He knew it, too. Knew what to do to drive her wild with need. Hell, she was already halfway there, and they were just getting started.

Just getting started. A great shiver of anticipation raced down her spine.

He dragged the remains of the shirt down over her shoulders, but only to her elbows, effectively trapping her arms as he gathered the fabric together with one hand at the small of her back, twisting the folds into a knot that he pulled tight.

She wiggled experimentally, and sure enough, in this position he had her virtually immobile. Her arms were forced behind her, thrusting her breasts forward, on display for him, a position Baron wasted no time taking full advantage of.

His mouth was already latching on to one rose-colored nipple, his tongue teasing the hypersensitive bud while his free hand plucked at the other. The ruthless torment sent delicious lightning shocks of pleasure through her, and she felt her knees weakening, her legs turning to rubber. They weren't going to hold her any longer.

She needed a bed. What luck, there happened to be one just a few steps away.

Max tested the restraints, pulling her arms against the cotton that bound them. She took a step back, trying to force him to let her go so they could move to the bed.

He released her nipple, his hot breath caressing the tight peak. "Ah ah. No, you don't." Baron smiled, but his voice was hard, offering her no mercy. The hand still holding her arms behind her back tugged a little more, tightening the cotton around her elbows and Max groaned.

He leaned in close, the sound of his voice low and gravelly in her ear, making her shiver. "You're going to stand there nice and still and let me do exactly what I want. You don't move until I say you can move."

She moaned softly, her head falling back as she arched her spine, pushing her breasts higher, wordlessly urging him to touch her and taste her again. When he didn't move to take her aching nipple into his mouth, she squirmed closer. "Please, Baron."

"Not good enough, Max," he bit out, his amazing eyes turning a cloudy steel gray with the force of his desire. "Tell me."

She knew what he wanted, of course. And if she didn't comply, she thought he could hold out on her for a very long time. "Baron," she groaned, wetting her lips with the tip of her tongue. "You're very cruel."

"Tell me."

She twisted and writhed in his arms. Baron and Max had had one night together before this. One night of mind blowing, crazy hot sex. And while the after part had been one of the worst moments of her life, the during part had proved just how good the two of them *could* have been. Truly inspirational.

The two of them were the perfect combination of sexually dominant male and submissive female...and Baron knew it.

He knew just how far to take her, just how much to push her.

And Max knew exactly how much to give...and what to hold back and make him work for.

"I want you sucking on my breasts," she demanded, thrusting forward again, the ache between her legs intensifying. Almost unbearable already.

He chuckled. "That's my girl," he said. But instead of complying with her command, Baron leaned into her and just barely grazed the tip of one tight nipple with his raspy tongue, then came back for another, longer lick, his eyes locked on hers, never wavering.

The torture was exquisite as he slowly built the

tension higher, fanning the flame inside of her from an already lively spark to an inferno of need, first flicking, then swirling his tongue around her nipples, one then the other. When he finally took her fully into his mouth and gave a good hard suck, she couldn't hold back the scream that erupted from her lips. She closed her eyes, squeezed her fingers into fists at her back, and bit her bottom lip hard enough to get a small jolt from the coppery tang of her own blood.

Baron's hand dropped from the makeshift binding holding her arms behind her. She flexed her hands open and closed to increase the flow of blood back into her arms, allowing the cotton to fall unheeded to the floor.

With her hands free, Max eagerly explored the hard planes of Baron's super-ripped body as he did wicked things to her breasts with his mouth.

The man sure did take the term *beefcake* to entirely new levels, she thought as she slid her hands down his sculpted back and beneath the waistband of his low riding workout pants to squeeze his fine, tight ass.

He growled and thrust into the curve of her hips, working his mouth from her breasts back up the column of her neck before stopping, waiting for...something from her.

She obeyed the silent command, turning her head to meet his gaze. With a growl of approval and a flash of heat in his eyes, Baron leaned closer and sank his teeth into the delicate tendon of her shoulder in a blatantly transparent display of aggressive possession.

Max loved it. Her body was humming, throbbing, so in tune with him that she responded to even the gentle tickle of his hair on the side of her neck, shivering as he raised goose bumps on her skin that went all the way down to her toes.

She could feel her newly-formed vampire teeth lengthening in anticipation of putting them through his skin. The prospect was disturbing, but exciting at the same time, and she wasn't quite sure how to handle it. She was still too uncertain about the whole vampire thing to be comfortable even though Baron had already offered her his blood and seemed more than okay with the situation himself.

Max tamped the instinct down deep where she hoped it wouldn't rise again to intrude. But Baron had other ideas.

His lips burned a trail up the column of her neck, nibbling on her skin as he went. "Delicious," he rasped into her ear before biting down hard on the sensitive cartilage.

When he kissed her, his tongue probed deep, sweeping the inside of her mouth before he deliberately searched for the hard points of her incisors. She flinched as he ran his tongue along the sharp length of one, then the other, but he held her steady with his hand buried in the long hair at the base of her scalp.

Max started trembling, all of her senses ramping up—the sound of their breathing a cavernous echo in her ears, the taste of his kiss a sinful, moist sweetness, and the pounding of his heart a heavy, obvious thud against her own chest as she pressed her body ever closer. They all combined to torment her, not only with passion, but with the hunger that was getting steadily stronger.

"I like these new teeth of yours, Max." He practically purred her name, sending shivering spikes of heat down her spine and into the warm, wet place between her thighs. She couldn't help but spread her lips and bare her teeth to him with a short hiss, aware that they were throbbing in her mouth.

"Are you going to bite me again, baby? I almost came the last time, it was so good. I think this time I want you to do it with my cock buried deep inside you."

"Oh God," she muttered, closing her eyes tight and dropping her forehead into the curve of his shoulder. She was both horrified and horribly turned on by his

126

admission, and didn't know which was worse. "Just hurry up and fuck me."

He laughed, a wholly male sound meant to torture and intimidate her. "Oh, no," he taunted, tilting her face to his and waiting until she was forced to open her eyes or have him stand there staring at her for the rest of the night.

"There's no hurrying between us, Max. I am going to fuck you. Be sure of that. I'm going to enjoy every minute of it, too." His eyes held arrogant promise and a smug determination that she didn't doubt for a second. "You're going to come twenty times in twenty ways, and it's going to take—All. Night. Long."

He punctuated each word with a hot, wet kiss. Kisses meant to make her beg for mercy, beg for more.

And she did.

Max melted, twining her arms around his neck because her wobbly legs were about to fail her, plastering her body as close to him as she could get. His hands were everywhere, smoothing up her spine, wrapping around her shoulders, and then back down to curve around the globes of her ass through the loose joggers she still wore. He curled one large hand under her knee and lifted her leg up, settling it high on his hip, then stroked his palm along the back of her thigh.

Max was equally involved in an in-depth exploration of Baron's body, testing the width of his biceps under her fingers, tickling the rippling muscles of his abs just to see them twitch and bunch for her. She sighed and rubbed her cheek against the raspy stubble of his chin. The abrasion on her skin was rough and erotic, and made her think about how it was going to feel to have his face buried between her legs.

For long moments they simply enjoyed touching, tasting, learning the contours of each others' bodies. But soon their touches grew more frantic and urgent, their kisses more insistent and their breathing rapid. Hearts pounding in tandem, chest against chest.

Baron stepped back. With his eyes locked to hers he shucked first his pants and then the tight boxer briefs.

Max's breathing hitched and her eyes widened. God, he was beautiful.

His answering grin was cocky and sure—the man definitely had no illusions about his effect on women—on her.

Baron's heavy erection rose high and proud between them as he pulled her back into his embrace and hooked his thumbs into the drawstring waistband of her pants— which were really his pants of course—reinforcing just how big they were on her by how quickly he had them pooled at her ankles on the floor.

Max moved to step out of them, but he had already scooped her up in his arms, and then just as quickly, she was flat on her back, her body spread across the width of the bed. He held her down with a hand splayed wide across her belly and looked his fill.

"Baron, what are you doing?" She tried to rise, wanting to touch him. "I want to—"

"Hush. You'll get your turn." His voice was scratchy and hoarse, as if the words were hard to get out. "But I'm first." He moved his big body on top of her—chest to chest, thigh to thigh—and Max groaned at the delicious heaviness. She arched her back and gripped the tight muscles of his arms in an attempt to get even closer. They bunched and flexed as he held himself over her.

When he kissed her—a wet, open-mouthed kiss that said he could easily have gobbled her up whole—Max nearly wept. She wanted more. So much more.

He stopped, but only to gaze into her eyes with a dark, unfathomable expression she was afraid to try and decipher. "Baron," she whispered with a small shake of her head, pleading with him not to say anything. Not now. She just wanted to feel. Not to talk or think—that would come later, along with the regrets.

Maybe he understood. He dropped his gaze to her

mouth, swiping a thumb over her lips until she gently bit the tip and then eagerly sucked it inside her mouth. She was careful to refrain from grazing him with her vampire teeth, even though the urge to do it was almost too strong to resist.

"I'm going to taste you now," he promised her with a wicked smile. She groaned, his husky voice having just as much of an effect on her as his kiss and his touch.

Lazily, he made his way down her body, dropping kisses and sharp little nips along her sensitized skin as if they had nothing but time, when in reality she was going to burst into flames in less than a minute.

"Your taste has haunted me even after all this time, Max. I can't wait any longer to have your sweetness on my tongue again."

He pushed her thighs wide, and if Max hadn't already been so far gone, she would have protested—or at least blushed—at being so exposed, so open to him. Vulnerable. This was Baron after all and she should be wary. But Max was way beyond that. Instead she spread her legs wider, practically begging him to come to her, take her.

She thought he would simply dive in, but true to his word, nothing about what Baron had planned for her was rushed.

He started with light, fleeting kisses along the soft, sensitive insides of her thighs, kisses that moved higher and higher, but never quite reached the pulsing core of her.

Finally, with one finger he traced the slick line of her slit, drawing out the silky cream that betrayed her readiness, her eagerness. "God, Max, you're so fucking wet. I could take you now without any more play and you'd come with the first thrust of my dick, wouldn't you?"

She groaned, her body singing. She squirmed beneath him, and her breath caught when he slid one finger deep inside her.

"Wouldn't you?" he repeated.

Her head twisted back and forth and her hips arched into his hand, urging him deeper. "Yes...God yes," she whispered on the exhale.

He joined his finger with another, plunging them into her in a tantalizing rhythm. "Then come for me now, Max," he ordered. "Do it. I want to see it."

"Baron—" She knew she would do it. Just because he'd told her to. Her body was so ready, so primed. So eager to please and be pleased.

"Now, Max," he said. "Scream through it. I want everything. I want to feel you and taste you and hear you coming." He put his mouth on her, drawing her clit between his teeth, and she did scream. His fingers thrust in and out of her, his tongue worked against her, in her, and she screamed as she came. Hard and fast, her body convulsing on waves and waves of ecstasy.

He worked her until he had drawn every last thrumming pulse out of her and then he was pulling himself back up her body. Even though her eyes were tightly closed, she could feel the weight of his stare. "Look at me."

She shook her head. She didn't want to open her eyes, wasn't ready to face the challenge she knew he was throwing down. He grasped her thigh and pulled her leg over his shoulder so she was wide open and ready to receive him.

"Look. At. Me."

She could feel him poised there at her entrance, rubbing himself in her juices. She rolled her hips in an attempt to entice him, but he wasn't budging. He would have it his way...or he would have it his way.

She opened her eyes and drowned in his silvery depths.

He roared, a sound full of wild triumph and primal alpha satisfaction as he surged into her in one smooth stroke, filling her. His cock pushing so deep. She screamed again, digging her nails into his back and arching her hips, taking more, wanting everything he could give her.

Chapter Thirteen

Sliding into Max felt like nothing else in the world. It was coming home, finding heaven, and every other clichéd axiom that had ever been coined for what was simply the best feeling in the world.

He gritted his teeth against the overwhelming sensations—the pounding of his heart against his ribs, the throbbing of his cock thrusting into her slick, tight passage—knowing that if he didn't stay in control, it was all going to be over way too soon.

My God. This is Max. Maxine.

Finally.

"Max." His voice was rough, hoarse with desire and need. "I want your bite. I want your teeth in me while I'm fucking you."

"Oh God, Baron," she murmured against his mouth. She wet her lips, her eyes darting to his neck, to the pulse point thumping hard against his skin. She caught a short little breath, her teeth pulling on her bottom lip. He saw the flash of elongated incisor and his hips instinctively slammed into her harder, making her cry out.

"Are you sure?" He could tell the idea excited her just as much as it did him.

"Fuck yeah," he assured her. He wanted this. Not only because it was sexy and kinky, and he liked that. But also because he wanted her to know there was nothing about her that he didn't love, nothing about her that he couldn't accept. He wanted her to share with him what she wouldn't with any other man—hell, if he examined his motives under bright lights and with microscopic lenses, then he'd even have to admit that he wanted this act to tie them together so irrevocably that she never could go to another man.

He was the one who could fulfill all her needs. *He* was the only one.

And wasn't that ironic, coming from the same man who'd walked out on her and the life they could have had, without a word of explanation or even a goodbye.

Shit, he was screwed up.

But right now none of that mattered. All that mattered was Max and giving her what she needed. "Come on, baby," he urged, hips pistoning hard. He was losing control fast, his body already tensing, his balls tightening, every nerve ending ready to explode.

Then she did it. He watched as her eyes glittered with passion and instinct, her lips pulling back and her already long incisors lengthening into deadlier points.

She looked absolutely magnificent. Beautiful, powerful, sexy as hell.

She's mine.

The thought slipped through his subconscious before he could stifle it. *Ah hell.*

He brought his hand to the back of her neck, guiding her to him but was surprised when her lips settled not on his neck, but over his chest, her teeth piercing him right over the heart.

That was it. He couldn't hold on any longer.

"*Max*," he cried, one hand fisted at her waist while the other was propped in the pillow by her head. He held himself over her as his hips surged into the snug cradle of her body. Faster. Harder. Over and over. And then he felt her teeth withdraw, felt her coming again, her sex pulling at him, drawing him deeper with every one of her tight convulsions. He soared over the edge, roaring his release.

Baron held himself still, their hips fused. He wondered what she would say if he kept her like this forever.

With a sigh, he pressed his forehead to hers before leaning back to brush several long, damp strands of hair from her flushed face. She looked him right in the eye as her tongue darted out to catch a small drop of blood from the corner of her mouth, and he shuddered, his body reflexively thrusting forward one more time, wrenching a groan from his lips. He kissed her lightly on the mouth. The spicy, coppery taste of his blood lingered on her lips.

"Woman," he muttered, his breathing still ragged. "You are dangerous."

She smiled. Damn, he loved her smile. It had been so long that he'd almost forgotten how just that small tilt of her lips could bring sunshine and music spilling into the room.

Reluctantly withdrawing from the warmth of her body, he shifted to lay by her side. "How come I never knew that you were a private investigator?" he asked suddenly.

She looked surprised. "Because you never asked?"

"Well, I'm asking now? So why did you become a PI?"

"Why do you want to know?"

Baron hadn't actually meant to ask, but the question had come out and he found that he wanted to know as much about her as she would tell him.

He shrugged. He propped himself up on an elbow so that he could look at her and keep touching her. "I don't know, but I always thought that you'd be a great teacher, or maybe a nurse. Someone who would spend a lot of time with people. You have a way with people. They gravitate to you—young and old—and always seem better for having been gifted with your company."

When Max self-consciously reached for the bed sheet,

trying to pull it over their still sweaty bodies, he shook his head and yanked the smooth linen from her fingers, tossing it down to the foot of the bed. She sighed, glaring at him with mock aggravation, but snuggled deeper into the wall of his chest.

"I don't think I have that kind of effect on people," she denied, but continued when he would have interrupted to insist. "I guess I actually became a PI because of you."

He was stunned, his hands pausing in their relaxed exploration of her nakedness. "Because of me? Why?"

"Well, both you and Jackson." She laughed. "When I was eighteen, I caught you guys keeping secrets from me, and I made it the mission of my senior year to figure out what the hell was going on."

This was news to him. "Uh, I don't think I remember that. I'm pretty sure it was you and Jackson getting up to shit and keeping secrets from me, not the other way around," he chuckled. The two of them had always been concocting some wild scheme or another, and at the last moment trying to con Baron into being the muscle for their half-baked plans. Max would enlist his help and then conveniently fail to mention some key component or another, thereby making sure he was the one who ended up in hot water when things invariably went wrong.

"What do you mean?" Max's voice was deceptively innocent. She knew very well what he meant.

"What do you think I mean? What about Chicago?" He twined a finger around a lock of her hair and tugged.

Her laughter—so pure and fresh—touched him, warmed the heart he had believed to be long dead. "Chicago? But that was a fabulous trip, we all had a blast."

He snorted his disagreement. Of course, she and Jackson had a great time. They had played cards in the backseat of the car while Baron had done the two hour drive. They had watched movies in the hotel and laughed together while Baron tried not to notice that Max was wearing only a skimpy pair of boy's boxers and a belly-baring tank top to sleep in. The two of them had fallen into blissful dreams with the deep exhaustion of excitement spent, while Baron had lain awake, his brother snoring loudly beside him and the sound of Max's soft breathing in the room's other double bed.

Baron still remembered just how easily they had suckered him into that one.

Because of his illness, Jackson hadn't attended school all year. Instead, he had his lessons sent home with a tutor so he would still be able to get his GED with the rest of the class.

It was two months before the fiasco of Max's senior dance. Baron was finishing his first year of college and was home early that Friday because their mom was going out of town on business for the weekend.

As soon as he'd walked in the door, Max approached him with her liquid, solemn blue eyes—eyes he'd been trying to avoid for months—and asked if he would take them to Chicago, assuring him they both had permission to go if he would agree to drive.

In his defense, Baron hadn't actually bought that line of bullshit. But she'd started in with a sob story about how Jackson was missing out on so much, including the senior class trip to Chicago because of his illness, and he really wanted to go to the Field Museum of Natural History. Suffice to say, Baron hadn't been able to say no to her.

He tried, but Max had an answer for his every excuse. Jackson had been in remission for months and was cleared by his doctor; they even had a note—which he found out later had been forged by Jackson himself on a "borrowed" sheet of his physician's prescription pad. The hotel room had already been reserved and paid for. The two of them had saved enough money to cover all expenses.

He'd taken them.

136

He'd gotten in so much shit when they got back, his mother refused to speak to him for a month afterward.

Baron shook his head at the memory.

"You had a blast. Jackson had a blast," he corrected her. "*I* had a coronary."

"Hold on." He remembered something now. "This secret you're talking about...was that about the same time you started following me to football practice, but when I asked why you were skulking around and wouldn't just come watch in the bleachers like everyone else, you denied even being even there?"

She laughed, her voice full of bright, impish amusement that caused his chest to tighten painfully. "Yep," she chuckled. "Are you kidding? Like I would ever admit to watching one of your games, admit to being like one of your groupie cheerleaders." Max put her hand to his chest, flexing against his bare pec like a cat testing her nails before settling down for a nap. "That was just the time you caught me, though. Did you know I also followed you to work at Jerry's Hardware? I would park my bike around back in the alley beside Mrs. Marshall's café and sit at a table, pretending I was on a stakeout while I did my homework. And did you know that I paid your friend Steve Krendell to go through your locker in the men's change room?"

He blinked, speechless.

"No, I guess you didn't," she laughed and licked her index finger, then dragged it down in a line through the air between them. "Point for me. Even back then, I guess I was a pretty good detective."

He didn't doubt she was a good one now—not many people could have found Baron Silver after he'd decided to disappear, but Max had done it.

"So you want to tell me what that was all about?" Baron still couldn't figure out what secret she thought he and Jackson had kept from her.

"Well, it's kind of embarrassing now," she hesitated,

but with a cheeky smile.

"Spill it woman, or I'll have to use my extraordinary talent at sexual torture to get you to talk."

Her smile widened and his heart lurched. If only things could always be this way. If only he could always make Max feel safe and happy enough that she would smile like that.

"Okay, okay. Well, my cousin Sally—do you remember her?"

"How could I not," he said with a groan. "She was dating that guy who thought he knew so much about cars. He was trying to sell me his beat up Honda for almost a year. Finally some other poor sucker bought the piece of crap off of him."

Max grimaced, her expression rueful. "Yeah, his name is Stan. They're married now and he's still trying to pass off crappy cars to everyone in town, since he started working at Lou's Used Car Dealership about two years ago."

Baron barked with a shout of laughter. "Really? Well, at least you know better than to buy anything from him."

"Uh huh. Well, that's another story," Max muttered under her breath. "Anyway, I started following you all around town. It was funny, because I think everyone else saw me but you. It got to be a running joke now that I remember. People knew I was offering a reward to anyone who could give me good intel on your movements whenever I had to be in class. God, some of the stories I heard about you..."

"You what?" Damn. Baron tried to remember what kind of shit he was getting himself into that year that he wouldn't have wanted anyone else to find out about. Luckily, he had been pretty focused on school—it had been the one thing that managed to distract him from the constant guilt, and distract his hormones from Max's too tempting self.

"Anyway, Sally came to me one day and said she'd

seen you at the mall with Deb Dewson and that you two had been pretty chummy in the jewelry store."

She was watching his expression, waiting. But for the life of him he couldn't remember—

Oh, shit.

Now he remembered.

"You following along so far?" Max must have seen the flash of recognition in his eyes because she nodded her head and continued. "Right. I still didn't know if it had anything to do with the secret you and Jackson were keeping, but I thought it was interesting. I mean, not many boys would have actually admitted to dating Deb 'the Skank' Dewson, and they certainly wouldn't have taken her out in public, much less to a jewelry store, at least not unless she was blackmailing them with something. So I watched you guys. Figured even if I didn't find out what I had been hoping to...it would still be eye-opening to discover just what you saw in a woman like her."

"Geez, Max."

"What? Like you wouldn't have done the same if the situation had been reversed."

His eyes narrowed, and he growled. Baron didn't want to think about what he might have done if he'd had to watch Max with some pretty boy, maybe letting him kiss her and feel her up in a public place. Thankfully, that had been the least of his problems. Max had never seemed interested in spending time with anyone but Jackson.

She laughed at him again and swatted his fingers, which had been drawing invisible circles on the inside of her elbow. "Don't get your chest hairs tied in a knot. Or don't you want to hear the rest of this?"

"Go on." He grabbed the hand that had smacked at him and started rubbing her palm with his thumb, feeling oddly content in a way that he hadn't in a long time.

"I even had your mom spying for me. She was my eyes and ears every time you picked up the phone."

"Holy crap." He couldn't believe that he hadn't had a clue. Then again, now that he thought about it, Baron had been dealing with some pretty heavy shit back then. He'd been trying to decide whether he was going to go ahead and enlist, or continue with his college program, knowing that if he did ship out, he was gone for good.

"I was getting desperate because as far as I could tell, there was nothing going on. Besides that one time when Sally said she'd seen you with Deb, I couldn't find any evidence that you had anything up your sleeves."

"That's because there wasn't anything going on," he pointed out.

"Ah, but then everything changed. I actually caught you two in a lie."

"What lie?" When had he lied?

"One day Jackson said you had gone to work, but I followed you to the mall. I figured I was finally going to catch you in the act...of what I didn't know...but you just went back to the jewelry store."

Baron smiled. Now he had a good idea where this story was heading.

"I didn't dare go in after you, but I did notice that Debbie wasn't anywhere in sight. I was walking back out of the mall when I caught up with Trevor Daniels. He asked if I was there to shop for a dress for the spring formal. I was stunned. I think I freaked him out because I just stared at him blankly for about two whole minutes."

Baron watched the animation in her expression, the laughter in her eyes, in her voice. It was captivating to him the way she relived these memories with such clarity and enjoyment. "You see, in all the intrigue of spying on you, I had forgotten all about the dance. I was too busy trying to catch you sneaking around that I didn't realize I had followed you to the tuxedo rental place and the flower shop, and your mom filled me in on a conversation she overheard you having with your buddy James where he promised to let you use his Fiero for that Friday night."

He chuckled, turning her body into his so he could spoon in behind her with his arms around her waist. "So is that when you figured it out? I was positive Jackson and I had caught you off guard."

"Aha, so you do remember!" She turned and glared at him, but he just kissed her sweetly. She sighed. "You did catch me off guard," she admitted with a wry grin, wiggling her rear in his lap. "Well, you were a college boy after all. I figured Skank Dewson had worked her way through the high school boys and was broadening her horizons. I thought that your trip to the jewelry store was to get something for her. I was already planning my smear campaign. I was going to tease you mercilessly."

"I'll bet. I can't believe you thought she and I were getting it on. Didn't she go out with half the football team?"

Max chuckled. "At the same time, too." She paused, and her smile faded. "When I went to see Jackson that afternoon, and he started trying to talk me into going to the dance, that's when I realized what all the secrecy had been about. I still can't believe you guys even bought me a dress."

"Mm. It was that ruffly pink thing. It looked great on you. I remember it perfectly." He actually remembered taking it *off* of her—at least as much of it as he could manage in the cramped confines of his friend's sporty car.

By the end of that night, Baron's self-control had snapped, despite the good intentions he started with. Somehow, the bodice of her dress had ended up pulled down to her waist, revealing her perfect breasts to him so that he couldn't not kiss and lick and tease her nipples until she squirmed and whimpered beneath him. And somehow, the three or four layers of crinoline and silk had been pushed up around her thighs, and his fingers were sliding past the silky barrier of her panties to delve into the incredible wet warmth of her pussy. He'd kissed as much of her as he could reach, and they'd steamed up all of the windows until the car was practically a sauna.

They both felt awkward and uncomfortable afterward, but it had been beautiful all the same, because that night had been full of magic. Full of love. Full of youthful promises—all of which he regretted later, none of which he had lived up to—but which he would never forget.

"You looked beautiful that night, Max. And I guess you were able to figure out why I had been in the jewelry store," he said, smiling.

"Yes." She frowned and looked down at her hand, which was bare of any jewelry. "I stopped wearing it after you left. I know it was supposed to be from you and Jackson—a friendship kind of thing—but I felt...I knew you had picked it out, and..."

She shrugged.

He didn't like it. But at least she wasn't wearing another man's ring in its place.

He cleared his throat and buried his face in the clean scent of her hair, unsure of what to say.

"There's one thing that I never figured out," she continued.

"What's that?" His hand smoothed her hair back behind one ear, so that he could nibble his way down the column of her neck.

She shivered prettily and angled her head to allow him better access. "Were you ever really with Deb Dewson in that jewelry store?"

"Well..."

"You were weren't you?"

"I was in there looking at rings, and I had picked the one that I wanted for you—that Jackson and I wanted to get you—but I didn't have a clue what size you would wear. Debbie just happened to walk in and offer to try it on for me so I could see what it looked like. I think she was trying to get me to tell her who it was for."

Max craned her neck to look at him and grimaced. "Ew. Are you telling me that Skank Dewson had her mitts

142

on my ring before it was given to me?"

He frowned. "Um, is that bad?"

She just laughed and shook her head, turning back around to cuddle in closer, her back to his front. "You really are an ass," she said, but without any real heat.

"That was a long time ago," he defended.

"Right. And your point is?"

"I've learned a few things since then." He shifted her in his arms so that she was facing him, her thighs cupping his thick, heavy erection. He palmed her breast in his hand and dragged his thumb over her sensitive nipple, watching for her hiss of delight. His kiss was as desperate as if he hadn't just had her under him, his body just as hard.

"Again?" she said, chuckling as she wiggled in his embrace, clearly up to the challenge.

"I warned you," he answered. "All. Night. Long."

Chapter Fourteen

Baron watched Max as she slept. He hadn't been able to sleep himself, so he just held her in his arms, listening to her feminine snores and waiting for the dream to end.

He knew morning had come and was glad for the windowless room. It was easy to forget that his childhood love was now a vampire—what with Max laying so peacefully beside him, her body warm and pulsing with life even in sleep—but it was true nevertheless, and he wanted to make sure that she was kept safe from the sun.

There were so many things that he should be doing right now, not the least of which was going out with Alric to search for Devon.

And still, he stayed.

He stayed and he remembered.

Baron had spent so many years doing everything possible *not* to think about Max or about what he had thrown away by leaving her. Now those memories bombarded him.

Surprisingly, it was a lot of little things that popped into his head. Like the way she had to peel off not only the skin, but every piece of white stuff from her orange before eating it, or that she liked peanut butter and banana, but not peanut butter and jam. He remembered how Max had looked at his mother as if she hung the moon. He thought of the way she was with Jackson, never treating him like an invalid because of his illness, but showing him all the love and compassion of a true friend.

It was because of all those things that Baron thought it would be best to stay far away from her. Especially after his transition. He had known that if he stayed, he and Max would eventually get together. He wouldn't have been strong enough to resist her for long—even for Jackson. So he left, and he tried to pack the void where his heart used to be with other women. Lots of other women. But it hadn't made a difference, just kind of dulled the pain and filled him with more self-loathing.

After his transition, Baron poured all of that frustration and energy into his training with Rhys and Alric and the twins, and it seemed to work for him a little better than fucking every skirt in town. He focused his pent up aggression and regret into gutting demons, and found he was damn good at it.

When he heard about his mother's stroke, he couldn't not go home. But even then he had known it would be for the last time.

He hadn't planned to even see Max while he was there, but he should have known it would be impossible not to.

She was too capable and strong not to be right there with Jackson taking care of everything. Lorraine Silver hadn't technically been her family, but that was just biology. All of them had taken Max into their home as a part of their family that first day she showed up with Jackson's homework under her arm and made him her friend. Lorraine had once told her son she thought it was a miracle Maxine had grown into such a lovely woman, given the home she had been raised in. Baron had known it was probably a combination of Max's determination and strength and Lorraine's acceptance and love.

When Max's own mother died, it had been Lorraine who helped her with the arrangements, and Lorraine who told Max she could cry—even though to Baron's

145

knowledge, Max never did.

That's why he had been so surprised when he walked into Jackson's hospital room that day and Max started to weep in his arms. She who never cried over anything, who hadn't cried for her own mother, had cried for his.

He'd been holding onto his own pain by the thinnest of threads, and it had been all he could do not to fall apart then, but he'd known Max would force herself to push aside her grief and be strong for him, and he couldn't let her do that.

Instead, he brought her home and made wild, passionate love to her all through the night.

God, what a mistake that had been.

But he couldn't regret it.

In the morning, nothing had changed. He was still an Immortal; she had still been human. He couldn't stay.

Max had already been deprived of so much. Baron didn't want to be the one who took more away from her. She deserved a good man, and he hadn't wanted to disappoint her even more when she eventually found out he wasn't one and there wasn't a hope in hell he ever would be.

Maybe he had been wrong.

Now that he had Max here, now that she knew all there was to know, including what he was and what he'd done, did he dare ask her to stay? It wasn't something he thought he would ever consider, but now...

She needed him; there was that angle to work with. She dared not take blood from anyone but him. His Immortal constitution could safely feed her needs, could easily satisfy her hunger without bringing danger to anyone else.

She would fight it, he knew. But if he wanted her, what other choice did he have?

Baron had been forced to admit the truth the moment he recognized her broken body lying on his front step. He didn't know what the future held for them, but he already knew if he let her go again now, he might not survive it.

He glanced down at her face and found her watching him. "Hi there," he said.

She smiled. "Hi yourself."

Baron heaved himself out of bed, dragging her up into his arms. She squealed prettily in surprise, and he chuckled.

"Hey! You big muscle-bound jerk, what do you think you're doing?" she cried.

He tossed her over his shoulder, ass in the air, and smacked her bare, fleshy cheek. "I'm going to wash out that mouth of yours and see if you show a little more respect."

"You just try it, buddy."

"Oh, I'm going to," he promised, enjoying himself immensely. "I'm going to try a lot more than that." He started walking to the adjoining bathroom with Max pounding playfully on his chest. He set her down right inside the glass enclosed shower stall and turned the water on.

Max screeched and shivered as the cold droplets hit her skin. "Oh! I'm going to get you for that."

"I'm looking forward to it," he taunted, stepping into the shower behind her when he was sure the water was hot enough.

She turned to him with a smile, and he thought she was going to continue their verbal sparring, but her smile faltered. "Baron," she started, hesitating. "We can't stay like this forever. Sooner rather than later, both of us are going to have to deal with those skeletons that are overflowing our respective closets. And while this has been an enjoyable interlude, it isn't real. You know that, right?"

"Shh, there'll be time enough for reality later." He knew what she wasn't saying out loud. She still didn't trust him. And while he couldn't blame her for how she felt, surprisingly, he was hurt by it nevertheless.

He hushed her with a finger to her lips, then leaned forward and replaced it with a long, wet kiss.

They went slowly, using the water and the soap to lather and tease each other. He ran his hands over her breasts, palming their weight in his palms and teasing her nipples to hard sensitive points. He loved how she sighed and whimpered under his tender ministrations, how her body blossomed and trembled from desire that she couldn't deny.

She traced the hard planes of his chest, abs, waist. Her eyes hungry as they followed the progress of her slick, soapy hands. She headed downward, and his cock kicked up against his abdomen in anticipation of her touch. Her laughter was throaty and teasing. He tipped her face up to his so that he could kiss her nice and deep, working her with his tongue.

When she wrenched her mouth from his, her eyes were dark like cobalt and her breathing came fast. "You said I would get my turn," she warned with a coy smile that jumpstarted his heart.

He couldn't help but marvel again over his colossal stupidity of the last two years. What the hell had he been thinking to give this woman up without even a fight?

She was light and laughter; she was air to him.

"So I did. On your knees woman," he commanded.

Max kissed her way back down his chest, the warm water sluicing down both of their bodies in long rivulets. When she settled before him on her knees, she ran her hands slowly from his calves up his thighs, her thumbs inching inward as she reached his groin. Her breath teased his curly hair. God, she loved his body. Big and powerful, he was all hard planes and smooth sculptured muscle, every inch of which called her to touch and taste.

Closing a hand around him she squeezed, making him

groan. She leaned in to taste him and he shot an arm out to brace himself against the glass wall of the shower enclosure, which made her laugh wickedly before she swirled her tongue over the tip of his cock, then closed her mouth over him. She cupped his sac in her hands while her mouth moved on him. For several minutes she indulged herself, using her tongue and her mouth to torture him like he had so recently done to her.

"God, Max," he moaned, one hand in her hair, holding her to him. "Harder. Suck me harder."

She complied with pleasure, her hands enfolding him, up and down, while her mouth pulled on him hard. His hips began to move, his cock thrusting into her mouth, and she took all of him, happily.

It wasn't long before he drew her up by her arms, and turned her abruptly to face the clear glass of the shower wall. He let out a low growl and ran hot kisses along the length of her spine. With the cold tile pressed against her breasts and Baron's raging heat at her back, Max was more than ready. His urgency excited her, and she arched her back toward him eagerly. When he pulled her hips into the cradle of his thighs, she braced herself, putting her hands flat against the glass.

"Spread your legs." He kicked them open himself.

She felt him poised at her entrance, waiting, and she tilted her ass higher to accommodate him. "It's going to be hard and fast, Max. I can't do it any other way right now."

She laughed, desperate for him to fill her. "Why would you think I'd want it any other way?"

His hand was at the small of her back, rubbing in circles. "I just...I haven't exactly been gentle with you, and..." Though his voice was apologetic, his hard body was insistent as he pushed inside her from behind, entering her just a fraction of an inch. She couldn't help the hiss that blew past her lips, and she rotated her hips in an attempt to entice him in further.

"Do gentle later." Her voice came out rough and gravely. She tilted her hips up and back, sliding her body onto him, taking him as deep as she could without any help from him. The water pounded down upon them both, steam rising from their bodies, though she thought they probably could have generated enough of it on their own without the water's help.

"Oh fuck, Max," he groaned. "That's so fucking good." In one long thrust he surged into her, sliding right to the hilt. His thighs slammed up against the backs of her thighs and her breasts jiggled with the delicious force of it. She kept her hands braced on the wall as he pulled almost all the way out, and then pushed home again. And again. He reached around her for her breasts, his fingers pinching her nipples to hard points.

"Yes. God, yes." She was a creature of sensation, insistent on her own pleasure, unable to form a coherent thought or sentence except to demand more. "Baron, touch me."

His grunted reply was followed quickly by the slide of his hand between her legs. A shot of electricity through the very core of her made her weak in the knees, and she felt her legs wobbling, ready to collapse beneath her. Baron wrapped his arm tightly around her waist as he continued to stroke her, continued to pump in and out of her, his movements turning frantic as they both crested the ragged edge of release.

She could feel his breath over her shoulder, hard and heavy as he kept up the frenzied pace. Max shouted as the wave hit her in fierce pulses, and she tilted her head back, feeling the water streaming over her closed eyelids and into her open mouth. Behind her Baron stiffened with his own release and then he folded himself around her, both arms holding her close, his face buried against her neck.

Long moments later, he turned off the cooling water. They stepped out of the shower and went back into the bedroom, both of them wrapped in great big terrycloth towels.

Reality started to settle in as she again realized that she had no clothes to wear but for the pants and ruined shirt Baron had lent her earlier. It was time to go home.

"What time is it?" she asked.

Baron glanced at her sharply, obviously picking up on the strained tone of her voice. He checked his watch, a nice, obviously waterproof Swiss Army job that looked expensive. "Early," he said. "Six a.m."

Wow. Had they really spent the whole day together? The whole night? Talking and arguing and making love? It was definitely more than she thought would happen when she started out to find Baron. But now it didn't seem enough. Was this all she would have to last her through the days and months and years ahead?

"I had better be going." She pulled on the oversized pants she had worn earlier, and started looking around for a shirt. "Jackson wants you to come home. He's sick, Baron. He's dying. And there isn't a lot of time left."

Baron simply watched her, his face a stone mask.

Max didn't know why she should be surprised. "Fine. You obviously don't care, since you haven't even asked about him. So whatever. You can come or not."

He gripped her shoulders and turned her to face him. "Max, you can't go."

"You can't stop me."

He was going to try and argue with her, she could see it in his eyes. But maybe he had seen something in hers as well, because he didn't. He stood down. Stepped back. With a sigh he said, "Maybe, maybe not. But the sunlight sure can."

Max flinched. Damn it. So that wasn't part of the myth. She really wasn't going to be able to go out in the sun. She felt the loss sharply like a dagger to her breast. "Ever?"

His eyes were sad as he shook his head and reached for her. "I'm sorry, baby."

151

She jerked out of his grasp and stalked away, arms crossed in front of her chest. Where the hell was that shirt? "Don't call me that. And don't you dare say you're sorry." She could feel the tears threatening at the backs of her eyes. Damn! She hadn't been this close to crying so freakin' often since...well, she never cried. And she sure as hell wasn't going to start now. She would die if Baron saw tears in her eyes.

"Look," he said, "for now...just wait. I know you need to get back, but I can't let you go with the vampire still out there. He's keeping his eye on all of us right now, trying to gauge our reactions to what he's done, and he'll use you to hurt me again if he thinks he can."

Max blinked once to clear her vision of the pesky, useless tears that she couldn't seem to get rid of, and clenched her jaw tightly. Her laugh was a brittle, sharp sound. "Well, then I might as well go tell him right now that he's wasting his time," she snapped. "Because we all know everyone is dispensable. He couldn't possibly use me to hurt you."

She thought he winced, but otherwise Baron didn't rise to the bait. She didn't know whether to feel relieved or disappointed. Part of her still wanted that lock down drag out fight to relieve the tension between them. But that was just asking for trouble, since Max and Baron both knew how close she had come to losing what was left of her humanity the last time her emotions took a swan dive.

"Max—"

She shook her head. "Forget it, Baron. Just leave me alone."

He sighed, and after a long, silent moment, he turned toward the door. "I asked Diana if she wouldn't mind lending you something to wear. You're a bit taller than she is, but she said she probably has a few things that would fit you." He paused. "I'll leave you alone for a while. Don't leave the premises."

She snorted, her indignation plain. Yeah, as if she could.

He glanced back, his expression cold as his gaze raked over her before he walked out the door without a word. Max swore as she realized she was still standing in the middle of the room with her arms crossed protectively over her naked breasts.

Damn.

Chapter Fifteen

Max paced. The rug was going to have a hole worn through it if she didn't stop soon, but she was too wired, her nerves strung out so bad she felt like a junkie who'd gone without a hit for one too many hours.

She had to get out of here.

It had already been proven to her in graphic, wet, naked detail that her carefully established firewalls would not hold against Baron any longer. In fact, given the last several hours, she was surprised she hadn't already fallen at his feet and begged him to give them another chance together.

Thank God she hadn't done that...at least not yet. But she could feel herself losing ground in the battle to remain detached and get out of Chandler without losing her heart to Baron all over again.

She was still angry as hell at him, but surprisingly, a lot of the old hurt just wasn't there anymore. And okay, he had saved her life, let her drink his blood, and finally spilled the sordid story of why he left.

But that was no reason to simply forgive all of the pain he had caused. Max couldn't forget that if she hadn't been forced to come to Chandler looking for him in the first place and ended up a late-night snack for a vampire instead, then she would still have no idea what Baron had been doing all this time. No idea why he had ditched his only family...and the ridiculously foolish girl who had once found herself falling in love with him.

Well, she wasn't that girl anymore, and it would take more than a sob story and some acrobatic sex to change her mind about him. Whatever his issues, the truth was he hadn't trusted her enough, hadn't wanted her enough, hadn't believed in them enough, to give them a chance at a real love. Instead, he had made excuses for why they couldn't be together, excuses why he couldn't be the man she needed.

And that was fine. Let him wallow in his excuses, because she *didn't* need him. Max would go back to her life and forget that Baron ever existed.

Hell. Even she didn't believe that.

She cocked her head to the side. Someone was coming down the hall...to see her. Odd, she knew it was Diana; somehow she could sense the other woman. There was a light knock at the door. Max hesitated, but then went to open it and sure enough, Diana stood there smiling, her arms overflowing with a selection of women's clothes.

"How are you doing?" she asked.

"I'm going stir crazy, to tell you the truth." Max stepped aside to let Diana come into the room. "I'm not used to being cooped up like this."

"I understand how you feel." Diana put her pile of folded clothes neatly on the bed and turned to face Max with a smile. "There have been a few times when Alric believed it wasn't safe for me to be alone at home and initiated what he calls the lockdown procedure. And I know Amy's been through it with Rhys a few times, too."

"I guess being an immortal demon hunter could give a guy some control issues," Max joked. "It must be frustrating to live with such...overbearing men."

Diana grinned. "Oh, sure. But you'd never believe the perks." Her teasing wink left Max with no doubt whatsoever of the kinds of perks Diana was talking about.

"It's like that is it?" She laughed.

Diana sobered and said, "Baron told me that you're anxious to get back to your friend. Is he doing okay?"

Max bit back the nasty comment that sat on the tip of her tongue. It probably wasn't a good idea to vent her frustrations with Baron to his friends, no matter how understanding Diana seemed. "I just got off the phone with his doctor. There isn't a lot of time. But for the moment he's stable."

Max sensed Diana's anxiety. She could tell the woman was nervous. Nervous because...Diana knew Max could read her thoughts and was worried about distressing her.

Oh jeez, a*s if my thoughts aren't distressing enough.* Max doubted anything Diana came up with was going to faze her.

The sensation of having someone else's fears and worries running through her head was very disconcerting, and Max put her fingers to her temple in an attempt to block them, but then quickly dropped her hand, not wanting to make it obvious that she was reading Diana like an open book.

But how was she even doing such a thing? How could she be picking up on another person's thoughts? Obviously, it had something to do with the vampire inside of her—Max still refused to think of it as a *part* of her. She wasn't ready to face those kinds of truths just yet.

"Thanks for the clothes, Diana. Baron said you had a few things that I could borrow. I appreciate it. I don't know what happened to my bag after..."

"It's really no problem." Diana waved her off. "I just brought you a pair of jeans and a fresh shirt, and I thought you'd probably appreciate a bra and some underwear. I bought a nice set last week that I haven't worn yet, so you can keep them."

Max felt like the worst sort of beggar for having to accept the other woman's charity, especially Diana's pretty pink lingerie, but she would take the garments nevertheless. The only alternative she had was to keep wandering around in Barons' clothes, and that was unacceptable. She had to get away from the scent of him somehow. It was too intoxicating, distracting her thoughts, making her...want. "I'm sorry to be an imposition, but thank you."

"Don't worry about it. Baron is a good friend, and I'm glad that I can help you both even if it's only by going shopping. Some hardships are necessary." She smiled.

Max chuckled. "I can reimburse you for everything once I get back home."

"Uh, sure, but don't feel obligated. Consider it a gift." Diana dropped her eyes to the floor and Max frowned. Well hell. Diana was trying not to think it, but she clearly didn't believe Baron had any intention of letting her go home.

Max could have told her not to bet the farm on Baron's ability to keep her here when she decided to go, but felt it would be prudent to adopt the more diplomatic course and keep her mouth shut. Her battle was with Baron, not Diana.

"Can I ask you something?" she asked. This mind reading thing was really freaking her out.

"Of course," Diana replied. "Ask me whatever you like."

"Well..." How was she going to put this? "Don't take this the wrong way, but..."

Diana smiled. "You're reading my thoughts, aren't you?"

"I'm not trying to," Max protested with a frustrated sigh. "I don't even know how I'm doing it, and I can't seem to stop it. More specifically though, my question is *why* am I doing it with you? I can't seem to read Baron's mind, and I didn't notice that I could with Alric earlier either. When we met yesterday, though, I think I got a wave of something from you—although I didn't understand what it was at the time—but then it seemed to just stop, so I didn't think much about it." Max turned to sit on the bed.

Diana laughed. "I know, and I'm sorry about that. If it's too much for you, I can leave you alone."

"No," Max replied hurriedly, not wanting to lose the other woman's company just yet. "I just don't understand what the hell is going on. With any of this."

"It must be difficult for you." Diana came forward and sat primly on the edge of the bed beside Max, conscious of the hem of her pencil skirt. "You can read me like that because I'm human. It's harder with the boys, since they're Immortal. An older vampire like Devon might be able to pick their brain, but they have strong psychic barriers that a newbie vampire like yourself wouldn't be able to breach."

Immortals, vampires, and psychic barriers. Max had to wonder how Diana, as a human, had found herself caught up in all of this, and how she was able to speak so matter-of-factly about things that no person should be talking about except in reference to the latest Hollywood blockbuster. "Okay, I can understand that...I think," she nodded. "But what happened yesterday in the kitchen? Why did the live mind feed suddenly just stop?"

Diana smiled. "I think Baron probably noticed what was happening and blocked your ability, so that you wouldn't be able to read my thoughts."

"Baron?" Baron was able to do that? "Is that some kind of monkey trick all the Immortals have then?"

She shook her head. "No, actually. Although all Immortals end up with some kind of psychic ability when they come out of the transition, it's different for each of them. For example, Alric can move things around with his mind, which is kind of nerve racking when you walk into a room to find the TV remote coming straight for you." She smiled. "Rhys gets visions of the future in his dreams—warnings really. And Baron has the ability to sense another's psychic talent and take control of it temporarily."

"Take control? Well that's something he conveniently failed to mention," she muttered. She shouldn't be surprised. It was so like him to dole out only little tidbits of information, but to never give anyone the whole unvarnished truth. Damn that man.

Diana's look was sympathetic. "I know how you must feel. The men can be pretty overbearing at times—okay, pretty much all of the time. It's in their nature I think. They operate like a military unit—as if everything is need-to-know and we don't have proper security clearance. But they mean well, and you find ways of getting around them if you really want to."

Diana might find ways around it, being married to Alric and all, but Max didn't have the patience to be so discreet. She would end up busting her way through those pig-headed inclinations of Baron's and demand answers.

Actually, no, she wouldn't. She was leaving. Gone. For good. And Baron's obstinate, mistrustful nature could rot in hell.

"Well, I'd say playing around with my mind is something that should have been on his Max-needs-to-know list," she protested.

"I know, and I agree. But at the same time, I'm sure he thought he was helping." Diana apparently saw from the look on Max's face that she wasn't buying it. "Really. He probably only did it because he could tell the sensation was distressing to you. He knows that you're going to need some time to build up an internal buffering system before you'll be able to keep the psychic waves from overwhelming you. Simply walking down a busy street right now would be very difficult for you. The din from even the most innocuous thoughts—like someone running through their grocery list in their head, or humming a tune they heard while stuck in an elevator—

when combined with thousands more..."

Max grimaced, feeling a headache coming on at just the thought of all those voices in her head. "Yeah, I think I get the picture." She was starting to realize how precarious her new place was in this world—and just how much Baron had been shielding her from that reality.

"So he knew I had this...ability?"

"I would assume so. He did a lot of reading the night you were brought to us." She hesitated but must have realized that if she didn't say what was on her mind, Max was going to pull it from her head anyway. "You know, he was really devastated when he saw what the vampire had done to you. I've never seen him get like that before."

Max could see in her mind what Diana still wasn't saying. "I'm sure." Max winced inwardly as she heard the sarcasm in her own voice, but at least sarcasm would mask the hurt that tightened her chest. "Don't worry about it. It isn't as if I didn't already know the guy is a sleazy man-whore." Max tried to act like she didn't care about all the women, but she doubted she was having any success.

Diana snorted with laughter, and clapped her hand over her mouth. "Sorry, I don't mean to sound insensitive. It's just that I think I said something along those very lines to Alric only a few days ago." Her grin softened and her voice turned gentle. "Max, don't take my thoughts out of context, okay? I don't know what happened between the two of you before Baron came to us, but—"

"Nothing happened between us. Nothing of any consequence anyway." Max's laugh was harsh and self-deprecating even to her own ears, and she winced. "Just a quick pity-fuck before he disappeared from my life for good."

Amazingly enough, she sensed that Diana honestly cared. Not just about Baron, her friend, but about Max. She looked the other woman in the eye, trying to find ulterior motives for her kindness, but there weren't any.

The woman was just that sweet.

Max sighed and gave up trying to hide the evidence of her pain and anger because she knew she was an emotional wreck and it wasn't working worth a damn anyway. "You tell me how you would feel if the boy you loved all through high school left town and deserted his family just to get away from you."

"Oh, Max—"

Max shook her head, refusing to meet Diana's eyes. "You know, Baron has taken so much about this situation in stride, I think the only thing that's really bothered him is the fact that he can no longer pretend invisibility. He would rather have me think he was dead, so that he wouldn't be forced to see me again."

Diana put a hand on her arm and Max could feel the waves of understanding rolling softly from the woman's gentle spirit, almost as if she had been through a similar experience herself.

It was nice of her to want Max to feel better—too nice actually. Max didn't need any sympathy. She didn't want understanding. What she wanted was to not have to feel this way at all. What she wanted was Baron out of her life for good so that he couldn't torture her like this anymore.

"I know you don't want to hear this, and it isn't really my place to get involved either way, but..." Diana paused, considering how much she should say. "I've known Baron since he came to us after the transition. I know he uses women. I know he doesn't care about much. While I may not have psychic powers, I know a man trying to escape his past when I see one—and they don't do that unless there's something to run from."

Max didn't want to hear anymore. None of it mattered any way. She knew very well she never had any claim on Baron. Their history was pathetic in so much as it was virtually non-existent. Max knew she had no right to judge his life choices, and the fact that she continued to let herself be hurt by them was her own fault.

Except when it came to Jackson.

Jackson was her friend, and he was too nice and too weak to hold Baron accountable for his actions. She did and would judge Baron an asshole for the way he had let his brother down.

"Do you mind my asking how you and Alric got together?" Max's attempt to divert the kind woman's attention from her own disgusting misery was obvious, but what the hell.

Diana shrugged her shoulders. Max could tell that the request had made her tense for some reason.

"That's okay, Diana. I'm sorry, I shouldn't have asked. I don't want you to feel like I would purposely pry into your personal life just because I can't handle my own."

"You aren't prying, and I don't mind. It's just that...those memories are really close to the surface lately for some reason. I was just thinking about it last night. Really, if you want to know, I have no problem telling you." Diana seemed to understand that Max was going nuts in this bedroom and was generously offering her own history as a distraction.

"Only if you're sure." She felt guilty, but too curious to demur. She wanted to know more about these people who seemed so perfect for each other.

"No, it's fine, and I like the idea of having a woman around to talk to. Alric and I don't usually stay here. We have our own place across town, and I find myself alone there quite a bit. Especially at times like these when he's off fighting, um...well, in any case, there aren't too many women who could understand what I feel."

"Now?" Max asked. "Are they out there..."

"Ah, yeah. I mean I think so. They're looking for the vampire."

"Do you think they could get hurt?" Did she sound too concerned? Max had been going for a casual, indifferent sort of curiosity, but judging by the canny look on Diana's face, she seemed to have failed in that.

The other woman settled back with a grin. "They're both very good at what they do, Max; don't you worry."

Diana's grin turned to a private little smile, and Max felt the love Diana had for her husband, the pride she felt, and the confidence she had in him.

It was nice to know that some people had good, healthy relationships with one another.

"You know, I used to be a welder for a pretty big construction outfit here in town,"

"A welder?" Max eyed the slight, delicate, so very feminine woman up and down with skepticism. "You're kidding me right?"

Diana laughed, her voice clear and ringing with humor. "No, not kidding," she said. "It's funny how often I get that same look from people when I tell them."

Max shrugged her shoulders. She wasn't exactly in a female-dominated profession herself, so who was she to judge? "Sorry, I didn't mean anything by it."

"That's all right. The reason I entered that line of work to begin with was because of my latent insecurity issues with my father, who was also a welder. I was always trying to find ways to be closer to him, but he wanted nothing much to do with me and my sister. She learned early on to ignore him, but I guess I never really could."

"I can understand that." Max had never had a father, since hers had taken off while her mother was still in the hospital giving birth to her. She mostly pretended that it didn't matter, that she had never cared one way or the other, but as a kid she would have jumped at the chance to have a father, even one who practically ignored her existence.

"Anyway, about four years ago I was on a job down in the subway tunnels. I came across Alric. He had been chained to the stone, trapped behind a wall of rubble."

163

"Oh my God." Max could tell that Diana was understating what really happened. Max purposely tried to shut her mind down because she didn't want to spy on the woman's memories, but she got a good, clear image before managing to get a barrier up, and she was horrified by what Alric had been through.

"I'll never forget that night." The light in Diana's eyes went out while she relived the dark memory of that underground tunnel. "Alric's life has been...hard, which is a hell of an understatement. His father raised him from childhood to be a warrior, and he had already been fighting every day of his life before he became an Immortal."

She paused and a shadow passed over her face. "Hundreds of years of evil, Max. That is their legacy. They fight it every damn day, and there's never an end in sight. Who could blame them if they should falter, just once? Make a bad decision?"

"What happened, Diana?" Max felt an overwhelming urge to take Diana's hand in hers and offer the woman comfort, but she knew if she did that, the images would be even harder to control.

"He was betrayed." There was a world of implication in that statement that Max didn't want to touch.

"How long was he trapped down there?" she asked.

Diana's eyes turned brittle with remembered anguish for Alric. "When I found him he had been there almost one hundred years," she answered.

"Oh my God. A hundred years? How did he survive?"

"He didn't have a choice. I think if he could have chosen, he would have picked death, but he is an Immortal. There are some things that can kill him, but starvation and insanity apparently aren't among them."

"But why didn't anyone find him in all that time? Weren't there other Immortals who would have noticed him missing and gone to look for him?"

"They weren't as close a group as they are now. It

164

was only recently that Rhys got these guys to band together and pool their resources to more effectively deal with the demon threat here. Before then, it was an every Immortal for himself kind of arrangement." Diana ran an index finger with preoccupied inattention over the front seam of her skirt. "The others didn't know Alric well enough to wonder about him when he stopped coming around. They knew he was alive because there hadn't been any new Immortals called by the Guardian. They assumed he'd moved on and was fighting demons somewhere else—which is exactly what Alric's enemies had planned on."

"So who is this 'Guardian' character?"

"That one's a little harder to explain," Diana frowned. "I get the impression that the Guardian is some kind of otherworldly being. Apparently the Guardian directs the power from a dying Immortal, to the one who gets chosen to take his place."

"Sounds like an interesting guy."

"Alric likes to call him the 'absentee landlord', because other than loading them up with power and sending them out to fight, the Guardian practices a strict hands off policy with the Immortals, and few have seen what he looks like."

"So what did you do when you found Alric? You must have been terrified."

"Yes, but I got him out of there," she replied. "I mean, what else could I do?" Diana probably didn't even realize it, but for her to even think that way proved just how amazing she was. Not many women could have faced the terrifying visage of an Immortal man left to rot underground for a hundred years, and not only try to rescue him, but also manage to bring him back from the brink of madness—because Max had no doubt that's exactly what she had done.

"I was scared. And Alric was out of his mind...I must have been insane myself, because I took him home with me." She sent Max a rueful smile. "It was a crazy thing to do, but I knew if I took him to the hospital they would put him in some psych ward and maybe strap him down to a bed, and I couldn't bear for that to happen to him, not after..."

Max knew she was staring, but she couldn't help herself. She was seriously stunned by the incredible strength and compassion of this tiny woman. Alric must know just how lucky and blessed he was to have found her. He had just moved up a few more notches in her esteem.

"Alric was not exactly cooperative," Diana admitted. "And it was a trial just to get him out of the subway tunnels and back to my very tiny bachelor apartment—which he promptly proceeded to trash in a violent fit." Diana's grin was unapologetic. "But I'll have you know I kicked some serious Immortal butt that night getting him to settle down," she said with pride.

"I don't doubt it for a moment." Actually, she kind of did. Diana was just too delicate looking for Max to ever be able to see her as a bad ass.

"Hey, I had been working side by side with some of the roughest men in tool belts you'll ever come across, and there were plenty of times I had to defend myself from unwanted advances. Not to mention the fairly consistent 'tests' that were supposed to prove I didn't belong because I was a woman and, therefore, couldn't hack the job."

"I understand completely," Max nodded. "As a PI, I get a lot of flack from the local police who think I should stay home and knit or some shit."

"Exactly," Diana smiled. "And who the hell actually knits anymore?"

The two women shared a laugh at the expense of all men. "So I guess Alric couldn't help but fall madly in love with the woman who rescued him from eternal torment?"

Diana let out a loud snort. "Hah!" she said. "It wasn't so cut and dried as that. We both went through hell and back before love ever entered the picture." She folded her arms around her midsection, as if to protect herself from the misery of that time.

"Then he left me."

Max's mouth dropped open with shock. "What? Why?" The two of them were so much in love, Max could see that plainly even without paranormal assistance. How could Alric have ever left her?

"Alric was convinced our relationship was a fast train on a direct route to an exploding bridge, and so he turned on the brakes before we even reached the pass. He was very protective, and the safety issues seemed insurmountable. He didn't think he could protect me when the nature of his job put him in the line of fire opposite the world's most evil creatures on a nightly basis. Then there was the human/immortal thing, which loomed over us in a big, dark way. A cloud that rained down uncertainty and doubt whenever we found a moment of peace or happiness. Because in Alric's mind, there was always the possibility that one moment was all we'd have—that I could be gone at any time. He didn't seem to understand that I felt the same way about him. He might be immortal, but that doesn't mean he's invincible. It became a huge issue for us."

"How did you get past it?"

Diana paused.

They haven't gotten past it. "So it still bothers you?" Max asked, her voice gentle with shared pain.

Diana shrugged her shoulders. "Sure, it bothers me. I can't pretend it doesn't. The fact that I know the gray hairs will start sneaking onto my head in another few years, and that I won't be able to have Alric's children bothers me a lot. It bothered Alric enough that he thought the pain would be less for us both if he left."

Max was reminded of Baron's similar decision, and

she had to wonder whether it had as much to do with Jackson as he pretended. Or if maybe Baron had felt something for her after the night they spent together, but decided it wasn't worth the trouble because he had just found out he was an Immortal—and Max was still only human.

"So what happened? Did he come crawling back and beg your forgiveness? I really hope he crawled."

"No, I tracked *him* down and talked him out of himself. I convinced him of the rightness of our being together and told him he would always regret it if he wasted the time that we do have together being an ass. I fought for my life that day. Because the alternative was not having him with me at all, and that was not an option I was willing to consider."

Max couldn't help but be impressed by the woman's determination and strength of character. She could see why Alric had given in to her, why he was willing to have his heart torn from his chest every day as he watched her age right in front of his eyes—because while she lived, Diana would shower him with enough love for twenty lifetimes.

Chapter Sixteen

That afternoon, Baron and Alric met with Kane and Roland at the twins' offices downtown. It was a large corporate building in the heart of the city. A monstrosity of steel and glass that fit their corporate image well enough. Kane and Roland's company was a multimillion dollar operation that had its paws into everything from government contracts and medical research to computer technology. Its ultimate purpose was to supply funds to the Immortal cause, but also to make it possible for the twins to continue their scientific research into Immortal genetics.

Baron hadn't liked the idea of leaving Max alone, but it was mid-afternoon and at least he knew the vampire couldn't get to her...and she couldn't leave either. It was probably for the best that he put some distance between them in any case. The more time passed, the more desperate Max was to leave...and he couldn't let her go until the most immediate danger had been taken care of.

But Devon wasn't their only problem. Whether or not Max was still a danger to herself—or others—was an issue that he had to address before it was too late and someone got hurt.

Baron turned to the three Immortals. The day before, Kane and Roland had driven out to where Max said her car had broken down, but they hadn't found any sign of the vehicle.

"Our boy Devon wouldn't want a lot of attention focused on his neck of the woods, which an abandoned car showing signs of violence would surely have generated, even if the area doesn't get much traffic," Roland said. "I bet he pulled it into the woods or something."

"You're probably right," Baron agreed. "And I don't want to waste time trying to find the car, but that area is ripe with abandoned mines and caves, and we should scour every one of them until we find out where the vampire is holed up. He knows we're hunting him, but I think he's having fun playing with us. He thinks he's going to get away with it, and that means he's going to try something else. Soon."

"Kane and I did a walk through of the area, and the most likely place for Devon to be hiding is here," Roland pointed to the map that was spread out across his desk. They were looking at a section of rocky, cavernous terrain.

Baron let out a low whistle. "That's right where Duncan was killed."

Duncan had been one of them—an Immortal—but he was killed by a powerful demon almost two years ago right at that very spot. It was his death that was the triggering event for Baron's own transition, and Baron wasn't likely to forget it, since he had lived every moment of the demon's brutal attack and Duncan's bloody death in the visions that went hand in hand with the passing of his Immortal powers to Baron. "That spot sure is popular with the evil scum of this town."

"Maybe Devon's drawn to it," Kane nodded. "He would be able to sense the taint in the ground there and it gives him a feeling of security."

Alric nodded. "I wouldn't doubt it. I've been in places like that before, and the foulness is palpable. It would drive away any sane person."

170

Baron eyed him carefully, noting the far-away sound of Alric's voice. Part of him was in another time and another place entirely.

"Devon would think it gives him added protection because humans aren't likely to wander there during the day when it's harder for him to protect himself."

"Okay, then." Baron wanted everyone back on track, focused on what had to be done tonight. "Alric and I will go out there now and search the caves and tunnels. That way if we find something, we can deal with it before the sun sets." He turned to the twins. "Will the two of you stay close to the compound and keep an eye on Max and Diana?"

"That's no problem," Roland answered. "And we'll get on the horn to a few guys who can get into Inferno and Hell's Harem, to see if Devon's been spotted there."

Baron shook his head and frowned. "Alric and I have already been to both the blood clubs. We couldn't get anywhere. The vamps are a pretty closed-mouthed bunch and don't want us poking around."

Roland smiled. "One of their kind owes me a favor, so I'll contact him and see what he knows."

"Okay, good."

"But that doesn't mean we'll get anything useful. Devon's not going to be broadcasting his location even to his own kind, for fear of attracting the attention of their enforcer."

"I understand. Just do what you can. I want this guy dusted." Baron's gaze settled on each of the older Immortals, and he suddenly realized that he—the junior man of their group—had just given all three of them direct orders, and that he had every expectation that those orders would be carried out.

He didn't want to step on anyone's steel-toed shitkickers, but at the same time, he wasn't backing down. This was too important to him to let someone else call the shots.

Alric must have seen it in his eyes because he clapped Baron on the back and chuckled in that low, growly bear's voice of his. "Don't worry, boy, we're all in this together," he reassured Baron. "We're not here to argue rank or authority like a couple of straight-laced military boys hopped up on their own egos—we just want to help you get this bastard."

Baron released a breath and nodded, drawing a hand raggedly through his hair. "Thanks, guys," he said, acknowledging Kane and Roland's matching nods of assent. "Let's get this vampire once and for all."

Baron and Alric were on their way back to the warehouse. Their hunt through the deserted uranium mines had been successful, but only to a point. Following the deepest tunnels a long way beneath the surface, they came across the desiccated corpses of several small animals and a human male littering the dirt floor of one cavern. The human was an older man—a Mr. Thomas Sheffield from the identification that was still in his pockets—and it was likely that, like Max, he had been dragged from his car sometime late last night.

Devon himself was long gone. He'd no doubt known they would be hard on his tail, and decided it was time to find a new hole to hide in. Baron and Alric had taken care of the body—no one would find the late Mr. Sheffield, and though he felt sorry for the family who was right now worrying, wondering what had happened to their husband, father, brother, friend, given the obvious, unspeakable violence that had been committed against the man, it was better that his body stayed lost.

By the time he and Alric were done with the chore, the sun was getting low in the sky and they had both agreed it was pointless to waste any more time there.

Baron could tell just how impatient Alric was to be home from the way he navigated the Lincoln recklessly through the busy rush hour traffic. But Baron didn't say a word. He was just as eager to get back to Max and make sure she was still cooling her heels, safe and sound. Alric had called ahead and Diana said everything was fine, but Baron's nerves were dancing a Scottish jig all the way down his spinal cord, making him edgy and nervous.

He knew time had grown very short. The vampire still eluded them, and that meant Baron was going to have to find some way to convince Max to stay at least another night. The trouble with that plan was—Baron had called the hospital back in Rockford and they didn't hold out a lot of hope that Jackson was going to last much longer. He struggled with needing to hold Max close, and the guilt that he felt as a result of that need. Keeping her with him meant that he was once again putting his wants and desires above everyone else's, above his brother's.

Baron made note of the time and saw the dirty look Alric threw his way.

"What?"

Obviously fed up with Baron's brooding, Alric barked at him to snap out of it. "What the hell's eating you?"

Baron clenched his jaw and turned to look back out the window. "Nothing."

"Fuck nothing," Alric sighed. "Am I going to have to beat it out of you, or what?"

"You wish." Baron rubbed a hand across his eyes. "I don't know what to do about Maxine," he admitted.

"Ah."

Baron threw Alric a dirty look of his own. "What's that supposed to mean?"

"Nothing."

"Fuck nothing," Baron threw back the other Immortal's earlier smart ass remark. "You think you've got it all figured out? Well, why don't you enlighten me then, 'cause I sure don't have a clue."

"No kidding." Alric barked out a laugh, but

173

annoyance with their sluggish progress showed on his face, trapped as they were behind a slow-moving, but sleek, silver Beamer. Alric glanced in the rearview mirror and quickly slid the SUV into the left-hand lane behind a speed-demon soccer mom type driving a green minivan. "It's pretty simple my friend. You love her, right?"

Baron hesitated, then nodded. He couldn't lie, not to his friend, not to himself. Not anymore. "I've loved her forever." The words surprised him, coming from somewhere inside that hadn't seen the light of day since he'd left his home town and any future that might have had Max as a part of it.

"But it isn't that simple." He thought of his brother, dying in the hospital, and winced.

"Sure it is. Take it from someone who knows, man. If you love her, then all the reasons why you can't be together don't mean shit. Take the chance. Isn't love worth at least that?" He glanced over and met Baron's eyes, his expression thoughtful. "You know, I once told Rhys the same thing after he'd made a stupid decision like the one you're contemplating."

Baron remembered. Rhys had fallen hard for Amy, but she'd almost been killed and he had convinced himself she would be better off without him and all the danger and demons that came with the kind of life he led. He sent her away and then proceeded to slowly die inside. Baron saw the parallels to his own situation. He couldn't help but see them since they were practically screaming at him to stop being such an ass.

"So you were the one who talked Rhys into going to Amy and begging her to take him back?" Baron asked.

"Hell no," Alric laughed, checking his mirrors again and then sneaking in ahead of a rusty old Ford. "I just explained to him what I'm explaining to you—that if you want to stay sane in this world that we're living in, it helps to have someone willing to hold onto you and ground you to what's really important—give you a reason to keep on keepin' on, as it were."

Was it so simple?

God, of course it was.

After all these years, after all of the men he'd seen fight and die in service to their country, all of the innocent humans who had fallen under the slash of a demon's claw. After all the brutality and violence he'd witnessed since leaving his family and his heart behind—how could he have never before seen just how wrong he'd been?

All of his excuses about not wanting to horn in on his brother's girl—while true—where still just that. Excuses.

Baron had always known Jackson would have understood how Baron felt and even wished him well. He knew this, because he knew Jackson was a much better man than Baron.

Sure, he'd been willing to let Max go, but he hadn't been able to do it gracefully. Instead, Baron had dropped out of both of their lives completely so he couldn't change his mind the first time he heard Max's sultry voice, was forced to meet her deep blue eyes, or caught himself ogling her tight ass walking across a room.

For a while, he'd kept in touch with his mother and with Jackson through the odd phone call, but that meant shit. The reality was that he'd checked out.

Now his mother was dead, his brother dying, and Max was a vampire who hated him.

And what did he have to show for all his misplaced ideals?

For all of his practical jokes, Baron was a bitter, hardened, cynical man. He was forced to face the awful truth—that he was a coward, afraid to be happy.

In the back of his mind had always been the rationale that, if someone so good and innocent as Jackson could be made to suffer so much, then why should Baron be allowed to squeak through life unscathed?

What made him worthy of a forever kind of love?

Nothing.

Baron hadn't ever done anything to merit Max's love or his brother's unswerving devotion, and he'd known that if he tried to accept what they offered, the punishment for daring to think he deserved it would be severe. The loss, when it came, would destroy him.

What he hadn't realized was that there just wasn't anything he could do about it. As powerful as he was, as strong and capable and *immortal* as he was, Baron still had no control over those things that had the greatest ability to hurt him, because the damage was already done.

He was still going to love Max with all his heart, and it still wouldn't change the fact that he was far from being the kind of person she needed and deserved. Jackson was still going to die young of leukemia no matter how much Baron wished he could take his brother's place and bear his brother's pain.

Now, he thought of what losing Jackson was going to do to Max, and Baron knew she needed to go. And surprisingly enough, he wanted to go with her, to be there for her–if she would let him.

"Shit. What do I do now?" He turned back to Alric. "I screwed up so bad."

Alric laughed. "You do what all men have to do at some point when they're involved in a relationship with a smart and righteous woman." Alric swerved into the right lane and stomped on the gas, flying onto the off-ramp. His crooked grin never faltered. "You get down on your knees and beg."

Alric opened the door to find Diana curled up in a chair reading one of her mysteries. She looked at him and smiled, and he felt his heart constrict within the confines of his chest.

"Hey, princess." He stripped off his trench coat and the scabbard that held his blade to his back. Diana waited until he was done before rising from the chair to greet him with a soft warm kiss.

"Did you find the vampire?" she wrapped her arms around his waist, her head coming only to the middle of his chest.

"Not yet," he answered with a sigh. "We found where he had been hiding out, but he's already gone."

Alric rested his chin on the top of her head and drank in the familiar scent of lavender and lilacs. It was an utterly feminine scent that was both perfect for her and a contradiction at the same time. She was soft; she was feminine. His Diana was a girly girl who loved getting her hair done and always made sure that her nails were perfectly manicured. She could out-shop Paris Hilton and looked dynamite in a slinky black dress, or nothing at all, and would rarely be caught in a simple pair of jeans and a t-shirt.

Yet Diana was so much more than that, too. She had a core of steel that would tolerate no bullshit, and she wouldn't let anyone push her around. She had more courage than twenty seasoned warriors and a sense of right and wrong that could not be corrupted.

God, he loved her.

His arms tightened and he lifted her off her feet, ignoring her protests and bringing her with him into the bathroom. "I need to shower," he said. He had an entire mine's worth of dust and grime in his hair and all over his skin. "Will you join me?"

Diana smiled, reaching for the holster that held his gun. He stopped her, not wanting her to touch it, and unclipped it from his waist himself. He placed it on the countertop and Diana reached for his belt buckle. "Only if you promise I can wash you," she answered with a sexy, playful glint in her eyes.

She unbuckled him and pulled his dirty wife-beater from the waistband of his leathers. Alric lifted his arms and let her push the cotton up his chest. Her hands burned a path over his abs to his pecs and then up his arms as high as she could reach.

Instead of leaning down to let her pull the garment right off, Alric reached behind him and peeled the crusty shirt over his head, then dropped it to the floor. He grabbed a handful of her pink satin blouse and dragged her closer, leaning down to touch his mouth lightly to hers.

He needed to be gentle with her tonight. Needed her to know it was all about the love, so that later when he asked her—

He mentally shook himself.

One by one he slowly undid the buttons of her shirt, though his hands itched to tear it from her. When the slinky fabric fell open, acting as a gauzy frame for her magnificent body, he groaned and let her see the admiration in his eyes.

Her breasts were small and perky, her nipples already hard, poking through the tiny gaps in the black lace of her bra. His hands went to her shoulders and smoothed the sleeves down her arms, until she shrugged it the rest of the way off.

When he just stood there staring at her, she pressed her body against his and reached a palm up to softly caress the side of his face. "What is it Alric? What's the matter?"

He shook his head. Not now.

"Nothing," he lied. "It's just...you're so beautiful. You know how much I love you?"

She sighed, knowing him too well. "Okay, don't tell me," she said. He was always amazed by how accepting she was of his moods and quirks. No resentment colored her voice, only loving patience.

Her lips pressed to his heart and Alric smoothed a heavy hand over her head before he cupped her face and tipped it up to his. "You know how much I love you?" he repeated.

Her gaze was steady as she met his. "Of course I do."

178

He lifted her and walked her back until he could sit her down on the bathroom counter. He pushed her black skirt up to her hips and held the firm globes of her ass in both hands, forcing his way between her legs so that his heavy erection pressed intimately against her through the thick layer of leather that he still wore. With a persistent grind of his hips, he kissed her slow and deep, his tongue dragging the inside of her mouth over and over again until they were both panting, their bodies hot with need.

Alric finally forced himself to step back. He wasted no time stripping off his pants. Naked, he waited as Diana stood and reached behind to the zipper of her slim skirt.

Her eyes told him how much she was looking forward to this, but she teased, pulling the zipper down slow and lowering her waistband over her hips an inch at a time. Alric growled in response, fisting his cock in his hand, not even bothering to hide the evidence of his raging desire for her. She smiled sinfully, letting the skirt fall to the ground. Only her black lace bra and matching thong remained. God, he loved it when she wore a thong.

She moved to take off the bra, but he stopped her. "Leave them on," he growled. She dropped her hands and he stepped to the shower. When the water was nice and hot, he pulled her in with him and pressed her to the wall. The water sluiced over them both as they kissed and touched. Alric palmed her breasts, plucking at her nipples through the wet lace, glorying in her little moans and sighs of pleasure.

"I thought you wanted to get cleaned up," she teased, her voice breathless and sexy.

"I changed my mind. It feels too good being dirty with you."

She smiled, and slid under his arm, leaving him staring at the ceramic tile. "Where are you going?"

She moved behind him and ran her hand down his spine, her touch slippery with soap.

He stood still for her as she washed him, taking

comfort in her gentle, loving attention. "Bend," she ordered, and he laughed, ducking so that she could wash his hair. When he was rinsed, she turned off the water and stepped out, handing him a thick towel to wrap around his waist.

"Hey." He shook his head vigorously, sending water droplets flying across the room to make her shriek with mock outrage. "I wasn't done in there." His plans of taking her against the shower wall were fast disappearing before his eyes.

"Oh yes, you were," she said with a smile. "The water is getting cold." Diana wiggled out of her wet bra and panties, and Alric's eyes grew wider, watching. She slid him a sideways look as she pulled her robe from the hook on the back of the door and slipped it on.

Diana knew something was up with her man. She wanted him to spill his guts, but after five years, she understood him well enough to know he would only do so when he was good and ready. She also knew that whatever bothered him must be very serious if he was letting her see how much it affected him. If she pestered him and tried dragging it out of him before he felt ready to share, it would be like watching a dry field of brush go up in flames. The outburst of temper would burn hot and quick.

The better course would be to help Alric calm down. Something she had no problem attempting, and every intention of enjoying herself.

She knew he would follow her out the door and back into the bedroom. A sultry look sent his way and a little twitch of tail would ensure his response.

It wasn't their usual sanctuary. The room was smaller than they were used to, but not uncomfortable. The bed was a queen, and with Alric's size it seemed more like a twin, but Diana didn't mind. Anything that kept Alric close to her was a good thing.

Sometimes she got so scared for him that if she could have kept him tucked in her bed for the next fifty years she would. He might not appreciate her as much as an overprotective fishwife, but if it was the only way to stop him from coming home with blood on his clothes and death in his eyes, she thought it would almost be worth it.

Turning back, she set her hook, drawing him closer with half-lowered lids, her lips pouty and slightly parted. Diana didn't play the femme fatale often, they were usually too desperate for each other to bother with games, but tonight she got the distinct impression he needed a little distraction from whatever was plaguing his mind, and she intended to give it to him.

"Why don't you come over here and let me take care of you," she purred, staring pointedly at the huge erection tenting the towel wrapped around his waist. Diana's breath caught at the sight of his wide, sculpted chest and the bulging arms, tiny drops of water still glistening on his smooth skin.

Alric groaned and shook his head. "I can't handle you teasing me tonight gorgeous," he warned. "I need you too much."

"Oh, Alric. You're such a big strong man, I'm sure you can handle whatever I decide to dish out."

"Fuck."

"Oh, we'll get to that." She chuckled, enjoying herself.

He laughed and dropped the towel, revealing himself to her in all his huge, eager glory, and she was glad to see the devastated look in his eyes starting to fade. "All right, then, woman. You want to play?" His grin was evil, ripe with sexual intent, and so damn sexy her thighs quivered and her core grew wet. "Let's play."

Ah, now this was much better. Gone—at least for the moment—was the brooding Alric, the Alric with a heavy weight riding on his massive shoulders. Instead, if she played her cards right, Diana would be the weight flung over those shoulders in another few minutes.

His desire was plain as he stalked her across the little room. It didn't take much, with two strides of his long legs, he had reached her.

Not to make it too easy on him, Diana lunged across the bed, but she didn't make it to the other side. Face down, he had one of her ankles in his hand and tugged. She turned over, her robe twisting and riding up her thighs.

His hand smoothed from her ankle up her leg, sliding the cotton higher up her hips. "You should have run faster," he murmured, leaning forward, pressing the long length of his body to hers. His warm breath whispered in her ear. "Because I'm not letting you go now."

Diana just smiled, putting all of her love for him in that smile, all her passion and all her faith in him. She wanted him to know that whatever happened, whatever problems weighed on his soul, she was here to support and to help. "Well, darn," she teased. "I guess I'll just have to give in gracefully then."

He snorted and bent his mouth to her neck. "Yeah right," he murmured with a growl and a soft, teasing bite. "You got exactly what you wanted."

"Well, of course, silly. Did you doubt that I would?"

"Not for a moment." He lifted her in his arms and stood up from the bed.

"Wait a minute, what are you doing?" She wrapped her legs around his waist, hands gripping his shoulders.

He grinned and splayed his hands under her rear as he walked her across the room. "This is me getting what *I* want." With her back hard against the wall and her legs around him, he put his mouth to her breast at the same time he slid his heavy, swollen cock inside her.

"Oh," she moaned, her body stretching to accommodate him.

His mouth tugged at her breast, sucking hard, and she

ran her fingers in his hair, holding him to her. He pressed deeper, his hips anchoring her in place, ensuring she felt every inch of him inside of her.

"Alric." His name was a challenge on her lips. She took from him, all that he could give, and then demanded more.

His tongue lapped at her breasts, then swirled over her tight, puckered nipples. His teeth nipped at her, teasing. "Alric," she repeated, pulling on his hair until his head lifted and gazed back at her, his gleaming silver eyes filled with predatory intent.

She leaned forward, very aware of the tightening of her core around the heated, thick length pulsing inside of her. She took his mouth, her kiss wet and desperate, challenging. She dug her fingers into the hard muscle of his shoulders, urging him to give her more. She wanted his tongue in her mouth, wanted her breasts smashed against his chest. She wanted every part of him enveloping her in heat and need as she pushed her heels hard into the small of his back.

"Diana," he growled. He was close, she could tell. He wouldn't be able to deny her much longer.

"Now, Alric," she ordered. "Give it to me now. Hard." Her voice was thick with her desire. She felt everything. Every throbbing inch of his cock as it jerked inside of her. The almost painful points of her nipples rubbing in the hair of his chest. She felt his breathing heavy on her neck, and the hand that he lovingly ran through her short-cropped hair. "Now," she repeated, urgent.

"God, I don't want to move. I don't want it to end. Not yet. Just let me—" His body quivered around her and his jaw clenched. She squirmed and arched against him, desperate. Alric moaned into her mouth as he took it in another blistering kiss. Slowly he pulled out, then thrust inside her again. Hard. Oh, yes. So long and hard. Perfect.

"Yes, Alric. Yes," she cried, throwing her head back.

She couldn't move a muscle, this was all him. His biceps flexed beneath her fingers, his thighs supported her weight, his hips surged back and forth, pressing her into the wall.

Alric's lips pulled back from his teeth as he took her, his expression reflecting a combination of torture and pleasure as he pumped faster. Diana could only let her body accept what it was given. She was lost in sensation, drowning in the pleasure centered between her thighs.

She came apart with a scream moments before he did, her convulsions squeezing him tightly until he shouted in her ear with his own release.

They remained like that for a few moments, Alric's forehead pressed against the wall, his chin resting on her shoulder. She loved that he could take her weight like this and make it seem completely effortless. Just thinking about it got her hot all over again, and she tightened her inner walls reflexively.

Instead of letting her down—which probably wouldn't have been a great idea anyway, since she doubted she could have stood on her own—Alric carried her to the bed, their bodies still connected, and pressed her into the mattress. She sighed blissfully, loving the feel of his weight on top of her.

He kissed the top of her head, and she met his eyes. The return of his drawn, worried expression made her want to weep with sadness for him. "Will you tell me now what this awful problem is that makes you so melancholy?" she asked.

He shifted and pulled from her body, leaving her thighs sticky and wet. Lying back, he threw an arm across his eyes, and Diana started to get really worried. The only other time her warrior had been so darkly introspective was when he tried telling her that his life was too dangerous and they couldn't be together. Changing his mind from that decision had been one hell of a fight—a fight she had very nearly lost.

Sure, his job was dangerous; he hunted demons for God's sake. But they dealt with it, and she was sure he had ever regretted making the decision to give them a chance with each other.

Or maybe he had.

"Come on, Alric. Spill your guts," she urged. "You're starting to scare me here and you know how much I hate that."

He lowered his arm, his expression hard and resolute with some mysterious decision that he was obviously struggling with. Pulling her closer he looked deeply into her eyes like he was searching her soul for the answers he needed.

"Diana." He kissed her lightly on the mouth. "I never want to lose you."

She kissed him back and drew a finger along the deep worry line in his forehead. "I know that," she answered softly. "Tell me what happened today."

"It's not...nothing happened." He squeezed her in a tight embrace. "But I want you to listen to what I have to say, okay? Don't say no until you've really given it some thought."

"Say no to what? Why would I say no?"

He hesitated, clearly worried about her reaction. "I want to ask Maxine to turn you."

Chapter Seventeen

Baron stood motionless in the hallway facing the closed door of his room. He had checked all the security cameras, and the computer system, called Kane for an update, anything not to end up where he was right now.

He was uncertain about the wisdom of entering. Diana had spent a long time with Max this afternoon, and like most men with a healthy instinct for self-preservation, he knew it was always a bad thing when two women got together with nothing to do but talk about their men.

So was he Maxine's man, then?

If she would have him, he would thank his lucky stars and the twist of fate that convinced her to give him another chance.

But he had serious doubts Max felt the same way he did. She had been clear as crystal today, making sure she pointed out that what happened between them was all about the sex, and nothing else. It was about an escape from fear and uncertainty and a release of mutual tensions.

It was probably better that way anyway.

So why did he want to howl his fury at the moon?

He had done a lot of thinking this afternoon about Max, about the two of them, and about his past choices. He flipped back and forth between wanting to keep her close and letting her go.

Damned if he knew anymore what decisions were the right ones. Years ago, he'd been certain he was making the only choice available to him. But he knew now that his decisions had been based more on fear, guilt and the insecurities of a boy who hadn't yet matured into a man.

That wasn't to say that Baron had enlisted in the army simply as a way to escape. It had always been his intention, his dream, to serve his country—and in that respect he'd gotten even more than he bargained for when he'd been recruited as a Delta Force operative—but he could have found a better way, one that didn't involve walking out on the people who loved him and relied on him.

Thing was, his fear was still there, the guilt still roiled in his gut, and he still wasn't good enough for her. He had nothing to offer Max but a life of danger and killing.

And he still couldn't face his brother.

Baron sighed and reached for the door handle. Before he even turned it, he knew Max wasn't inside the room. Her distinctive scent—an alluring mixture of citrus and fresh cool seas that he would never mistake as belonging to anyone else—lingered, but it was faint.

"*Shit*!" Where the hell could she have gone? The security system had been fully armed all day.

He stormed from the room and stalked down the corridor, leaving the door wide open. "Alric," he called loudly. "Alric!"

The Saxon stuck his head out of the guest room at the end of the hall and stood in the doorway buttoning his pants. "I'm here. What's going on?"

"Max is gone."

"Shit." Alric glanced behind him into the room and then nodded before turning back to Baron. "Diana says Max seemed pretty upset earlier."

Diana slid past Alric, throwing an inscrutable look his way. She was pulling a robe closed around her. Alric went back inside the bedroom, but returned quickly, dragging on a shirt, his gun belt hanging from an arm. He pulled Diana in for a hard kiss on the lips, but when they parted it wasn't with their usual lovey-dovey gooing and gawing. The tension between them was so heavy that even Baron, who was admittedly distracted, could sense it hanging in the air.

There was something going on between those two—but whatever it was would have to wait.

Baron continued down the hall with Alric following close behind. Shit, he had reviewed the security cameras and seen nothing. Where was he even going to start? Where would she have gone? She had no car.

"Baron?" Diana called.

He stopped and looked back, the dread a heavy ache in his chest.

"I'm sorry," she said. "I knew that Max wanted to leave. I should have—"

"It's not your fault, Diana," he reassured her. And it wasn't. It was his fault.

Halfway to the garage, Baron stopped short. He sighed.

Alric looked at him, then clapped a heavy hand on his shoulder. "If you need me, you know where I am."

Baron nodded, his gaze trained on the closed door of the gym. "Thanks man."

He waited until the other Immortal had rounded the corner before he approached the door, needing time to will the wild thumping of his poor heart back down to a level that wasn't going to cause him to suffer a heart attack.

She was in there.

He didn't know how he could tell; he just knew, like he'd known that she wasn't in his room. Maybe because his blood was in her, flowing through her veins; it called to him and he would always be able to sense when she was near, or maybe it was because she was the keeper of his soul and would always carry a part of him with her.

The view that met Baron when he opened the door robbed him of speech.

On the treadmill, Max was running full tilt to nowhere, fast. Sweat poured from her face, her breathing heavy, and she had tied her long hair back into a slim ponytail. He'd seen her body before—naked in his arms only hours ago in fact—but the sight of her now made him just as hard as he'd been with his dick buried deep inside her.

He couldn't take his eyes from her flawless, toned body engaged in the smooth, perfectly synchronized movements of her workout. Diana must have given her some workout clothes, because she had on only a skimpy training bra that left bare the smooth expanse of her belly and arms, and nylon bicycle shorts that stretched tight over her drop-dead amazing ass. Her long, sleek legs gleamed with perspiration, the muscles of her calves and thighs subtly sculpted, mesmerizing him as he was reminded of just how good they had felt under the slide of his hands and wrapped around his waist.

She knew that he was there, but she hadn't yet deigned to look at him.

That was fine. He was in no rush.

Max kept running. Normally, she would have been tired by now—long ago actually—but the strength in this transformed body of hers continued to amaze her. It seemed her resources were limitless, although she knew that probably wasn't true.

She had expected Baron to come for her, and so she wasn't surprised to see him. What did surprise her was the instant, powerful reaction she had to his presence, especially since she had gone to so much trouble earlier talking herself out of wanting him.

He hadn't returned to face her before leaving with Alric to go vampire hunting, so Max hadn't seen Baron since their argument. Which was probably just as well, because if she had been forced to carry this picture of him with her all day long, she would have found it even harder to stick to her resolution to leave him and this place tonight.

She would not waver. Max repeated the mantra, trying to reinforce the walls she had just finished rebuilding. But he looked so damn hot, and even though her footing on the treadmill remained sure, inside she was sliding.

He was warriored-up from head to toe in black leather, from the thick shitkicker boots on his feet to the knuckle-cut driving gloves smoothed over his hands. His heavy, muscled legs were encased in leather, and he had a long leather trench coat still draped over his shoulders.

She'd never seen him in his army uniform, had rarely seen him in anything other than casual attire. And she had thought he looked good then, but this was something altogether different. Primal, powerful, dangerous. For the first time, Max could clearly visualize Baron as the Immortal who took on demons. The youth who had teased her mercilessly as a child was gone, buried behind hard crystal eyes and deadly purpose.

He looked fearsome, breathtaking, and so damn good; her mouth went dry as she surreptitiously eyed him and hoped he didn't catch her doing it.

He wasn't going anywhere.

He leaned his back against the wall and watched her with heavy-lidded eyes.

She could feel her body growing hot, and not from the vigorous workout. Finally, she couldn't stand his gaze on her any longer and flicked a couple buttons on the treadmill's console, reducing her speed to a brisk walk in order to cool down.

He took it as a signal from her, doffing his jacket and the gloves. She glanced at him sharply with wide eyes as he pulled the snug black tee over his head.

"Uh, Baron?" She couldn't make herself look away.

"Come here, Max," he said, his voice low with single-minded intention.

Her breathing heavy, Max turned off the machine and stepped down, shaking her head as she grabbed for her towel.

It wasn't technically a "no", and from the way he stalked her, Baron knew it. The thrill of conquest gleamed in his silver eyes. He reached her in three long strides, taking her up in his arms before she could so much as whimper a protest. Truth to tell, Max wasn't interested in protesting. She wanted him, and recognized that this might very well be her last chance to have him.

His kiss was fierce, a reflection of the hard body he pressed close. "You scared the shit out of me," he muttered before taking her chin in one big hand and forcing her head to tilt to the side, giving him better access to her mouth.

Despite the succulent taste of him, Max's hackles rose at Baron's tone, and she tore her mouth from his. "What?" she gasped. "I didn't do *anything*. I couldn't—I've been trapped here all day like a prisoner, while you were out gallivant—"

He laughed, and some of the tension he'd been carrying in his eyes since he walked through the door bled away. He rested his forehead against hers and breathed deeply. "I'm sorry, baby," he whispered. "When you weren't in my room, I just..."

"You thought I left," she finished for him, stepping back and throwing her towel across the back of her neck. "Well, don't get excited, because I am leaving."

"Max..." His body turned stiff with agitation once again.

"Don't start. I have to go back, you know that." Max

took another step. "He's been alone for days now. Can you imagine what that's doing to him?" She looked at him, letting him see plainly all the hurt that pulled on her soul. She couldn't help it. She couldn't shake this feeling that he'd betrayed her again with his callousness. "He's your brother for God's sake. How can you not be rushing to his side?"

"Fuck." He walked away from her, running a hand through his hair. "We talked about this, Max. And what the hell am I supposed to say to him?" He shook his head and met her glare with clear, cold eyes. "He doesn't need me."

"You're such an asshole. Who are you to say what he needs?" she spat, crossing both her arms over her chest. "Fine. But he needs someone."

"I know. I just want you to wait one more night until we get this vampire and then...then I'll go with you."

She sighed. Would the extra night be worth it if she could show up at Jackson's bedside with his brother like she promised? Max didn't know anymore. Her feelings were too twisted, her emotions too raw. She could no longer trust herself to know if her decisions were being made based on what was best for her dying friend or what her heart wanted for herself.

"I need to take a shower," she muttered, moving past him to the doorway.

Chapter Eighteen

Max tilted her face into the hot spray, letting the water sluice over her face and down her body. Her mind felt fractured, emotion and uncertainty causing her to lose focus.

Her vampire abilities were increasing, getting stronger, but her mind continued to flounder.

She was afraid.

Staying here with Baron was like being cocooned in a little bubble of his protection, a place where she could pretend that her world hadn't disintegrated, that she wasn't a monster. But she had to leave. There was no way around it, even if Jackson hadn't been waiting, alone in the hospital. She couldn't stay here with Baron any longer. Her heart wouldn't stand it.

But could she leave? Really? She was so unsure of herself. Unsure of whether or not she could be trusted with her new powers, the extent of which she wasn't even certain of. And it would mean trusting herself enough to control the hunger.

The hunger that even now raged inside her again.

Shaking with it, Max stumbled out of the shower and found herself facing her reflection in the foggy mirror. For several long moments she stared into the glass. Careful not to look at the slicked back, wet hair dripping water onto the floor, the frightened blue eyes that shone with a peculiar light, or the pointed incisors that peeked from the feral snarl curling her lips.

An eternity passed before a small sigh escaped and Max blinked her eyes, coming back to her surroundings. The water in the shower was still running. She stood stark naked in front of the sink, her body cold and wet—but she was in control. Thank God, it seemed to get easier to hold onto herself each time the hunger reared its ugly head.

That didn't mean she was off the hook. She knew it would still have to be appeased...and soon.

Using her nifty inner vampire clock, she estimated it was still early evening by the time she exited the bathroom looking for something to wear. She should have brought her clothes in with her, but she'd been too impatient to put a closed door between herself and Baron at the time, it hadn't occurred to her until she was already naked, which kind of defeated the purpose.

Now Baron was waiting for her in the bedroom. She found him leaning back in bed with his hands tucked behind his head. His eyes were closed, but Max knew he was awake; his prone form was throwing off too much intensity to lull her into believing he had fallen into harmless sleep.

He still hadn't put a shirt on.

Max was very aware that she wore only a fluffy white towel, and she sidled past the end of the bed carefully. She would grab her borrowed clothes and go back into the bathroom to dress.

She started when his arms came around her, encircling her from behind in his warm, solid strength. So silent and swift, she hadn't even heard him move.

"I need you, Max," he whispered, his hands pulling at the soft white terrycloth she held in a tight fist to the vee of her breasts. "Come be with me. This one time—let us have this one time together without any bitterness, guilt or spite, without anger or fear, without the shadows of the past to get in the way."

He tugged again, and she released her grip on the towel, watching it tumble to the floor. Her inhibitions and earlier outrage tumbled down right along with it, and on a low moan, she let her head drop to the side, encouraging the small kisses he set along the column of her neck.

"This one time." His words teased the wispy strands of drying hair that curled over her shoulder as he pulled her closer against him. "Not as a contest of wills between us, not as vampire and Immortal. But as man and woman. As Baron and Maxine. Let me worship you. Let me love you."

She couldn't resist him. His scent, his warmth, his hard body against her—all combined to drug her with passion. "Yes, Baron," she whispered. "Oh yes, that's what I want, too." She turned to face him, but he held her still, his hands gripping her hips.

"No, stay where you are," he murmured. "Just let me touch you." His callused palms slid over her acutely sensitive skin. Unbearably slowly, dragging heat and sensation first up her sides, then back down her arms. He took her hands in his and raised them above her head. Leaning her head back against his shoulder, she bent her elbows, dropping her arms behind her to his neck. Urging him closer, she was aware that the position pushed her breasts higher, that she was begging him to touch them.

Baron touched his open mouth to her neck. He smoothed his hands over her belly, and Max's muscles twitched and jumped in response. Her breathing hitched as his hands continued up her abdomen and his thumbs grazed the soft undersides of her breasts. She arched her back and moaned, the sound scratchy and desperate, and was rewarded when he finally turned his attention to her breasts, rolling the aching, pointed nipples between his fingers.

"Ah, Max." His low voice rumbled in her ear, a

practiced seduction all its own. "God, I love how you respond for me. The soft sounds you make when I touch you, and the way your body flushes and welcomes me. You're so perfect in your passion, has anybody ever told you that?"

She shook her head and bit her bottom lip to keep from crying out as he pulled at her nipples. God, he didn't really expect her to answer that? Max couldn't even remember either of their names at this point. Both of her prior experiences had been utterly forgettable. Only Baron had ever touched her as deeply, disturbed her reason so completely, roused her passions so thoroughly.

Her body felt heavy, hot, and she squirmed, pushing back into the cradle of his thighs, rubbing her behind along the hard length that strained urgently within the confines of his leathers.

"Jesus, woman," he grumbled. "You're going to be the death of me."

Max's answering chuckle was throaty and seductive, "I think you can handle it, Immortal."

Baron spun her around to face him, and she gasped at the heat blazing in those molten silver eyes. "Oh, I intend to do my very best, babe, don't get me wrong."

"Good." She gave him a slow smile. "I expected nothing less." On tiptoes, she leaned in and kissed him, her mouth open, her tongue searching, wet. He groaned and crushed her close before lifting her high in his arms and carrying her unerringly to the bed.

He laid her down carefully, almost reverently. Looking into his face, she saw fear and uncertainty in his eyes. She saw Baron, the real Baron—a strong, powerful man with a shattered soul.

He'd always felt as if he were unworthy of health while his brother was so weak, that he was unworthy of happiness while his brother suffered. What he didn't realize was that all of his guilt had effectively crippled him. The result being a life more bereft than Jackson's

196

had ever been. And Baron just accepted that as his due. Max felt a surge of tenderness and love for him so strong and profound it brought tears to her eyes, which she quickly blinked away, not wanting him to see.

She gave him an encouraging smile and was glad to see the hint of hesitation melt away. He rose to strip off his boots and his leathers, and finally stood naked before her. He was magnificent. Strong, dynamic, sexy, and she loved that in this he had no shame; he was completely comfortable in his own skin, confident and sure, and...yes, just a little bit arrogant.

When he moved to join her on the bed, she stopped him, crawling to her knees and placing her hands flat against the rock hard planes of his thighs.

"Not so fast," she said teasingly, watching as his eyes grew dark, passion evident in their shadowy depths and in the hungry twitch of his penis straining tall and proud between their bodies. Taking him in her hand, Max leaned over, touching her tongue to him, loving the way he twitched and grew in her hand. She licked at the drop of wetness that had gathered at the tip, savoring his groaning response. Then she kissed and licked her way down his thick length to the base of his shaft, and back before taking all of him inside her mouth.

"Max." His hand twisted in her hair, halting her progress and urging her to rise and face him for a long, deep kiss full of the passion and love they had denied each other for so long.

His kiss was hot and potent, his touch tender but insistent as they fell back on the bed. He cupped her breasts in his hands, then smoothed his palms down over her quivering belly and slipped his fingers into the soft curls covering her pulsing core.

"Open for me sweetheart," he urged. His teeth pulled gently on her ear as he reinforced his request with his hand on her thigh. "Let me touch you."

Eager to comply, Max sighed and let her knees fall

open, desperate to have his touch ease the fire raging within her. He moved into position between her thighs, but held himself above her, still inches away from touching her heated flesh. Her body burned, a conflagration of need that threatened to overwhelm her, and she arched her hips high in a wordless plea.

"Now tell me exactly what you want, baby," he coaxed, running light, maddening circles along the insides of her thighs with his thumb, and blowing a teasing breath across one tight, puckered nipple.

Max groaned even as her body responded to his torture, pulsing and throbbing deliciously. "Ah, Baron," she gasped, swirling her hips in a circle and throwing her head back against the sheets. "Please."

"Is this what you want?" Max bit her lip against the frustrated scream that threatened as he flicked her nipple once with his tongue and dragged his thumb over the sensitive bud of her clitoris. "Tell me."

"Yes," she moaned. "Yes...please."

"More, Max. Tell me more."

"Ah..." Fine. If that's the way he wanted it. She opened her eyes, levelled her gaze with his, wet her lips. "That's what I want. Touch me, Baron. Kiss me. Fill me. I want your cock stretching me, thrusting hard and deep. Make me scream when you take me. Do it."

"Ah, God. That's it. That's what I want to hear." Baron groaned and latched onto her breast, sucking hard as he parted the swollen lips of her sex and slipped across the slick evidence of her readiness. He penetrated her with one finger and she thrust against him, rolling her hips into his hand until he added a second, plunging in and out, while his tongue flicked and teased her breasts.

He brought her right to the very edge of orgasm and left her hanging, only to start over—again and again, until she was writhing and pleading for him to take her.

Baron slid his tongue between her lips for another drugging, sensual kiss. Max sighed, cupping his face in her hands. He raised his head and their eyes met. Max knew this moment would be the one she tucked away in a safe, secret part of her heart. "I love you," she whispered. Surprisingly enough, she wasn't afraid to say it, wasn't afraid to let him see it shining in her eyes. "Even if this is all we ever have, I wanted you to know that."

He was slow and gentle as he entered her, his eyes never leaving hers, joining their souls as they joined their bodies. He didn't return her declaration of love, but suddenly his mind was opened to her and she was flooded with thoughts and images. He was purposely letting her see into his memories. All the pictures of her that he kept near his heart. Like photographs. Of two teenagers teasing each other mercilessly, of her laughing with Jackson, of her dressed up in that frilly pink prom dress, of her naked with her head thrown back in the throes of passion.

"Max," he started, but she hushed him with a finger to his lips. The words didn't matter. Not when his body spoke volumes.

"Love me, Baron," she told him, wrapping her legs around his waist and leaning up to his kiss. He groaned and thrust deeply, wringing a shout from her lips as she dove right over the edge into exquisite climax.

With her body pulsing and quivering around him, beneath him, Max widened her senses, wanting to hold onto the mental connection as well as the physical one between her and Baron for as long as she could.

The assault was swift and thorough. As if he had been lying in wait for just the right moment.

Devon.

The vampire ripped through her mind with vicious brutality, settling in before Max could get any of her barriers up. An insidious presence inside of her, too powerful to oppose, though she tried desperately. Taunting and whispering, he dug at her control, clawing it away. He purposely fed the hunger she had struggled to hold at bay until now, lending it strength against her until her stomach tightened painfully. She felt the ache of her vampire teeth growing long and sharp inside of her mouth.

Baron surged above her, shouting his release as he reached orgasm, and inside her the demon roared.

Chapter Nineteen

Baron sensed the change in Max, the sudden swell of venom and power, but was physically incapable of halting the orgasm that burst forth from his body with a ragged shout of pleasure. With his seed pumping into her, he watched the glint in her eyes turn red, saw the sharp points of her teeth as she let loose an unnatural snarl.

He fought to bring his body under control, shattered as it was from their lovemaking. He managed to lever himself away in time to avoid the sudden swipe of claws now sprouting from delicate fingers that had only moments ago clutched his shoulders with eager passion.

Oh shit.

"Max!" he shouted. "Max, fight. You have to fight him, baby."

The perverted stink of psychic energy surrounding her clogged the air between them, impenetrable. Like before, only ten times stronger this time. He wanted to howl. Rage choked him, closing his throat. How dare that monster violate Max—and in such a way, hiding behind her mind like a coward.

Ignoring their nakedness, Baron turned his attention inward, focusing his energy. He worked to put his power between Maxine and the vampire in an attempt to shelter her and help her drive it out. He forced himself into her mind. Connected to her as he was, Baron could sense not only the vampire's insidious presence, he could also hear Devon's laughter. The natural vampire hunger that Max had been learning to control was being stirred up, heightened to severely unnatural, uncontrollable levels. Devon baited her relentlessly so that when she couldn't stand it anymore and caved under the pressure, Baron would be the one she attacked, looking for blood to appease the demon set loose within her.

If Max did attack Baron, went for his vein while in the midst of a frenzied madness, if she took his blood without the sanction of his offering, then she damned herself—which is exactly what Devon was hoping for.

Baron stared into Maxine's glowing red eyes as his mind worked double-time to find a chink in the vampire's psychic screen. His Immortal gift allowed him to sense Devon's energy. If he could just zoom in on it, if he could tune his mind to the same extrasensory frequency, then he could turn that power against the vampire and force it out. But Devon was a fog in her brain, drifting everywhere at once, fluid and murky, and dissolving into another corner of her psyche as soon as Baron thought he finally had the bastard in his grasp.

Intent on the silent battle taking place within, Baron was unprepared for Max's physical attack.

"Shit!" He jerked back as she swung again, but this time he wasn't quick enough to avoid being clawed, and his chest showed three bright lines of crimson as proof that the demon still had control of her mind.

He danced backward again as she lunged forward with a feral snarl of rage and hunger, her lips pulling back from the long, pointy incisors and going right for his throat.

"Max, don't." He held her back, just barely. But she fought wildly, hissing and scratching and lunging, trying to get at him with all of her considerable strength. His breathing was soon labored and ragged with the amount of energy he expended trying to keep ahead of her without hurting her. Baron had fought countless battles against hundreds of demons, but it was an altogether different story when you were trying *not* to annihilate your opponent.

"Shit, shit, shit," he muttered, angry with himself for letting the situation get so out of hand. He should have sensed Devon's presence as soon as the bastard had tried to tap Max's mind. Especially after the last time. That he hadn't and they were now in this position was entirely his own failing.

Max crouched, circling him with predatory intent. She hesitated slightly, and Baron thought he saw her eyes flash back to blue, but then it was gone, and she let out a low hiss.

"Max." He called to her, hoping to reach her with his voice and his touch, since the vampire controlled too much of her mind. Holding out his hands, he took a careful step forward, then stopped. Conscious of the blood dripping from the jagged claw marks she'd drawn across his chest, he changed his tactics. It probably wasn't a tremendously brilliant idea to get too near to her, after all. Inundating her with the scent of his blood wasn't going to help matters any.

He spoke to her in soothing tones, urging her to be strong. With his mind, he relentlessly pursued the vampire, and tried to help her control the growing hunger.

Long moments passed. Maxine stood stock still, her head lowered, her breathing heavy and uneven. Baron finally sighed.

Thank God. She's winning.

When she looked up, her eyes were clear. Crisp and pure blue. And full of tears.

Ah, hell. Anger and ridicule he could deal with from Max. But her tears were foreign to him. No matter what happened, Maxine Deveraux always held it together. Through her mother's drunken binges and rejection, and the ridicule of the entire town. Through death and...undeath—Max had faced it all with such courage, strength and without shedding a single tear.

It was about damn time.

She sank to the floor, the tears streaming down her face as she stared, horrified, at the blood staining her hands. Gone was the growling, wild whirlwind. She looked frail and vulnerable, her face pale, her nude body curling in on itself.

Baron grabbed one of his t-shirts and went to her, kneeling before her on the floor. She threw up a hand in protest. "No. Get awa—"

"Shut up. You know that's not going to happen." His tone brooked no argument from her.

He dragged the cotton shirt over her head. Still naked himself, but unable to walk away from her long enough to find a pair of pants, Baron took Max in his arms, folding his body around her like a cocoon.

She fought to be free, but his embrace was stubborn and inflexible. Her struggles subsided, but the tension in her shoulders and the way she refused to look him in the eye, told him she was far from accepting of his comfort.

Suddenly, he stiffened, alarmed. He felt something, a whiny ringing in his ears as if he were getting radio feedback from an earpiece. Max felt it, too. She flinched, and he heard her gasp.

But Devon had given up his hold on Max, at least for the time being. Baron had known the moment the vampire removed himself from her mind.

Which meant...*Shit.*

"Shit. He set this whole thing up as a decoy. To fucking distract me from what he was doing right under my fucking nose. *Shit.*" Baron reluctantly let Max go, and went to the dresser for something to wear. He would rather not have to go into another battle tonight naked as the day he was born. Max stood along with him, her legs a little wobbly. She started pulling on a pair of joggers.

Dragging the zipper of his jeans, Baron grabbed his

gun belt and strapped it on before he turned back to her.

Looking at her devastated face, he hesitated, but Max swiped at her eyes and shook her head. Like him, she knew whatever Devon had planned was already in motion, that it might even now be too late.

"Baron! I need help!" The desperate shout tore through the eerie silence. Down the hall.

Baron immediately jumped for the door, with Max close on his heels.

"Fuck," he said, turning back—torn between keeping her safe should the vampire attack her again, and needing to go help his friend. "Alric."

"I know. Let's go."

He shook his head as he jerked the door open. "Not a chance," he said. "I want you to stay here."

Hell, she had that steely, stubborn look on her face, and he didn't have time to tie her down or argue with her. "Fine."

He met her eyes. There was no time for delicacy, to beat around the bush, so he just spit it out. "Be sure, Max. If you come in that room, you need to be in complete control. I need to be able to trust that you can handle whatever happens."

She caught her breath and her body stiffened visibly. "Can you do that?" he demanded. "Can you shut it all out? Because I can't afford for you to be a wild card." He softened his voice then, "Baby, don't feel bad if you can't do it...but make the right decision and wait here."

Her expression was hard, closed to him. Hell, he had probably hurt her with his callousness...again. But it couldn't be helped.

"No. I'm coming," she said.

"Okay, good." It would have to be. "Come on." With one last look, he nodded and pulled his glock before sprinting down the hall to Alric and Diana's room.

Chapter Twenty

Shit. Devon had carefully and deliberately taken him out of the equation tonight. Baron knew it in his gut. Divide and conquer. The oldest, most basic strategy of war. He'd used it himself more than once.

Which is exactly the reason why he should have expected something like this to happen. What was he, some kind of amateur? Some seriously bad shit had gone down right across the fucking hall—and he hadn't sensed it because Devon had used his power over Max as a smoke screen to disguise what he was really doing.

He'd been handled.

Maybe he was wrong and Alric and Diana were fine. Hell, he didn't really believe that.

This was going to be bad.

Shit. Shit. Shit. He said it over and over in his head as he flew down the short hall and practically slid into the open door of Alric's room.

The room was empty. But God, there was a lot of blood. All of it drying in ominous black circles on the light parquet floor like splattered blots of ink on a white page.

"Bathroom," Max whispered. Her voice was hoarse and her body tense. She was very deliberately not looking at the blood. He paused for a moment, using his mind to test her psychic shields. She was doing well so far, holding it together. Damn, he had to admire the woman's courage and strength.

They followed a splotchy trail of blood that started in the center of the room, and ended at the entrance to the ensuite bath. Even before they reached the doorway, Max knew what they would find. She could feel Diana's pain.

The sight within was enough to tear Max's heart out.

Alric knelt on the hard tile of the bathroom floor in a pool of what could only be Diana's blood. They were both covered in it, and Diana herself was cradled in Alric's arms, her pale, pale face so still.

"Oh God—*Diana*." Max made a conscious effort to ignore the blood, and ignore the disgust she felt for herself that such a thing had to be done.

Alric turned on both of them with a low growl that ended in a wild hiss. He held Diana closer, pulling her up and into the great wall of his chest. Max watched Diana's head roll back on his arm like a rag doll's.

Very slowly, Baron stepped forward. "Alric. Man, it's me—Baron. Baron and Max. We're here. We want to help."

Alric's eyes blazed with a terrible black fire, and Max realized that behind the agony coming to her from Diana's subconscious mind, she could also feel the intensity of Alric's violent emotions. His defenses were down and he wasn't able to keep his mind closed to her. God, so much rage, anguish, guilt, all of it seething and burning a hole in his heart, in his very sanity.

Baron took another small step forward, showing no reaction to Alric's desperate animal-like snarls. "It's okay, Alric. Everything's cool now...we just want to help you. Diana's hurt. She needs medical attention. You saved her—you did—but now you need to let us get her patched up, okay?"

Max thought that Baron's words had finally gotten

the warrior's attention, his head seemed to clear just a bit as he gazed down at the woman clutched desperately in his arms. After a long moment, his hold on her loosened.

"Baron?"

"Yeah, man. I'm here."

Alric met Baron's eyes, his expression reflecting all of the pain that Max was feeling through him. "I couldn't stop her, Baron." His voice broke on each word. Max gasped, closing her eyes tightly as his mind unknowingly broadcast to her what had happened...in vivid, horrific detail.

Baron shot her a sharp, warning look, and Max forced a nod, plastering her hand to her mouth to stop the scream.

"We were arguing," Alric continued, shaking his head. "We were arguing and I was angry and I stomped out on her. If I hadn't... If I had stayed with her, been watching over her, then she wouldn't have been able to get to the knife—"

"Wait a minute. What happened here Alric? Did Diana...did she do this to *herself?*" Baron asked, the shock evident in his voice.

He jerked around to look at Max, but she barely noticed. The images were coming from Alric fast and hard and it took everything she had to keep from crying out. She knew what their argument had been about. She saw the desperation in Alric's eyes as he tried to convince Diana to take Max's blood, and the frustration that made him finally leave the room. She knew he'd spent an hour frantically pumping iron in the gym in an attempt to release that frustration before going back to say how sorry he was. Only to find Diana in the bedroom with a long, long knife in her hands.

"She cut herself the first time before I even had a chance to blink." Alric held one of Diana's bloodstained and crudely bandaged wrists so gently in his own massive hand. "Before it had even sunk in what she was doing, she was going for the other wrist." He stared, lost in his feelings of recrimination and self-hatred. "I couldn't...it totally threw me—" He choked the last words and paused. Max thought he wouldn't be able to continue, but the words started pouring out of him. "I knew I'd never reach her in time. She'd already cut herself again—so I did the only thing I could, I yanked the knife from her with my powers." He stopped and spared a tortured glance at them, his silver eyes filling with tears.

"God, the blood...Baron, all that blood. And then...then she started laughing. It was almost the worst part. That laugh...it wasn't her. The vampire was looking out at me with her eyes, laughing at me *through* Diana. I can't stand the thought that he got inside of her, that his sick, twisted mind was linked like that with her."

Baron knelt on the floor by Alric's feet. "It's okay now; he's gone. He can't hurt her anymore."

"No, it's not okay, Baron. He's done something to her. I know it. Something in her mind. Why won't she wake up?" Alric's expression turned black with rage. "I should have been prepared," he said. "I *fucking knew* that bastard had something up his sleeves. I could have handled any direct attack...but this—there was nothing for me to fight."

Alric brought Diana's body closer and pressed a kiss to her brow. It worried Max that she still hadn't made a sound or moved a muscle, and Max started to think Alric was right about Devon having done something else to her. She just lay there, unconscious and pale, locked in a well of pain deep inside of herself.

"So much strength, Baron, you know? But what the fuck is any of it good for if I can't even..."

"Alric, don't. You can't play that game. It won't help her." Max was amazed at Baron's calm, rock-steady manner.

She realized again that no matter the history between them, this was still a man who in many ways remained a mystery to her. There had been so much of his life that she had not been a part of, that she had no idea of. He had been exposed to an untold amount of violence and death. She supposed it was really no surprise that he would know what to do in a situation like this.

Max bled for Diana and for Alric. They had already been through so much together.

She bit her lip and struggled to control the torrent of images being thrown at her by Alric, as well as the pain that radiated from Diana. She felt the despair rise up inside of her in response and cursed herself and the powers that she still fought to control.

No more. It was time that she stopped being a victim, time she took a stand against Devon and the evil he had infected her with. Because she wasn't of any use to anyone like this. Afraid to act, afraid of herself...*afraid*.

She was a vampire. So what.

Admittedly, it was a problem. But she wasn't the only one in the world—hell, she wasn't the only one in this room—with problems, and Max swore this would not be the thing that broke her. She would be strong for Baron and his friends. She would deal with it like she'd dealt with every other hurdle and trial life had thrown at her— by pushing aside the fear and tackling it head on.

With that in mind, she closed her eyes and redoubled her efforts. Immediately, the bloody, painful images started to recede to the back of her consciousness.

When she was certain she had it under iron-tight rein, Max opened her eyes and approached Alric and Diana.

"Alric." She kept her voice low and soft, as soothing as possible, since she knew just how close he was to the edge. "Alric. I'm going to take Diana now, all right? You've done the best you can, and you saved her life, but she needs to rest, okay?" Reaching deep into herself, Max called on her vampire abilities on purpose for the first time, hoping she had enough power to subtly push Alric into letting Diana go. She was weak, her ability unfocussed, but Alric was distracted enough that it just might work.

His own powers must have given Baron the ability to sense what she was trying to do, but he didn't stop her and for that she was grateful. Given her track record, he had more than enough reasons not to trust her, but it seemed he did anyway.

"Take her," Alric choked out finally. "Make sure she's okay. Please."

Max stepped forward and lifted Diana into her arms. Alric resisted for the length of a heartbeat before he let his hands fall and released the love of his life to her care. She felt humbled by his trust.

At least these new vampire abilities were proving useful in some ways, lending her strength where before she would have struggled with Diana's weight. Diana was admittedly a tiny woman by any standard, but with her newfound strength, Max felt as if she held a small child.

She gingerly carried Diana back into the adjoining bedroom, but paused at the doorway. She didn't want to lay her down in here, not with all the blood still staining the floor. Instead, hoping that Alric wouldn't come charging out of the bathroom after her like a raging bull, Max took Diana down the hall to Baron's room—making sure to keep the door wide open—and placed her gently on the clean linen bedspread.

She had been worried that the close proximity with Diana would trigger her blood hunger, but so far, she was able to keep that at bay. She felt clear headed and was focused on getting Diana cleaned up and comfortable, hoping it would help to settle the other woman's mind and bring her back to them.

Max quickly dashed into Baron's ensuite and rifled through the cabinets until she found a very comprehensive first aid kit. One thing was for certain, Immortals sure knew the value of a high quality medicine cabinet. Probably came with the territory.

Returning to Diana, Max carefully removed the bandages that Alric had desperately wrapped around her delicate wrists, wanting to cry at the damage to her poor arms. Thankfully, the bleeding had almost stopped, but Max knew the gashes would still have to be stitched, and the woman would live with horrible scars for the rest of her life.

A nervous glance at the medical supplies confirmed there was indeed a suture kit—several of them actually. But that didn't solve the problem of how in the hell she was going to do this.

"It's okay, Max; I'll take it from here." Baron approached the bed and placed his hand overtop of hers, taking the needle from her. "Not that I don't think you could, but I have some experience with this type of thing."

Max let out a sigh of relief. "Oh, thank goodness," she said, rising from the bed to let Baron sit down with Diana. "Where's Alric?"

"I told him to clean himself up. Said it was because I didn't want him to scare Diana when she woke and he was covered in blood, but really, I need him out of the room until we get her patched up. With his head being where it is right now, the less he sees of her like this..."

"I understand." She handed him supplies as he worked, both of them silent and reflective. Baron did indeed have some experience; his stitches were smooth and tight, his hands steady. Max breathed another sigh when the deed was done and the first of Diana's wrists had been bandaged up all clean and tight.

"How did you know how to do that?" she asked.

He kept his head down to his task and shrugged his shoulders. "It's something you learn pretty quickly when you start carrying a gun twenty-four/seven," he answered. "I've stitched up my fair share of gunshot and knife wounds in my time. I even had to suck poison out of one guy's inner thigh once when he got bit by a Palestine

Viper." A wry grin turned his upper lip. "That was definitely an experience I could have done without in my lifetime," he joked. "No matter how long that life might end up being."

"I can imagine." Max handed him a gauze pad and watched as he deftly wrapped Diana's other wrist and secured the dressing with a tidy knot.

"And, well...while we Immortals may not die as easily...that doesn't mean it bleeds any less when we screw up and some demon gets a shot in."

Max closed her eyes on a wince that she couldn't stop but tried to hide nevertheless. She obviously failed, since Baron swore under his breath and reached for her hand. "Hell. Max, we should talk about what happened earlier," he said.

She managed to avoid his touch by making a grab for the basin of pink water they had used to clean Diana's wounds. Not trusting her voice, she got up without a word and disappeared into the bathroom.

Carefully avoiding any glimpse of her reflection in the mirror, Max rinsed the bowl and then let the water run in the sink, staring down into the gentle whirlpool swirling down the drain. This was her fault. It was through her that Devon had managed to find a way to Diana. She had unwittingly let him use her to distract Baron so that he wouldn't be able to help his friends.

After a long time, Baron knocked on the door. "Max?"

She leaned her forehead against the smooth wood finish. "Is Diana going to be all right?" she asked.

"Physically...she'll be fine, I think." Baron paused. "But she still hasn't awakened, so...I don't know. Alric's got her now."

"How is he doing?" In the short time she had been here, Max had come to like Diana and her bear of a husband very much, and it hurt her heart that something so horrible had happened to them—because of her.

213

He didn't answer right away. She heard a hollow thump of sound against the door, and imagined that his forehead was pressed against it just opposite hers. If not for the barrier between them, she might already be in his arms...ah, but the division between them was so much thicker than a bathroom door now, wasn't it?

She heard Baron's sigh and closed her eyes tightly against the visual of him that rose in her mind and the surge of longing that went along with it.

"I don't have to tell you that Diana is his whole world," he said finally. "If she died...or dies still...I think we would lose him, too."

Chapter Twenty-one

Baron reluctantly left Max closeted inside the bathroom, sensing she needed time and knowing that forcing his way in would only makes things worse. But it grated. He wanted to break down the door she'd shut in his face, and the larger wall that had grown up between them like a wild tangle of thorny vines.

Unfortunately, the night was ticking by, and every minute that passed was one minute less he had to find Devon.

He let his senses flare open, searching for any hint of the vampire's sick psychic signature, but he couldn't pick up anything in the immediate vicinity of the compound. Now that the damage had been done, Devon was no doubt already headed for some slimy rock to hide under.

Grabbing his cell phone where it rested in its charging dock on the dresser, Baron flipped it open and dialed Roland's number.

"Baron, we're already on our way," Roland said. "How's Diana?"

Baron sighed. He was relieved not to have to explain the situation. "Kane have one of his visions?"

Roland hesitated, then said, "Yeah. We know what happened. Look, we're heading in; be there in two minutes."

"Good, I'll meet you in the garage." Baron hung up

the phone and grabbed for his coat and weapons. He strapped the sword to his back and clipped his holster to his waist, then swung the long, heavy trench coat over his shoulders. He paused, glancing toward the closed door of the bathroom, but there was no choice now. Maxine would have to wait.

The twins showed up just as he was grabbing a set of keys. Kane got out of his car, looking wiped. Dried blood smudged his forearm and a nasty looking gash cut a line across his temple. "Sorry, man," he said. "We had trouble tonight. A whole pile of watchers hit the university looking for a good time. It was a bad scene."

Baron didn't bother asking if they'd been able to take care of the situation; he knew the twins too well for that.

"Alric?" Roland asked as he came around the back of the car and joined his brother. He, too, looked like he'd been in a war, and Baron bet that wasn't too far from the truth. There must have been a football team's worth of demons partying it up on campus if these two warriors had taken such a beating.

Baron nodded and ran a hand through his hair. "Alric's with Diana. She's...she's hurt bad, but she should live. Anything else is completely up in the air."

Kane just nodded. Roland eyed Baron and said, "Your girl?"

Baron felt his back go up at the careful tone of the other Immortal's voice. "She didn't take anyone's blood, if that's what you're asking."

Roland's gaze was direct, his expression tight. "Baron, I needed to know," he said. "If she's crossed over—"

Baron leapt for his friend, his hands fisted in the collar of Roland's shirt as he backed him up against the Ferrari. "You stay away from her," he growled. "*If* she crossed and went rogue, and *if* she had to be dealt with by

216

anybody, it wouldn't be by you." Baron knew he revealed too much with his reaction, that his vehemence belied the casual and imperturbable persona he had carefully cultivated with the others since becoming a member of their motley group. But none of that mattered any longer.

"Max is *mine*. My responsibility. And if anybody lays so much as a baby finger on her, I'll cut him in two. And as much as it pains me to say it, man, that goes for you, too...both of you."

Roland, who was usually a pretty laidback kind of guy himself, glared at Baron with murder in his eyes, ready to throw down right here, right now—something Baron wouldn't back away from. His blood boiled, and he found himself looking forward to the fight. He could use the kind of physical and emotional release a good smack-down would give him—whether it be his or someone else's ass that got kicked.

Before he and Roland had made it past the glaring at each other stage, Kane was between them. "Hey, you two," he said with his customary unlimited patience. "Save the theatrics for another time; it isn't helping the situation any." Turning to face Baron, he continued. "Listen, we're not here to take out your girlfriend. But just know that, if it comes to it, and if you're too close to the problem to *solve* the problem—"

Baron shook off the twins and walked round to the driver's side door of Alric's Navigator. "It won't come to that."

He stood, staring at Kane and Roland over the hood of the car, daring them to contradict his decree. Finally, Roland shrugged. "Good. You make sure of that and we got no problems." He opened the door. "So, where the hell are you going?"

"It's early. I have a vampire to hunt. You guys in?"

Their foray into the city's deepest, darkest, rankest

217

holes in the ground proved futile. But at least Baron had gotten his earlier wish. He managed to expend some of his pent up anger and frustrations on three unlucky watchers hanging out near Hell's Harem—which itself had been conspicuous in its vacancy. They cornered the demons as they'd been sneaking out the back alley, trying to escape the Immortals' notice. One of them confessed to Baron they had heard all the vampires were laying low because word had it the Enforcer had come to town. Baron believed him—he made sure his interrogation technique left no room for misinformation.

The three of them returned to the warehouse, only to find that Baron's Ducati was missing.

And so was Max.

"Whoa, Baron." Roland whistled. "Your girl sure has some guts. I can't believe she stole your ride. And how do you think she knew to reprogram thc system?"

A quick check of the security console revealed that Max apparently initiated a timed reset of the system, giving herself a short, two minute window during which the cameras and alarms would shut down and she could escape without the whole house knowing about it.

"She's a private investigator," Baron explained distractedly. He knew that didn't really explain much of anything. He felt his throat closing on him and a cold sweat caused the hairs along the back of his neck to stand on end.

What time was it? It couldn't be more than an hour before sunrise. "Shit." Gripping the back of his neck with one hand, he tried to think. "I don't know how she did it, but she's always been very resourceful. I wouldn't doubt it if she picked up that kind of knowledge on a job or something and socked it away just in case it should come in handy the next time she felt she had to escape an Immortal stronghold."

"Well, given since the security system didn't even register a blip of disturbance, it seems your Max definitely has a knack for retaining certain kinds of useful information." Roland's tone said he was seriously impressed.

Baron was, too, but he was also furious with her and scared shitless. "Yeah, she's got a knack for a lot of things," he said with a heavy hit of sarcasm.

"No kidding. Why do you think she reprogrammed the system to arm itself, instead of just shutting it down and making a break for it?"

Baron knew exactly why Max had made sure the system was back on when she left—because no matter how much she worried that becoming vampire had transformed her into a vicious killer, the truth was she was still the same compassionate, kind-hearted person he'd always known. "Because she cares for Diana and Alric. She knew they were in no condition to defend themselves from another attack tonight and didn't want to leave them high and dry."

Dragging a fist through his hair for what had to be the hundredth time that night, Baron swore. "Something I should have thought of myself. *Fuck.* I shouldn't have gone out. I shouldn't have left them alone."

"Maybe not. But if we're going to take care of this vampire, we have to get out there and look for him, take the fight to him," Kane said. "We can't keep waiting around for Devon to attack someone else. Either way, should haves are pointless. We need to act." He closed his eyes, and Roland immediately stepped closer to his brother in what looked like a protective gesture. After a brief moment, Kane shook his head. "I can't see her. She's not close enough to me, for me to recognize her pattern."

Roland turned to Baron. "Where do you think she's headed?"

Baron sighed, knowing that there was really only one option. "She'll be heading home."

"How do you know that for sure?"

"Because her best friend—my brother—is dying, and she wants to be with him."

"Your brother? Man, I'm sorry. We didn't know."

Baron clenched his jaw and shook his head, dismissing Roland's expression of sympathy. He started down the hall back toward the garage. The twins followed close behind. "Yeah, well that's where I think she's going. And I'm going after her myself. You shouldn't leave Alric and Diana alone with Devon still hanging around."

Baron grabbed a set of keys from a console on the wall and headed toward a large black Yukon. He stopped and closed his eyes against the guilt that rose thick in his throat. "Alric might need the backup if Devon decides to take advantage of another opportunity like the one he created tonight. And be careful. He gets off by fucking around with other people's heads."

It would probably be a good idea to take at least one of the warriors along with him, but Baron still wasn't going to do it. If he had to go home, it was something he was going to have to do on his own.

He got in the car and punched a code into the custom console to open the large bay doors. Kane and Roland watched as he drove out, their faces showing identical expressions of concern and not a little bit of wariness, but they hadn't tried to stop Baron from going.

He stomped on the gas. A feeling of urgency had his heart beating at a fast clip. His eyes strayed to the horizon, which was still dark for the moment, but Baron knew it would soon begin to lighten with the start of a new day.

He hoped to God Max didn't let her impatience to get home, or her eagerness to run from him, tempt her into staying on the road any longer than was safe.

The only consolation he had was the knowledge that if Devon had decided to follow her—like the sick, foreboding sense of doom inside his racing heart told him he had—at least the vampire would be stuck by the daylight, out of commission for just as long as Max was, while Baron had the advantage of being able to travel all day.

He knew where she was going. He just hoped to hell he got to her before someone else did.

Chapter Twenty-two

Max flicked down the tinted face shield of Baron's motorcycle helmet, covering her sensitive eyes. Through the protection of the thick plastic shade, she eyed the horizon line ahead of her, searching the sky for the slightest evidence that it had started to turn a lighter shade of black.

The sun was there; she could feel it. It was sitting under the horizon, just beyond the point where its rays could start to stretch across the land. Thankfully, darkness still reigned on this part of the earth—but only for another hour at most.

Maybe it hadn't been such a good idea to leave Chandler tonight. Perhaps she should have waited—but Max just couldn't do it. She couldn't stand the thought of another moment spent in close proximity with Baron, not after what she'd admitted to him, followed by the horror of what she had done to him. And especially not after the danger she had brought to Diana and Alric.

She especially couldn't tolerate the idea of Jackson being stuck in that hospital by himself for one more minute longer than was absolutely necessary.

It meant a long drive with a stopover somewhere safe to escape the sun, but Max had been certain she was making the right choice—at least she had been, *then*.

Now, with the sunrise imminent and her eyes already

stinging, she wasn't so sure anymore.

Pulling over to the side of the road, she stopped to check her map. Realizing the ghastly déja vu factor of that, she took several deep breaths. Then she laughed. It started with an acrid, vitriolic snort which turned to uncontrollable cackles that had her gasping for air and fighting off hysteria.

When Max regained control of herself, she didn't feel any better for having wasted any of the few precious moments that were left of the night.

With an anxious sense of urgency, she turned her efforts back to finding a safe place to buckle down for the long hours of the day.

Max kicked the motorcycle into gear and revved the engine, listening to it roar with life, feeling the power of every one of the 1000 ccs that were at her beck and call in the aggressive vibrations which caused her thighs to pulse. Pulling back onto the road, she went fast. Her speed was dangerous, but her control of the bike was total. Leaning into the wind, she was as one with the top of the line piece of motorized equipment, utilizing the steel, fiberglass, engine fluids and mechanical functions, as she would her own body parts—arms, legs, heart and lungs.

With the cool, biting wind rushing past her face, and the black tarmac rolling beneath her feet, Max had to wonder if she was any different than the motorcycle—a machine. It was a perfectly built, harmonious coexistence of parts that had been carefully put together so as to work to its maximum potential on as little energy as possible.

Machines were theoretically error free, while humanity was lousy with imperfections and wasted potential. Max had already found that as a vampire, her body now utilized so much more of that innate potential; she was able to exploit so much more of the precision, strength, and natural fluidness of her body's incredible architecture than ever before, without the hassle of limited energy and aging cells to hamper her.

It almost made her wonder why she bothered to mourn her lost humanity. She had never really gotten anything special out of it after all. Just expectations dashed, disappointments up the wazoo, and dreams that she never realized, followed by a horrific, violent death.

But then, to be human was more than just shattered dreams and decaying faculties. It meant choices, and it meant love. Close friends and sunshine. And it meant growing old as your children grew tall. It was life, and yes, it was death.

Where did that leave her now? She'd already proven that most of these essentially human strengths and failings, rights and assurances, didn't apply to her anymore. She was vampire whether she liked it or not. There would be no more sunshine for her, no more friends, no chance for children. And as for choice, well she definitely hadn't chosen any of this.

Because her choices had been taken from her, she was no longer alive, although not really dead. either.

Ah, but she wasn't exactly a machine, not like the bike was a machine. She still breathed; she still...wanted...and loved...and perhaps she would still die.

Let's not have it be today, though. Okay? She shot another nervous glance toward the now grayish horizon line ahead of her.

The sun was coming fast. She could smell the morning's dew on the grass, that fresh, light scent. And even though she couldn't hear much past the muffling effect of the spongy head protection of her helmet and the consistent drone of the bike, Max imagined that a few early birds were already singing good morning to some very unlucky worms.

A few minutes later, she had almost come to the conclusion that she would be forced to drive off the road and find a dark place to bed down in the woods, when she caught sight of a slightly worse-for-wear billboard advertising a cozy, family-run hotel called the Sleepy Time Inn off of I-94. Thank goodness she'd had the presence of mind to take a look through Baron's coat and "borrow" the sixty bucks in his pocket. Otherwise, she'd be screwed worse than she already was right now.

Hoping to God she didn't get pulled over by a trooper looking to meet the last of his ticket quota for the night, Max gunned the engine and raced for the next exit.

Thank God.

Sure enough, with maybe fifteen minutes to spare before full-fledged sunshine started streaming into the sky in long, soon to be hot rays, Max was ensconced in a ratty, flea-infested hole of a hotel room that made her mother's old trailer look like a suite at the Hilton.

Choices. And yet again, she had been left with none.

She set her helmet and keys—*Baron's* helmet and keys—down on the scarred surface of the cheap bedroom dresser, a rickety piece of particle-board furniture that had been laminated long ago with a barely-wood colored veneer that was now rubbed down to almost nothing. She was afraid of what she would find living inside if she were to actually slide open any of the drawers, but that wouldn't be a problem, since she had no clothes to unpack and wouldn't be staying any longer than sunset.

However, the rest of the room might be a problem. The one double-sized bed had been positioned on the side wall of the room, perpendicular to the door and the one window—a window covered not with reassuring blackout curtains that fell nicely to the floor, but with a set of mini-blinds consisting of maybe a dozen rows of bent and broken vinyl strips. It wouldn't come close to keeping the deadly daytime sun from streaming right across the bed.

With a sigh, Max quickly realized that her safest option was going to be the bathroom. She might not get any sleep, but at least she wouldn't have to spend the day nervously tracking the motion of light as it moved across the room, or watch dust motes dancing on sunbeams as she contemplated the pathetic circumstances that had brought her to this pass.

Walking to the bed, she reached for the sheets and blankets and dragged them into the tiny bathroom with her. She didn't hold out hope they would make the cramped space any more comfortable, but it couldn't hurt.

Sitting cross-legged in the doorway on the cracked tile floor, she watched the sun slowly making its way inside the room. Watched until her eyes burned beyond what she could stand and her skin had started to redden.

Finally, she shut the door and placed a wadded-up towel against the shaft of light that still tried to sneak in by way of the space underneath.

A long while later, Max finally started to relax.

With no other place to rest, she set her back against the rusty porcelain tub. She tried stretching out her legs, but was hampered by the sweaty, yellowed toilet at the other end of the pocket-sized room.

With a crabby groan, Max swore and stuffed a pillow on the edge of the tub behind her neck. If she had thought her muscles were going to be sore after riding hunched over the bars of a motorcycle all night, she was already dreading the discomfort she would feel when it was time to get back on it after a long day spent cooped up on the hard floor.

Still, she had made progress. Some. She was on her way home. Taking back some control over her wretched circumstances.

Then why did she want nothing more than to let loose the sloppy tears that sat annoyingly close behind her closed eyes? Because she couldn't get Baron's face out of her head. And she couldn't get his scent out of her clothes. And she couldn't get his blood out of her veins. Whether she liked it or not, and despite all her efforts to erase him from her past, Baron was more a part of her now than ever before. She had fallen in love with him. Harder than before. And she feared there was no getting over it this time.

Chapter Twenty-three

Jackson opened his eyes, or tried to, since his lids were glued shut with crusty bits of eye gunk. His face was angled away from the door, but when he could focus, he noticed three things. First, it was dark. Both inside his room and outside the window, which meant he must have been out the whole day. The last thing he remembered was Nurse Betty trying to shovel oatmeal down his gullet like he was a two year old.

The second thing Jackson saw was Maxine's slender form reflected in the darkened window, and he immediately started fighting back tears. Not that he minded if she saw him crying, 'cause hell, she'd seen that often enough over the years, but he didn't want her to know just how much he needed for her to be here, didn't want her to feel guilty because she hadn't been here—especially when he'd asked her to leave in the first place.

And of course, he couldn't help but notice that she was alone. That caused a sharp pain in his chest, a twinge of regret. But he was so glad to see her that he pushed the other feeling down to deal with later.

Maxine was standing just inside his door, staring out the window to the darkness of the night beyond. She hadn't yet noticed he was awake. Her face was shadowed by the light coming in behind her from the hallway, but Jackson knew his friend. There was something wrong.

Something different about her. Something in her posture.

She looked sad.

Fuck. If his stupider-than-dirt brother had hurt her...

What? What could I do about it even if he had?

It wouldn't even be Baron's fault. Baron had made his wishes clear enough when he took off without a second glance. No, it was his fault for sending Max to Baron in the first place. For pushing them together not once, but twice. Obviously with the same disastrous results.

But he had been so sure he knew what he was doing.

Jackson might be sick, but it wasn't blindness he suffered from. He knew Baron and Maxine so well, and he knew how they really felt about each other. When he sent Max out looking for his errant brother, it had been with two goals in mind. He wanted to force the two of them to come face to face with each other without Jackson's presence to muddy the waters, hoping they wouldn't be able to resist the longing that had always been painfully evident whenever the two of them were in the same room together.

And secondly, he had wanted Max far away from this hospital room.

He hadn't wanted her to be here during the chemo treatments, especially the spinal tap and the radiation. The last time he had gone through it had been bad enough for the both of them, but Jackson had known this time would be worse. And holy hell in a hand basket had it ever been.

He didn't yet try to turn his body around to face her. He would need a lot more strength for that than he had right now. But he did open his mouth to urge her to come closer, around the bed.

"Hey," he called, his voice registering at barely a croak and making him wince. He could tell her it just sounded so bad out of misuse because there was no one to talk to in this sterile purgatory of torture, but he knew Max would see through his pathetic attempt at humor to the pain beneath, so he didn't bother.

Not like she wouldn't see through him anyway. Maxine Deveraux was the best friend anyone could have, and Jackson was lucky to have her as *his* friend. The thing was, she was too good a friend. She was so attentive; he felt guilty for still being alive because every extra moment he lingered on this earth was one more moment Max spent wasting her life away caring for him and worrying about him.

He watched her reflection as she made her way around the bed. "Hey, Jacky," she said, settling down in the chair beside him, her voice soft with concern as her eyes took in every new line in his pale face. "How are you doing?"

With a smile, he summoned all of his strength and reached for her, glad that his hand remained steady. Surprisingly, she hesitated before taking it, as if she didn't want to touch him.

Her skin felt cool against his, but that could just be his fever building again. He cleared his throat, hoping to get some force behind his voice, pretend to be more substantial than a feather on the wind.

"I'm fine," he lied. "So, I guess...no luck with Baron, huh?"

Her eyes went dark, almost black in her pale face. "I'm sorry, Jackson."

With a slow shake of his head, he said, "Doesn't matter. I'm just glad you're back." He sighed. "Even though you look like hell."

Max laughed and glanced down at her baggy men's clothes. She looked like she'd slept in them. Tugging at the front of the sweater, she shrugged her shoulders. "That's a long story," she said. She shook her head, her expression turning sad once more. "I'm so sorry, Jacky. I didn't mean to be gone so long."

He smiled sadly, his chest tight. "Oh, honey, don't apologize. Truth be told, I had hoped you would be gone at least this long." Straightening his legs beneath the sheets, he groaned. Sitting up was going to be a bitch, especially the rolling over onto his back part, but he planned to give it a shot.

Before he could even begin to struggle to a sitting position, Max was there with an arm around his back, as if she had read his mind. Supporting him until he could push the button that lifted the head of the bed.

"Jackson." Max sat back down in the chair, eyeing him with what seemed like careful consideration, almost as if she were seeing something in his face that hadn't been there before.

Did he look that bad then?

"You look fine, Jacky," she said with an absent shake of her head and a tight frown on her face. "I'm trying to decide how to kick your ass without the nurses running in here."

What? He opened his mouth to speak, but she kept going.

"You know, I understand where you're coming from." Max rearranged the pillow behind his head so that his neck was supported, before she continued. "But did you ever stop to think how I would feel, knowing you didn't want me here with you? Knowing you didn't think I was strong enough to help you through this?"

"Hey, Max. Hold up sweetie. Before you rake a dying man over the coals here—let me explain." Jackson squeezed her hand and smiled. "Trust me, it isn't that I didn't want you with me, or didn't think you could handle...*this*. But is it so bad to wish that you didn't have to? To wish you could remember me as I was before? And not as a shriveled husk of a human being?" He sighed. "Don't get me wrong. I love you more than anyone else in this world, but the last thing I need is for you to change my bedpan and watch me yakking up my insides into a stainless steel salad bowl. And the last thing I wanted was for you to see me wasting away,

231

transformed into this barely-alive skeleton. To watch me die before your eyes like Houdini in the tank."

She was silent, but her eyes were piercing. Jackson felt like she was digging into his brain, reading him like a book. A thin, transparent book with lots of helpful illustrations.

"I'm sorry he isn't coming," she said at last.

He wasn't the only one who was an open book. It didn't take a psychic to be able to see from her face that something monumental had happened between her and Baron.

"What did he say?" he asked.

She shook her head and looked away, out through the window again. Into the night. Finally, she shook her head. "Maybe he would have come," she said, although the tone of her voice suggested she doubted her own words. "But something happened, and I...well, I kind of took off without him."

She was scaring him now. He held her gaze. "What happened, Max?"

"I think she would say that *I* happened," laughed a deep, masculine voice from the open doorway.

He'd never seen Maxine move so fast. One moment she was sitting calmly beside him, and the next she'd leapt over the bed and put herself between Jackson and the stranger who was still snickering from the entrance.

"Get the hell out of here," she snarled.

Whoa. What the hell happened to Max's voice? The treble was a few octaves lower, like the protective growl of a mother lion.

The man chuckled once more, and it seemed to Jackson that the sound echoed inside of his head. "Ah, my dear. Not even a kiss hello for dear old dad?"

Jackson looked from Max, whose tension levels had visibly skyrocketed into the stratosphere, to the stranger, a dark haired, pale-skinned man who exuded nonchalance and a not-so-subtle sense of barely-leashed power.

He shot a glance toward Jackson then and grinned, showing long gleaming white canines. *What in God's name are those?*

"You stay the fuck away from him." With her back to him, Jackson couldn't see Max's face, but he caught the sound of her rumbled warning clearly enough.

"Ah, but I have no intention of doing any such thing." The man moved farther into the room, the folds of his greatcoat swishing in a wide, elegant swoop against the edges of the doorway. "While I did think that it would be enough to amuse myself with you for a time—to get back at Baron you understand—imagine my surprise and delight when I saw in that pretty little head of yours that Baron had a brother as well. Your coming here was fortuitous in more than one way, as it happens. I needed to get out of town, and I seem to have gotten the opportunity to kill two birds with one stone in the process." There was that laughter again. Jeez, this guy was a barrel of them.

Too bad Maxine didn't seem to agree. Jackson was confused as hell.

He started as the door closed, seemingly of its own volition. Just what was going on here?

Max tensed, throwing an arm out as if to block the man's path to Jackson. Was it just him, or were her fingernails freakishly long? He hadn't noticed when she'd held his hand earlier that she had decided to grow them to supermodel length talons. It seemed out of character for a woman who had always been so meticulous about keeping her nails neat and trim.

"I don't know what your history is with Baron," she said to the stranger, her voice tight, guarded. "But don't you think that you've done enough? It's only a matter of time. He and his friends are hunting you. They're going to kill you."

"Oh, I have no doubt they're going to try. They've tried a few times already, but I always have the upper

233

hand." He was very cocky this guy. What the hell kind of shit was Baron into to be attracting characters like this? And how had he gotten Maxine involved?

Given that Max had turned into his very own angel of protection, putting herself between him and the dark and mysterious stranger with suspiciously long, sharp teeth, Jackson felt like an extra in an episode of *Buffy the Vampire Slayer*. One of the guys who barely gets his name in the credits because he's killed off right at the beginning of the show.

Max shot him a sharp look behind her, and the man laughed. "Your friend is coming very close to the truth, my dear. Shall I enlighten him further, do you think?"

"I don't want you anywhere near him." Max moved as if to advance, but suddenly stopped. She turned toward Jackson, slowly, her face pale and drawn with fear. "No," she whispered. "Devon, don't do this."

"Well, you see, here's the thing," he drawled. "So far, you have refused to accept and embrace your altered biology, so I thought I would just help you along a little. It's a kindness really. Not to mention, I'm getting kind of bored, and it will present an interesting diversion."

Jackson's gaze lit first on the stranger—Devon—who smiled back, shrugging his shoulders as if to say, "Sorry, man, a psychotic maniac's gotta do what he's gotta do".

He turned to Max, who looked completely horrified. "What is it, Max?" He was getting more than a little freaked out here. "What is this all about? What's happening?"

She shook her head, the motion very controlled, and Jackson realized she was concentrating, so much so that whatever she was trying to do—*or not to do*—was costing her so much energy she had nothing left for speech.

"Do it, Maxine," Devon urged. He sounded like a kid on the playground pushing dope. "You know you want it. You can hear the blood flow in him, a little sluggish yes, but still sweet and warm."

234

Max growled, whether at Devon or at him, Jackson wasn't quite certain. He could feel the conflict in the air, the strength that flowed back and forth in waves. He locked eyes with Max. Worried about her. She looked more than drawn, more than strained. She looked...*hungry*.

As if he'd said the words aloud, her lips pulled back from her teeth in a hiss, and she bared long canines, pointed and deadly.

Jackson had the awful suspicion he had just been added to some inconceivable menu.

Chapter Twenty-four

Baron knew he looked out of place. He hadn't exactly dressed for a visitation.

He had dressed for battle.

This sick feeling in his gut had been with him since yesterday at about two in the morning when he found himself stopping at a Motel 6 because of the lingering scent of a psychic signature he knew all too well. The sight that greeted him in room 12C had confirmed his suspicion that he was not only on Max's tail, but Devon's as well.

The vampire was long gone from the motel by the time Baron arrived, and there hadn't been anything he could do for the dead woman and her child, but an anonymous call to the authorities from a few miles away would at least ensure they were found as quickly as possible.

Baron doubled his speed from that point, needing to get to Max before the vampire did. But as soon as he reached the doors of the hospital, he knew he was already too late.

Inside, he didn't have to stop at the nurse's station and ask what room Jackson was in, he just followed the rank scent of Devon's evil to the third floor and made his way to the end of the hall.

Pausing just outside Jackson's door, Baron realized

that although Devon had been here, he wasn't any longer.

But Jackson was in that room.

A memory slipped past his guards, and Baron remembered the day he found out his brother had Leukemia.

Baron rushed into the hospital, having carried Jackson the whole twenty blocks from the park. The nurses descended upon them as soon as they came through the doors, so Jackson didn't have to wait, but God, he was scared out of his mind. Especially when the only thing left to do was sit hunched in the hospital chair by his brother's bedside, and wait for their mother to arrive.

She whirled into the room and rushed right to Jackson's side. "Jacky. Oh Jacky, my poor boy," she cried. Baron winced. It sounded just a little overdone, but their mother was known to go heavy on the drama—an actress at heart who had never quite realized her true calling.

"Hey, mom," Jackson whispered as he tried to dodge her gushy kisses on his cheeks and forehead, and her searching fingers running over his arms and across his chest, looking for some visual sign of injury.

"What happened?" She turned to Baron and frowned. "Well? I thought you were supposed to be looking out for your brother. So how did he end up here?"

Baron straightened in his chair, bracing himself. He didn't bother to respond. His mom was just getting started. She'd drag this lecture out right nicely for a good five minutes getting it all out of her system—mom had to vent a little bit when she was afraid.

"Mrs. Silver?"

It was almost comical the way she twirled dramatically to face the doctor. "Dr. Saunders, how nice to see you again," she said sweetly. As a single woman in a fairly small town, Lorraine Silver was well aware of Dr.

Saunders' recent status as a divorcée and wasn't above using the current situation to let him know that she was ready, willing, and more than able to guide him through his difficult time.

Baron threw Jackson a disgusted look and rolled his eyes, causing his brother to laugh, which set off another round of coughing. Baron jumped from the chair as his mother turned back to her youngest son, helping him to sit up as he hacked his way through the fit. The doctor came around beside her and watched the bleeping numbers and lights on the equipment that monitored Jackson's condition.

When the coughing subsided, Lorraine leaned over and whispered something soothing into Jackson's ear, then gently laid him back on the bed before turning to Dr. Saunders. All flirting aside, her expression had changed to one of deep concern for her child. When it came right down to it, neither of the boys ever doubted they were her number one priority. "So, doctor, are you going to tell me what's the matter with my son?"

Baron caught Jackson's eye and silently mouthed an apology for having made him cough, to which Jackson just shook his head wanly. He reached out a frail looking hand to Baron, who took it and gave him a tight squeeze of reassurance.

"Now that you're here, we'll need to get your signature on some forms, so that we can run a few tests."

"Yes, I'll sign whatever you need—" Lorraine nodded and waved a hand in the air. "—just tell me you're not pulling at straws here, that you have some idea of what's wrong with him."

"Mrs. Silver..." The doctor paused, his eyes moving from Baron's mother to Jackson and then Baron, obviously unsure about whether or not he should say anything in front of the children.

"Doctor, please. My boys are old enough that I don't hide the difficult truths of life from them anymore. Just spit it out, so we can get on with things and I can get them home."

Dr. Saunders sighed, and all of a sudden Baron knew. All of a sudden it seemed as obvious to him as it was to this good doctor. His chest tightened and he glanced over at Jackson, who returned his look with a grim expression that said he was very much aware of just what the doctor was going to say, but he wasn't in the least surprised. From the look on Jackson's face, his brother had known for quite awhile that something was seriously wrong with him.

"I've called in Dr. Tysdale. He's an oncologist. I'm sorry to tell you this Mrs. Silver, but I believe that our tests and Dr. Tysdale's examination of Jackson will confirm my suspicion that your son has chronic lymphocytic leukemia."

Baron remembered the look on his mother's face when all those tests had come back. He remembered praying he would be a donor match for his brother and the disappointment that his mother tried to hide when they found out he wasn't. He remembered the chemo and the transfusions and every brutal agony Jackson had undergone before that first remission.

He should have been stronger. For Jackson. For his mother.

Instead, he had failed them all miserably, including Max.

And if Devon had gotten to them, then his failure was complete.

Worried about what Devon might have done, he opened the door and stepped inside his brother's hospital room.

"Oh thank God, Baron."

Jackson was sitting up in bed, looking drawn and thin and so damn young. Baron felt a sharp tug against his heart. This was his family, *his brother*. All of a sudden it seemed too wrong for words that he had let something so petty as his own insecurities and guilt keep him from doing right by him for so long.

Was it too late?

"Jacky," Baron said, falling easily back into his childhood role with the use of the familiar moniker. "Are you all right?"

Jackson shook his head, his eyes wide with panic and fear. "I'm fine, but Max—"

"What happened?" *Let her be all right*. Baron fought to breathe through the thick knot of dread lodged in his throat. "Where is she?"

"Baron, what the hell is going on with you two? What kind of people are you hanging with? Some spooky looking guy walked in here, talking nonsense, and all of a sudden Max's eyes started glowing red and she grew a pair of choppers on her that a cobra would envy."

"Did she hurt you?"

"*Did she hurt me?* What the hell is that supposed to mean? Of course she didn't hurt me." Jackson paused, his look uncertain. "There was a moment though... but it was nothing. The guy all of a sudden got this look on his face as if he heard something, and he took off. I figured that was a good thing, but then Max turned and ran after him." He scowled at Baron, who was still standing at the door. Trying to shift his body to face him fully, he said, "What did you do to her?"

"Ah, fuck." Baron ran his hand through his hair. "There's no time, Jackson. If I don't find her before—"

"Before what? Before *sunrise*?" Jackson finished with a chilling insight and unspoken incrimination.

Baron accepted responsibility. It was long past time he accepted responsibility for a lot of things. He clenched his jaw tightly, knowing the only thing that mattered right now was getting to Max before Devon got her. "Yes. Before sunrise. Before she does something that can't be taken back. Before she gets hurt. Or killed."

The steely light in Jackson's crisp blue eyes revealed the man behind the disease. His eyes showed clearly the strength and determination that had gotten him through countless treatments and tests, setbacks and dashed hopes. Revealed the man who had earned the respect and friendship of one such as Maxine.

A man who was done giving his brother the benefit of the doubt.

"Go then. You find Max and bring her back. And if anything happens to her, you better believe it's on your head."

Baron turned, stopped at the door. Without looking back, he said, "I love her, Jackson."

"I know you do, Baron. I've always known." He heard Jackson sigh. "Just find her."

Baron turned round and met his brother's gaze. "I promise. I won't fail her again...not like I've failed you."

"You never failed me, my brother. I didn't ask you to give up your dreams and hang out at my bedside. I was always proud of what you have done with your life."

They both studied each other for a moment. Silent. Baron finally nodded.

"I'll be back," he promised, leaving his brother behind once again.

Chapter Twenty-five

Max knew these woods like the back of her hand. Her mother's trailer, the sinkhole of sin she had wanted desperately to escape her entire youth, had backed onto them. And until her mother's death four years ago, Max had returned often enough to check up on her.

The vampire had moved quickly from Jackson's hospital room, and in the process, his hold over Max lessened and she was able to shake off some of the maddening bloodlust. She still hadn't been able to look Jackson in the eye. Instead, she'd taken off after Devon. She was done letting this vampire terrorize her and her friends.

She purposely delved deep inside of herself, tapping into the dark place Devon had created there, hoping she could somehow use it to track him.

Sure enough, if she concentrated, it was obvious, as if she had a laser beam trained right on him. He was heading deep into the woods. Something had spooked him, but she doubted it was Baron.

Not that Baron wasn't on his way, because he would come. She was sure of it. Maybe not for her, and not for Jackson, but she knew he would come for his revenge.

But right now something else had Devon on the run.

Beneath the heavy canopy of towering oak trees, the

darkness was complete, not even the light of the bright full moon penetrated to the ground where Max walked carefully. "This is by far the stupidest thing you've ever done, Maxine Deveraux." Great. Now she was talking to herself. No, she was actually lecturing, which was probably a step up from yammering away to her crazy-ass vampire self.

Max had come out here alone with desperation heating her blood, propelled by the harebrained idea she could take on Devon by herself and end this thing once and for all. Baron would freak if he found out, but then again what would that matter to her if she was dead?

When she'd seen Devon in that room, so close to Jackson, Max had felt fear. Deep, bone-chilling fear the likes of which she never wanted to feel again. And when he tried to compel her to bite her friend, tried to force her to turn on Jackson like a rabid dog...she knew that as long as Devon lived, that fear would forever be with her.

Max needed to take matters in her own hands. She was going to find the vampire and kill it herself. She didn't want Baron fighting this monster, not for her—he had enough evil to handle without Max adding to it. This was her responsibility, a way to take back some of the control Devon took from her when he took her humanity.

So...she was alone. It was better this way. The plan was hazy at best. Reckless. Stupid. Okay, there was no plan. She was acting on pure impulse, adrenaline.

Her focus kept her from screaming with rage into the night. It kept the thought of what she had done to Baron, what she'd almost done to Jackson, and how it was her weakness that had given Devon the opportunity to attack Diana, from overwhelming her with guilt.

Devon might be older and stronger and meaner than she was, but Max had a few tricks up her sleeve. Her chances of success were slim, yes. All right, if she were honest with herself, she'd admit the margin was more along the lines of slim-to-none. And she was also willing to admit she would likely be dead by morning. But if things went the way she planned, she could at least take Devon to hell right along with her.

It should have bothered her more, but curiously enough, it didn't.

Maybe because Max knew she should be dead already.

She had nothing anyway. Jackson was dying. Her mother was already gone. The official diagnosis had been cancer, but that was just medicine. Max knew the truth. A lifetime of drinking and smoking and drugs equaled suicide whether or not something else took you out before you could finish the job.

Max had never understood why her mother needed to load herself up with alcohol and chemicals, why she hated her life—and her daughter—so much.

But after the last few days, Max thought she could finally understand Charlene Deveraux a little better. A woman who'd gotten knocked up at sixteen, dropped out of school to shack up with Max's deadbeat of a father. A father Max had never met because he skipped out on them before she was two hours old. After that, Charlene worked two and three jobs at a time to keep them from starving, but as Max had gotten older, the drinking had gotten worse and the drugs more potent.

Thinking about it now, Max couldn't feel the same anger and resentment that she had always nurtured within herself. Instead, she felt something akin to pity and a deep sadness for the wasted life.

And she had to wonder if perhaps mother and daughter were not so different after all. Maybe blood really would tell.

Max didn't want to end up angry and alone, drinking herself into a stupor every night. But she could feel the bitterness rising inside of her, the same bitterness Charlene must have felt upon realizing that her dreams were nothing but wisps of smoke blowing away on the wind. And the feeling was getting stronger and stronger, choking Max with anger and shame and the knowledge that her life was never going to be what she had planned. All because of some rampaging mutt with dental issues.

The battle raged inside of her. The lure of the vampire's blood getting stronger as her anger settled in deeper, setting its hooks on her soul. She should fight it, but she felt the strength it gave her coursing through her veins, and she liked it; she needed it.

Baron's motorcycle was parked off the road along the shoulder. Max was nowhere in sight.

"Damn it," he muttered. "Where the hell are you?" He pulled over alongside the motorcycle and got out of the truck. It was hotter in Rockford than it had been in Chandler, the humidity making him sweat as he strapped the bike into the flatbed and bolted it down with a heavy padlock.

Let Max try to leave without him this time.

He tuned his ability, reaching out for any hint of psychic energy. He knew Max's powers were strengthening, and if she was anywhere close by, he should be able to—

Ah, there.

It was weak and distant. She had already gone deep into the woods. But for the moment anyway, she was alone. He wasn't picking up any other signatures.

Following the fine trace of energy that was more a wispy trail of smoke, Baron walked into the trees until he came to a small clearing and the entrance to a rocky cavern.

It was dark inside without even the moon to lend a reassuring glow, but that wasn't a problem for Baron's Immortal eyes. His sight was better than perfect even in the dark.

She was crying.

Max never let herself lean on anyone. Not Baron—who she'd hated. And not even Jackson—who she refused to burden with any more than he already had to deal with.

Instead, she kept everything inside. She was a superwoman who always had it all under control. It was enough to make a man feel more than a little useless.

But he had been proud of her. Proud of her strength and resilience in the face of her mother's alcoholism and drug addiction, proud of her determination to rise above that. Still, he'd felt a little like her damn appendix—a part of her life, sure, but not really necessary. If you had to cut it out, you wouldn't really notice the lack.

Maybe that's why he'd known he could just disappear from her life. Fact was, she hadn't come looking for him until Jackson asked her to.

Baron had accepted Max's front of disdain and distance as part of her defense mechanisms—something that was as necessary to her as breathing after the childhood she'd been forced to endure. But the last few days, he had hoped that maybe they'd broken down that wall, hoped that, for once, she would really let him in.

Instead, she had taken off like he'd done to her once before. It seemed Baron wasn't the only one of them who ran when things got messy and complicated. But now here they were; Max was crying, and it was tearing his heart out, and there was no way he was going to leave her ever again.

He took a step forward and stopped. Not wanting to frighten her, he called her name before approaching. "Max." He couldn't see her. His voice echoed off the rock walls of the cavern, sounding overly loud. Scary even to his ears.

He heard her breath catch and hold. She wasn't moving, wasn't breathing, and he started walking toward her again. "Max, it's me. Where are you?"

His eyes had long ago adjusted to the darkness. He looked left and right until he found her huddled on the floor against the dirt wall, arms wrapped tightly around her updrawn legs. His heart lurched at the sight of her there, looking small and lost like a frightened little girl.

Nothing else mattered to him as he went to his knees before her. Only Max. He knew his destiny in that moment with a crystal clarity that came to people rarely. He whispered to her as he rocked her in his arms. Words of comfort and love. Words he should have been telling her every day for the last two years but hadn't because of his guilt and his fear.

"It's okay, baby." He kissed her forehead, kissed the tears from her eyes, her nose and cheeks. "Please don't cry anymore."

For a long time they remained like that, Baron holding her as Max's tears flowed in a river down her face. He felt the drops fall, hot and hard on his soul, in his heart. They fell on his cheek pressed against hers, on the hands he used to soothe her with soft touches. They fell between his lips as he pressed his mouth to hers, desperate to take her pain into himself so she wouldn't hurt any more.

Baron kept his kisses light, but his body was getting hard all the same. She was close and soft and warm. Heaven in his arms, even in her grief.

He cursed himself even as his kisses became deeper, longer.

Max wasn't helping him to stop, either. She kissed him back, her tears finally slowing but not stopping, not even when she opened her mouth to his tongue.

Chapter Twenty-six

Max broke away from the kiss and took a deep breath, pressing her body closer to Baron, her face buried into the curve of his shoulder. When she'd come to this cave and realized Devon wasn't here, that she'd been following a ghost scent left behind—probably on purpose to confuse anyone trying to follow—she had lost it. Broken down and just started crying. And now she couldn't stop.

Why couldn't she stop crying? She rarely cried, and never like this.

This, this was endless. An outpouring of years and years of grief and pain and disappointment, all coming out of her in this one moment. She couldn't keep any of it in any longer.

"Baron please. What do I do?" she hiccupped, her sinuses waterlogged. "I can't stop it. It hurts so much, but I can't stop crying."

"I know sweetheart," he answered, his voice low, soothing. "It's okay." It was that voice which spelled her undoing. It always had. It tricked her into believing in him, into believing that he would be constant and true, and that he'd be there for her. Tricked her into thinking he cared, that maybe he even loved her.

But he never had. At least not enough.

Not enough to trust her with the truth, or to stay when things got tough. Not enough to give them a chance at what could have been something...so beautiful.

With that thought, she forced the tears back, pulled herself together. She looked Baron in the eye for the first time since he'd found her and recognized that he felt her misery and shared her pain as his own. Perhaps he did care more than she realized. But what did that really change?

She sighed and swept a shaky hand through her hair. "How did you find me?" she asked.

He frowned at her, disapproval and exasperation replacing his earlier expression of concern, and she thought it probably hadn't been a great idea to remind him that he had been forced to come looking for her in the first place.

"Luckily, I had a pretty good idea where you would go." He rose, brushing the dust from his thighs, and then held out a hand to her.

"Yeah, luckily." Max sighed as she took it and let him help her to her feet. "But how did you find me *here*?"

"My Immortal abilities allow me to sense the psychic gifts of others," he explained. He hadn't let go of her hand, and was now pulling her along with him back down the cavern corridor. "Yours are still weak and fledgling, but they're there."

"Ah, yes. The mysterious Immortal powers," she said. "The ones I had to hear about from Diana because you refused to tell me anything about them, or about you, or about—"

Baron stopped and jerked on her arm, pulling her against him so that their faces were only inches apart. "Don't," he bit out. He glared down at her, his eyes glowing silver in the darkness, his mouth a hard line. "Don't push me, Max. After the merry chase you put me to...I'm so close to the edge right now. And you do not want to see me go over it."

Max opened her mouth to shoot back a smartass comment, but in an uncharacteristically sensible move, she snapped it shut again when it became clear that Baron was itching for a fight. She had no problem obliging him, but considering where they were, this wasn't the best place or time for it.

Apparently, Baron didn't quite share the same assessment she did of their current state of affairs. "What were you thinking?" Both hands were on her arms now and he shook her as if trying to knock the sense back into her. "What if you'd walked right into one of Devon's traps?"

Max jerked her shoulders back, stepped out of his grasp. "That was the whole point, you idiot."

"Oh?" He sneered. "And what the hell did you think you were going to do after you found him then?"

"I'm going to kill him."

"Oh, fuck no." He grabbed her arm again. He started walking, pulling her along behind him. "Then it's even more imperative we get out of here. Right now."

She thought about resisting, but again, she knew it would do no good. He would haul her over his shoulder and continue walking out of here, and she didn't have the strength to stop him—at least not without using her vampire powers against him, which she swore she would never do again.

Still, she didn't have to like it.

"Why?" she argued. "There's no one here—not anymore." She was disappointed not to have found what she came here for, and Baron apparently caught it in her voice.

He stopped pulling her along like a bull mastiff dragging its owner, and turned back to glare at her again. "Fuck, you have some kind of death wish, don't you?" He spat. "Why the hell did I bother saving your ungrateful hide if you were just going to throw your life away like so much trash?"

"Ungrateful," she laughed. "Yeah, how impolite of me, Baron. Tell me something. When you found out about this Immortal gig, how *grateful* were you? I'll just bet you got down on your knees and said thank you to the guy who broke that news to you, huh?"

"You know, Max, you are absolutely right. I was horrified, angry. I wanted to kill the person responsible for taking away my right to choose," Baron said. "Is that what you want from me, Max? Do you want my blood? Do you want to hurt me? I can understand it—I know I've hurt you often enough. Do you want to get some of that back?" He held out his arms, showing her he was willing to take whatever she had to dish out.

"Fuck you," she snarled. "It's not always about you. I didn't ask you to follow me, or fight for me, or save me."

"Of course you didn't," he said, his expression turning cold. "You haven't ever asked me for anything have you? No, you're too strong for that. Max—the woman who can support her drunken whore of a mother at sixteen, take care of my dying brother, confront hundred year-old vampires, and apparently still have the time and energy to make sure I never forget that she doesn't need me."

"That's bullshit, and you know it."

"Is it?" he asked "Is it, Max? How did you feel when I never came home? Did you get angry? Yeah, I'll bet you were angry with me. But that's okay, anger's allowed, isn't it? It's all the other emotions that you won't allow, the ones that make you messy and vulnerable. The ones that make you hurt."

"Yes, I was angry!" she shouted. "I was angry because it did hurt. I was angry because I had to be. Because anger was the only thing that kept the pain of losing you from eating me alive." Her confession ended on a sob, all of her rage draining away. He was right, damn him. Without the anger, she was left with only the pain that she'd tried for so long to deny. "It kept me from asking why. My whore of a mother, as you call her, spent her whole life asking that question. Why? She never got an answer, and in the end, that's what killed her. I swore I'd never let myself be like her. I would be stronger than she was, smarter than she was. Never let anyone have that kind of power over me."

"But the truth is..." She lifted her eyes to his and knew he could see the tears that blurred her vision for the second time that night. "I am just like her. Because it *did* hurt."

"Max—" he started, but something grabbed his attention.

She knew their little confessions session was over. They had themselves some company. "Damn," he muttered.

"I'm sorry, Baron," she whispered.

He kissed her hard on the mouth. "Save your apologies for when we get out of here," he replied. "What kind of weapon did you bring with you?"

She blinked. "Uh...I kind of borrowed a 10 mm from your closet."

He smiled. A deep chuckle rumbled from his chest. "That's my girl. Take it out and make sure you're locked and loaded. If you're going to shoot, shoot for the head. It won't kill a vampire, but it'll sure make a mess." His tone was confident as he effortlessly took charge of the situation.

"Are you serious?" she asked. "A direct shot to the head won't kill—"

"Nope. You've got to sever the head clean off for the vampire to die, otherwise—" He stopped and winced, looking down at her. "Ah, shit. I'm sorry," he said.

Max shook her head. "Don't be. We don't have time for it." She pulled her gun and checked the barrel. It was habit, even though she'd loaded it herself before sneaking out of the warehouse. Max had never been so glad in all her life for the cool comfort of a weapon's heavy grip in her hand. She might not be able to kill Devon with it, but it sure would feel good to do some serious damage.

"Come on." Baron kept his voice low. With a nod of his head he indicated that he wanted them to keep moving forward toward the entrance of the cavern.

"Shouldn't we stay here and try to take him by surprise?" Max asked.

He shook his head. "We'll get him at the entrance to the cave. Staying here for that added element of surprise isn't worth the risk. Trust me. We don't want to get caught in a tight space against a vampire's speed and strength. Speaking of which..." Baron looked her over. "Keep that in mind. You're strong. Fast. You have power. Use it. Don't let any preconceived notions of what you think you can't do hold you back from doing what you have to. If that means you kill, then kill. If it means you run, I want you to run...even if you leave me behind."

"Baron, no. I couldn't—"

His expression was focused, unwavering. "You will do as I say, Max," he ordered. "It's the only way either of us has a chance of getting out of here."

Finally she nodded, even though she had no intention of leaving him. Had no intention of letting him take on Devon alone. Maybe she wasn't strong enough to kill the vampire herself, but she would make sure Baron had all the backup he might need so that Devon wouldn't walk out of here to hurt anyone else, ever again.

He must have seen her intentions in her face because he sighed before turning from her. "There are three of them," he whispered as they slowly and very quietly made their way to the entrance of the cavern. "Devon is with them. The other two are young, probably not much older than you are."

She hesitated. "They might not be...evil, right? I mean—"

Baron turned to her once again, this time taking her hand and bringing it to his lips. He placed a soft kiss on her palm, and his expression was regretful. "If Devon turned these two, then they're evil."

She gasped, jerking her hand back from his lips. "But—"

"It's different with you, Max." He looked like he wanted to say more, to convince her of his rightness, but there wasn't time.

She shook her head, disbelieving. How could it be any different? She was a vampire, just like these two poor creatures who had likely been victims of attack by Devon as well. She had been turned by the same vampire, she had the same blood urges and the unnatural strength.

God, the only difference between her and them was that she hadn't killed anyone...yet.

The three vampires were close now. Baron and Max stood just inside the rocky entrance, Baron's blade seeming black in the pitch darkness. Max tightened her grip around the handle of her own weapon, eyes burning.

The time for stealth was past. Max watched Baron surge forward, his motions quick and sure, his blade cutting through space and time to cleave the head of one vampire clean from his shoulders. It was so fast. Max's mouth opened on a silent cry as she watched the creature turn to dust. The particles hung weightless in the heaviness of the humid summer air until Baron tore through it again, this time with his body as he continued forward to face Devon and his remaining henchman.

The older vampire just laughed. Sliding easily out of the path of Baron's blade. "Ah. Once again life is proven to be a most circular concept. Here we are right where we began, although perhaps with a few exceptions." He goaded Baron with his sneering humor. "This time, I expect that it will not be *my* woman who dies."

Baron didn't rise to the bait. His face remained cold and hard. He approached the battle with calm surety and deadly precision, sword swinging with accuracy, catching Devon across the cheek before he could skip away once more. The vampire hissed and lunged for the Immortal, but Baron either anticipated the move, or he was just wicked fast.

Max labored to gather a deep breath into her lungs. She was going to need it. But oxygen was in short supply right about now. The universe had gotten too small in the last several minutes, the atmosphere too thin.

She shook herself, knowing she had to get out of her own head and help Baron.

Devon and his fledgling continued to dodge Baron's blade, coming ever closer to getting their sharp animal-like talons deep into his skin. Max flexed her own hand, and thought she could feel those same claws waiting just under the surface. It was a primitive, defensive reaction she had started to feel as soon as her body recognized the danger.

Taking a deep breath, she took care sighting her gun, wanting to make sure her aim was true so that she wouldn't hit Baron. She was a good shot—at least in target practice at the range. She could do this. Except that Baron kept moving, the vampires kept lunging forward and back.

She could do this.

Aim.

Aim.

Fire.

Max sighed with relief as soon as she realized her shot had proved true. One more vampire was down in the dirt, a bullet lodged deeply in his brain, a crater-sized bloody hole where his left eye had just been. He didn't pouf into dust like the first one, though. No, this vampire still lived, writhing and screaming, the sound piercing into her brain like a bolt of lightning. Baron must have felt it, too. He winced, although his attack didn't falter. He and Devon were moving, circling each other in the intricate steps of a dance. Together, apart. Each breathing heavily, seemingly matched in speed and strength.

Max aimed her weapon again, patient, waiting for her shot. Baron and Devon were moving fast, almost a blur of arms and legs, steel and leather, sharp fangs and deadly claws. She was absolutely terrified, but at the same time mesmerized. Baron was a fascinating vision to behold. Even though she had known him almost her entire life, she had never been witness to this part of him.

The warrior.

His silver eyes blazed with focus and purpose; his breathing was even and every movement was calculated. Powerful. She couldn't help but watch and admire the strength and beauty of this man that she...loved.

Ah shit, what a time to think about that—

As Devon's head came within her sights and she began to squeeze the trigger, Max sensed a shiver in the air. Cold. Biting. Icy. Another presence, someone else was close. And it wasn't some trailer trash wino walking off Saturday night's binge with a jaunt through the woods.

Shit! Her opportunity had passed, and Devon was dancing around Baron once more, in a desperate attempt to elude the Immortal's deadly blade.

Another vampire? Is that what she felt? Max couldn't be sure. She hadn't had this same reaction, this sense of terrified awareness, when the others had come upon them—but then again, she had been justifiably distracted at the time. Still, this felt very different. Stronger. Colder.

Keeping one eye on Baron, who was still holding his own against Devon despite the vampire's speed and despite the taunts and snarls thrown at him, Max searched the surrounding area, peering between the shadows, into the shadows.

Whatever it was came closer. Closer.

Although fear coalesced into a hard knot of ice in her chest, she clenched her fist tighter around her gun. Everything inside of her wanted to scream, but she clamped her mouth closed and dared not call out, knowing that Baron couldn't be distracted from his fight. Instead, she waited, all her senses alert. She focused her fledgling psychic ability on the icy power that thickened in the air. Strangling her. It was all around her now, driving away the humidity, creating a vacuum that left no room for anything but cold.

Him. He was here. Watching her. Watching Baron.

And waiting.

She felt him probing her mind, and she growled, the sound a primitive vocal protest as she frantically put up mental walls to keep him out of her brain. *Not again. Please not again.* But her resistance was like a butterfly's wings brushing against a window and had no effect. His mental powers were strong, so strong she knew she didn't have a prayer in hell of stopping him from doing whatever it was he had come here to do. *Oh, God.* She could hear his laughter, devoid of humor, a chilling rumble reverberating in her head.

Chapter Twenty-seven

Who are you?

Justice. The word whispered through her mind, and Max shuddered.

I am Justice.

Please. Her silent prayer was an entreaty that Baron be spared from whatever reckoning this creature believed should be meted out. *Please.*

As smoothly and easily as the cold presence had slid into her mind, it withdrew again, leaving her shivering and cold where she stood. Even as she felt relief, she knew that while he might not be completely in her head anymore, his fearsome power surrounded her. He wasn't finished with them.

Max swung her head around, searching for some visual proof of the intruder's physical presence, but there was nothing. He was still here, though. The cold was a palpable reminder of the new and powerful threat.

She set her teeth and tightened her grip on her weapon, feeling her claws stretching. She pushed aside the fear, determination setting her spine and giving her strength. She would not let Baron down; she would not allow this unseen danger to distract him from his battle.

A screech of pain drew her full attention back to the fight between Devon and Baron. Baron had scored another hit with his blade, a direct stab through the vampire's chest. Devon lurched back, pulling himself off the length of steel, staggering against a tree. It wasn't enough. Baron had to know it wasn't going to be enough to kill him.

Max took aim. As she was about to fire, the presence returned, and her movements slowed. Her arm felt heavy, sluggish. She couldn't do it. She couldn't move at all.

Devon—who had been about to lunge for Baron once more—stopped cold. His eyes grew wide and fear showed clearly on his face. Max knew he was sensing the same force Max herself had already been made uncomfortably aware of.

She blinked and gazed down at the wounded vampire, the one she had shot in the head. Had she really done that? He was struggling to get to his feet. Max was surprised to see the bleeding had already stopped. She realized that if he were to get away at this point, he would indeed heal and live to hunt for human blood another day. It was disconcerting to say the least.

As she watched, unable to move, she felt a rush of cold air from behind her, passing so close she thought it might very well leave the burn of frostbite along her arm. "Baron!" she cried in warning.

He paused, turning toward her, his blade poised in the air. The expression on his face hardened as he perceived that there was yet another threat, and his eyes narrowed, searching. He must have sensed the disturbance in the air, but like her, he wasn't able to see anything tangible.

Their eyes met, and Max wanted to run to him, but he shook his head very slightly, a silent order to stay where she was—she didn't bother to tell him that was something not actually within her control at the moment.

At a spot between Baron and Max and the now cowering Devon, they both watched as the air began to swirl, a mini twister that remained in one spot, but grew larger and larger. Within the moving currents, Max could see the shape of a man forming as if from the air itself.

It all happened in less than the blink of an eye and then Max gasped at her first look at *Justice*.

Holy crap, he was tall. Taller than Baron, probably about the same height as Alric...and just as gigantic. That in itself was enough to jack up Max's anxiety levels to the moon. But what freaked her out the most was the utter lack of humanity. There was nothing in those eyes. They were two glowing orbs of pitch black ice. Cold. Dead.

"Hey, nice trick. Wrecked any good trailer parks recently?" Baron's blade remained trained on Devon. His arm didn't waver in the slightest and his eyes looked as hard as their newly-arrived opponent's.

"Baron, shut the hell up." *Damn him*. Hand it to Baron to be his typical provoking, wise-cracking self at a time like this. He shot her a guarded, warning look and she felt like stomping her feet in frustration, but since she still couldn't move, Max settled for hoping that the horrified frown she threw back at him expressed succinctly what she thought of his silent orders and smartass mouth.

Max turned her attention back to the man...vampire...or whatever he was. The way he had planted himself right between them like a six-foot-eight wall of menace and muscle made her think that he wanted them divided, separated so they were less of a threat to him.

Yeah, that didn't make any sense, Max thought. This guy radiated so much power; she doubted very much that he saw either of them, both of them, or ten of them, as any kind of threat. It was more likely that he wanted Baron and Max separated so he could pick them off one at a time. Just for the fun of it.

Oh shit.

Power swirled in the air, seemingly caught on the dust still settling after the vampire's splashy entrance.

Baron didn't like the look of this situation one bit. He knew the newly-arrived vampire was holding Devon frozen in place, and Max as well. It was only by the concentrated effort of his own power that he managed to neutralize those same effects on himself.

He wished to hell that he could get closer to Max. He felt an overwhelming urge to put his body in front of hers as a shield. But even though she was only a few short feet away, with that vamp between them throwing off more psychic energy than the freaky little girl from the Stephen King book who built fires with her mind, the distance could easily have been measured in miles of scattered landmines.

Oh yeah, he knew who this was.

Enforcer.

"So, you're coming to the party just a little late, aren't you, Enforcer? Shouldn't it have been you cleaning up this mess—a long freakin' time ago?" Baron continued to taunt the chilly vamp, studiously avoiding Max's eyes as he did, hoping to keep the Enforcer's attention off her. From what Baron had been told, this guy only hunted rogues—vampires who broke the rules—but just who made up those rules? And what's to say that Max hadn't broken them simply by being turned in the first place? No, he wasn't taking any chances with her. He had to find a way to get her out of here. Fast.

But he couldn't just leave without taking care of Devon. He had to know for certain this bastard was never going to be a threat to Max, or anyone else, again.

"The vampires are mine, Immortal." The voice was low and deep, with a distinct Scottish brogue curling around the *r* in vampi*r*e and Immo*r*tal. An accent women would probably swoon over, if not for the fact that it was devoid of any emotion whatsoever. There was no life inside there at all. The Enforcer was simply a vessel, an instrument of death. "You will leave them for me."

The wounded vampire whimpered, its raw terror

streaming in rivers of blood-tinged sweat from its pale skin. Baron saw Max flinch, as if she believed that she, too, was being lumped in with the others. *Oh, fuck no.* He wasn't letting some heartless vampire bounty hunter get within a foot of her.

"I really don't think I can do that," he said. With a practiced move, and without taking his eyes from the glittering blue gaze of the Enforcer, Baron drew a long-handled dagger from his waist and sent it sailing like a dart into Devon's heart. It sunk in with a loud thunk, just as Baron twisted and sunk to one knee, bringing the longer blade of his sword swinging down to take the young, wounded vampire's head.

The creature turned to ash. Devon screamed. Max jumped. And the Enforcer growled, his displeasure at having lost one vampire to Baron's steel plain. He also looked pretty pissed that his nifty Simon Says "freeze" routine wasn't working as well on Baron as it did on the others.

Baron quickly raised his blade against Devon but before he could take that vampire's head as well, Baron was blasted. A surge of power barreled into him like thousands upon thousands of bees attacking with stingers the size of harpoons. Baron focused, and managed a small shield of protection around his face, but not before his eyes started to burn—and even that meager barrier was bowing fast under the onslaught of power being wielded by the awesome strength of the Enforcer.

They stood locked in soundless, motionless combat. Then, out of the corner of Baron's eye, he noticed Devon moving, slinking away. The Enforcer's power over the lesser vampire was obviously weakening as he was forced to expend more energy against Baron. Before Baron could do anything to stop Devon from getting away, Max had leveled her gun against him and fired.

"You don't go anywhere," she said, her voice cold. He saw her flex her fingers around the weapon and roll her shoulders, and was glad the Enforcer's power was weakening enough that she could move again as well.

"Max, run."

"Shut up, Baron." The look she tossed him was angry and determined.

He concentrated on gathering up more reserves of strength, converting some of the psychic energy swirling from all of the vampires to his own advantage.

He *pushed* with one forceful flood of power and dove for Devon. "I have some business to take care of with this animal here," he said, one hand in Devon's hair and the other holding the point of his sword to the vampire's neck. "And if I turn the dog over to you—granted, he'll probably pee himself with terror, which would be fun to watch and all—but I have no assurances that he'll be taken care of to my satisfaction. You see my dilemma, don't you?"

"This was not a choice that you were given," the Enforcer replied, his expression wavering not one bit. "This is not your business, and you will turn the vampire over to me. I decide how it is to be dealt with. It shall be in accordance with *my* law."

"*Your* law?" Baron spat. "You'll forgive me—or don't, I don't actually give a flying fuck—if I don't hold much stock in your law. It was your law that allowed this monster to prey on innocents in the first place. Your law that allowed him to turn a human without her consent and to torture my friends." Baron twisted his fist tightly in Devon's hair and dug the point of his sword into his neck, drawing a long line of blood.

The usually smug, cocky vampire had been awfully quiet through all of this, probably hoping to escape through the cracks when the conflict finally erupted between Enforcer and Immortal. The only thing that kept Baron from finishing the job right here and right now was the fact that Maxine was still in jeopardy. He wouldn't toss away his only bargaining chip until he could be sure she would get out safely.

Obviously having observed the direction of his thoughts, the Enforcer turned his attention to Max.

Shit!

Her eyes went wide and her body tensed as she visibly fought against an invisible assault. But she wasn't strong enough. The bastard was in her mind.

"*Fuck*! You leave her the hell alone," Baron shouted, immediately dropping the sword and pulling his glock.

The Enforcer started to draw Max to him, seemingly unimpressed by Baron and the hollow mouth of the gun barrel pointed at his head. Max's movements were slow and halting, obviously forced, but she took first one, then two steps.

Oh, hell no. This is so not going to happen. Squeezing the trigger, he swore when the slug didn't immediately take off the side of the supervamp's head. Instead, the bullet hung suspended in the air between them for a moment, then fell, harmless, to the ground.

Baron growled with frustration and fury. Turning his attempt inward, he gathered his ability, gathered Devon's and Max's abilities, and took more from the Enforcer. The power he held was massive, and as Baron grabbed onto it, he suffered a fleeting twinge of alarm.

What if it was too much for him and he couldn't control it?

Fuck that. He felt the intense energy flowing through him. Taking a deep breath, he opened himself up to it. The world seemed to pulse with his every breath, taking on a *Matrix*-like quality, and he felt just like Keanu as he opened his eyes and saw currents and shadows and energies all eddying in the hazy atmosphere.

He still held his glock, but Baron didn't have to shoot the Enforcer. He simply used the vampire's own power against him. Freezing him to the spot and forcing him to release Max. The vampire curled his lip in a rumbling, angry snarl, showing Baron a hint of gleaming white fang.

264

"Max," he said calmly, his voice even. "Max, get over here with me. Hurry."

Baron could feel the Enforcer pulling, struggling to take back control...and he was succeeding. Damn, the thing was strong. Just how old was this guy anyway?

Unfortunately, getting out of here was going to be tricky. Baron knew he couldn't hold onto all this power for much longer, and as soon as he let go...

"Now that I have your attention, why don't we make a deal you and me." Baron hoped he was right and this Enforcer character was technically a good guy, because otherwise this situation was about to head right into goat fuck territory—a term his army buddies had used when an op turned sour and everything went to hell in a hand basket.

Baron got a raised brow and a low growl from the vampire in response.

"Hey, drop the scare tactics, or I'm going to use this impressive array of abilities that you've so generously made available to me to do more than just keep you immobile," he warned, tightening his psychic hold.

"So look," he continued. "I'm pretty sure we're on the same side, that we're looking for same outcome, so there's no cause to get all caveman on my ass."

The guy was practically chomping at the bit. No longer looking quite so unemotional, his eyes blazed with ice-cold fury. He was looking more and more like the bloodsucking vampire he really was underneath all that talk of law and order.

Baron tucked Max behind him and said, "How about you don't touch the girl, and I'll let you go."

The vampire moved so fast, Baron didn't think he even disturbed the air around him. All of a sudden he was just there, right in Baron's face. Beside him, Max gasped and tried to step around him, but Baron grabbed her arm as the Enforcer's fist wrapped like a band of steel around his throat.

"You ever try a stunt like that again, Immortal, and you die," he growled into Baron's face, his eyes glittering with intent. "The only reason either of you still live now is because I owe a debt to one of your kind...and because your little vampire girlfriend here remains free of the taint."

"Wonderful," Baron retorted with a choked sound, heavy on the sarcasm. "Then if we're all going to keep breathing for at least a few more minutes, why don't you back the hell off?"

The Enforcer smiled then, a cold, toothy smile that managed to make him look even more savage than he did naturally. "You know, I could almost like you," he said, as he let Baron go and straightened to his full height. "You've got a great deal of power and a lot of balls for such a young Immortal. Not much brains...but yeah, a hcalthy set of stones."

"Yeah, yeah. Flatter me all you want, Dracula; you're still not my type." Baron shrugged and reached for Max, needing to bring her close. Her return grip on his hand was a reassuring vice.

"What did you mean just now?" Max asked. "What is 'the taint'?"

Baron wanted to knock the vampire's teeth out when he turned to Max, his nostrils flaring as he looked down at her. It would have been an understatement to say Baron was uncomfortable with the fact that she'd gotten the attention of a man whose sole purpose it was to eliminate vampires.

"The taint is the evil that starts to devour a vampire's soul when he takes blood from those who have not offered it of their own free will," the Enforcer explained. "That blood is often tainted with fear and anger, which will corrupt the already precarious balance that a vampire must maintain to keep from slipping into darkness and damnation."

"And it's your job to find these tainted vampires,

and...do what exactly?"

Baron squeezed her hand, hearing the anxiety in her words and wanting to reassure her that no matter what this guy intended, Baron was not going to let anything happen to her. She was *not* like Devon.

The Enforcer bared his teeth at her, long, sharp. He was obviously trying to intimidate Max, scare her, and Baron didn't like it one bit. He growled a warning and stepped in front of her.

The Enforcer returned Baron's stare with a long, deliberate look of his own. When he turned back to her, he smiled. "I hunt. I judge."

Chapter Twenty-eight

Maxine shared a long look with the Enforcer, and it was made very clear to her that she had already been judged.

She was still alive—for the moment anyway—so that was probably a good sign.

"Okay, we get it. Judge, jury, executioner. One nice tidy package." Baron interrupted with impatience. "Now, what about that piece of garbage?" He nodded in the direction Devon had gone. The coward had somehow managed to get a hundred or so yards away during their little rumble.

"That vampire is not your responsibility."

"Look, Enforcer, I'm not having a jurisdiction discussion with you," Baron sighed. "Whether you want to share or not, I *do* have a responsibility here, and I *will* make sure that bloodsucking demon is taken care of. For good."

The Enforcer—was his name really Justice, or had that just been his vocation?—must have turned some of his freaky mojo on, because she heard a high-pitched, keening cry echo in the night.

Baron growled and started forward, lifting his sword.

Max turned and grabbed his arm, holding him back. "Please, Baron. Just let Justice do his job and—"

"*Justice?*"

Max hesitated and Baron glanced at the vampire, who

gave him a mocking half bow.

"That's a bit like calling your Dalmatian '*Spot*', isn't it?" Baron said with a sneer. He turned a hard glare on Justice, who tossed one shoulder in a negligent shrug, seemingly unconcerned with the prospect of being compared to a dog.

Baron looked back at Max. "I guess I must have missed the introductions."

"Yeah, well I could have done without that kind of introduction myself," she replied. Justice's probing of her mind had brought back uncomfortable memories of the brain rape she experienced at Devon's whim not too long ago, and a cold sweat broke out on the back of her neck. "If I never have anyone inside of my head like that again, it's still going to be too soon.

Baron snarled, looking like he was going to lunge after the other vampire once more, but Max grabbed his arm and sighed heavily. "Stop. Just...enough. I hate to break it to you two, since you seem to be bonding with each other or something, but the sun's going to be coming up very shortly now, and I'd like to deal with this and get back indoors before I turn into charcoal. Anybody got a problem with that?"

She looked from one testosterone-laden male to the other as they silently waged their ridiculous ocular war. If glares could kill, they'd both be lying in the dust.

Moments later, the two men were still staring at each other.

Most of Max's fear having rubbed off along with her patience, she decided she'd had enough and shook her head, flipped open the chamber of her gun to double-check her rounds, then turned and started off through the trees after Devon.

Baron and Justice finally stepped back and Baron called out to her. He followed, but she refused to stop.

Justice stepped ahead of them and came across Devon first. The vampire was hissing and snarling like a wolf with its leg caught in a trap, unable to escape the powerful mind that held him immobile.

Justice slowly walked forward until he stood just inches from the vampire. The silence and stillness of the Enforcer was deceptive, because one look in his eyes and Max could tell there was more going on than she could see. Whatever Justice was doing to Devon had frightened the creature stupid until he couldn't do anything but drool and shiver. Even his snarl had turned into a pathetic whimper. Did they have mental hospitals for lobotomized vampires?

"What is he doing?" she whispered to Baron. Max couldn't keep her body from trembling and inched closer to him.

"I think it's kind of a Star Trek mind meld sort of thing," he answered, wrapping an arm tightly around her waist. "He reaches into thc vampire's mind to locate proof of the taint before he can dish out the penalty." Baron's voice was low, and he kept his gaze focused on the situation playing out with Justice and Devon.

Max could feel the coiled strength in Baron's embrace, the barely leashed readiness of his posture, and knew that he was evaluating the scene before them to determine whether he should step in and take care of the matter himself.

Max held her breath as she watched. Finally, Justice stepped away, back, and Devon's head drooped, his chin touching his chest.

"What did you do to him?" she asked.

"The vampire has been judged," the Enforcer answered.

She thought it was over, and let out a small sigh of relief. But that quickly turned to a gasp of horror as Devon started screaming. Smoke began to rise from his skin, skin that was charring, blackening as the fire burned through him *from the inside out.*

"Oh, God," she whispered, unable to keep from

imagining her own death in the same violent, painful, horrifying way.

When there was nothing but ashes blowing away on the wind and more dust settling onto the ground, Justice turned to them, nothing showing in his black eyes. "It is done."

Baron reached for Max as Devon burned, wishing that he could do something to vanquish the look from her eyes. Justice's expression remained unchanged. Hell, was he even breathing? The guy was cold.

The vampire turned and leveled a last, long look on Max. "I will give you this warning," he said, his voice hard. "This is not the human world, and I do not give second chances."

"Leave her alone," Baron warned. "She's been innocent in all of this, and I won't have you trying to intimidate her."

"Innocence is sometimes more a state of mind, and in her mind, she is no innocent. Already she fears succumbing to the beast." Justice kept his eyes on Max. "You've crossed lines you said you would never cross, already come so close to hurting the people you profess to love."

"You asshole!" Baron bit out, fury churning in his gut. "You know very well she hasn't broken any of your fucking laws, and you have no right to terrorize her."

Max tore her gaze from the cold, calculating condemnation in Justice's eyes. "He's right, though, Baron. Look at what I've already done—to you, and Diana and Alric. God, I almost bit Jackson—"

"Stop it, Max," he said. "You didn't hurt me or Jackson, and you had nothing to do with what happened to Diana."

Baron turned to the Enforcer. "This woman is the strongest and bravest person I've ever known. And if you ever come near her again, I'm going to stake you to the wall and enjoy watching you squirm until your shriveled heart turns to ash in the sun."

Justice nodded in acknowledgement of Baron's challenge. "I guess that means I shouldn't expect a card at Christmas?" he said with a turn of his lips, the smile was tight and fleeting, as if the vampire hadn't had a lot of practice with the movement.

"Fuck you," Baron returned, realizing the vampire hadn't really had any intention of hurting Max. He probably just liked to push people's buttons, to provoke a reaction—something Baron could relate to actually, he seemed to have the same propensity for courting danger. "We ain't buds, that's for sure."

With what sounded suspiciously like a snort, the vampire turned back to Maxine. "Be very aware of the line you walk, of the choices you make." His eyes looked like they were boring into her soul, and he saw Max shiver. "Do not make me come after you the next time."

Before Baron could step up and clock the bastard for talking to her like that, Max raised her chin and met Justice's stony expression with stormy eyes. "If you're done here, then I think you should leave," she said. "And I don't think we're going to see each other again."

"That's what I thought," he answered. Baron could have sworn there was respect and maybe even a sliver of real emotion reflected in the timbre of his voice. He turned and inclined his head to Baron. "Keep your sword in your own business, Immortal."

Baron cursed as he watched the powerful vampire do his freaky smoke and shadows trick once more. Then he was gone.

"*Damn*, I gotta learn how to do that," he said with a shake of his head. He glanced into the sky and took Max's hand, desperate now to get her out of here. "Come on, we have to hurry."

For once, she didn't fight him, and he was grateful for

small favors. That would have really put the icing on his bitch of a day.

They practically ran back through the woods to the road. Max raised a brow at him when she noticed the motorcycle had been strapped into the back of his truck. He had expected a sarcastic remark or two, but she circled round to the passenger side door without saying a word, and he knew then that she was already feeling the effects of the early morning hue lightening the sky.

Baron had just turned the ignition over when he heard the unmistakable sound of Roland's ridiculously super-charged Ferrari approaching from behind them.

"A little late for the cavalry," he muttered under his breath. He rolled down the window as the car pulled up beside them. "What the hell are you guys doing here?"

Kane leaned out the passenger side window. "We thought you might need the back-up. Tracked you through the truck's GPS."

"What about Alric?" Baron asked.

"Haven't seen him." Kane shook his head and glanced over at Roland sitting in the drivers' seat. "He left with Diana...but he never came back."

"And you didn't think to go look for him? What if—"

"They're fine. He called in, said they needed some time away for a while, and he was taking her to a safe place."

Baron sighed. It was probably a good idea that they'd gone. He was worried about Alric and Diana. There had been something big going on with the two of them even before Diana was hurt, and he hoped they were going to be able to get through it.

He sensed Max wanted to say something, but she was hesitating. "What is it?" he asked.

Without looking him in the eye, she said, "Alric wanted me to turn Diana into a vampire."

"What? No...he wouldn't—did he ask you?"

She shook her head. "I could see it in his mind. He

was torturing himself because they had argued over it just before...before the attack." She lowered her voice, as if she were afraid the Enforcer would hear her next words and return. "Couldn't I though? I mean, as long as it was something Diana was prepared to accept? Wouldn't that solve their problem?"

Baron was touched that she would even think to offer to try something like that. He sighed and shook his head. "I'm sorry, but it doesn't work like that. The truth is, you're too new. You probably won't be able to turn a human for at least a hundred years, maybe more. It takes a long time for a vampire to develop that kind of power, for your blood to be strong and pure enough. If you tried now, you and Diana would both die. You, because you're giving up blood that you can't yet afford to lose, and Diana because you would have to drink the human blood her body needs and replace it with weak vampire blood that isn't strong enough to fully transform her systems to those of a full-fledged vampire."

"What's going to happen to them?" she asked.

He didn't know what to tell her. There was no way for them. Even if they got through this obstacle, the matter of Alric's immortality and Diana's humanity had always been between them.

Baron glanced into the sky. Was it lightening already? "Look," he said, turning back to the twins. "The sun...I've got to get Max back. Are you two sticking around?"

Kane shook his head. "No. The threat here has been taken care of, so we'll head out and hold down the fort until Rhys and Amy come home." Baron didn't bother asking how Kane knew Devon was gone. That twin rarely missed a trick.

Baron made short work of the goodbyes in his eagerness to get Max indoors. She gave him directions to her apartment, and he pushed her down onto the floor of the truck to keep her away from the windows. The sun was balanced right under the horizon, its rays not yet bathing the sky with light, but definitely threatening to do so any minute now.

Even though Max was trying to hide it from him, Baron could tell she was feeling discomfort, and he didn't dare slow the truck until he'd pulled into the underground parking lot of her building and the garage doors were safely shut behind them.

Max sat up and took a deep breath, her smile more than a little shaky. "Remind me to invest in some celebrity style dark glasses and a couple of big floppy hats, okay?"

Hell. He couldn't return her smile no matter how much she might need reassurance from him now. That had been way too close, and he was rattled more than he wanted to admit.

With a curse he reached for her, pulling her over the seat. She was sitting in his lap, but it still wasn't close enough. Her mouth parted and he crushed his lips to hers in a furious kiss, tasting his own blood as one of her sharp teeth slit his bottom lip open. He didn't care. All that mattered was the feel of her solid, warm body, her wet tongue sliding against his, the proof that she was alive and she was safe. Maybe that would finally banish the god-awful desperate fear that still clawed at his insides, because nothing else had been able to do it yet.

"Too close, Max," he mumbled against her mouth, "Too fucking close. Don't do that again. Don't ever make me go through another night like this one."

She pulled from him, her eyes flashing with anger. "I really ought to kick your ass, you know that?" She braced a hand flat on his chest and squirmed out of his lap, maneuvering back into the passenger seat. She got out of the truck and slammed the door closed.

He sighed and followed her through the parking garage to the door of her building. They rode up the elevator in silence, the weight of words that needed to be said hanging in the air between them like balloons filled with hydrogen just waiting to explode.

The elevator stopped at the sixth floor, and Baron found himself curious to see what Max's personal space looked like. He realized that he had never really seen her in her own place before. When her mother was alive, she hadn't allowed anyone to come to her home. And the one other time Baron had come back to Rockford, they had gone to his place.

Three doors down from the elevator, Max stopped and shook her head. "Oh no. How stupid am I?" she muttered.

She touched the doorknob as if to test that it was really locked against them, before turning to him with a rueful smile tugging at her mouth. He chuckled. "You don't have a key, do you?"

She shook her head. "No. I don't. An important fact that I should have remembered before I dragged us here and effectively locked myself in this building for the day with nowhere to go but back to the parking garage."

He swept past her and approached the door of her apartment. "Don't tell me—" she started.

He pulled out a slim case from an inside pocket of his leather trench. "An Immortal is always prepared," he said with a grin.

She laughed, and Baron went to work. It didn't take long. In less than a minute, her door was unlocked. She raised her brows, and he shrugged. "Don't tell me you don't know the same trick. Isn't that lesson number one at private investigators' school?"

Her chuckle was low and husky, sexy. His cock hardened instantly.

She moved to walk past him, but he grabbed her arm and stopped her before she could open the door. "Do you keep the shades drawn when you're gone?" he asked.

"Oh!" She took a step back and looked at him with wide eyes, as if she were afraid the sun could reach her through the door. "I wasn't thinking. I have a wall of windows in the living area, and the curtains were all open when I left."

He squeezed her arm and motioned for her to stand to the side of the door. "It's okay Max. This is just going to take some getting used to."

She grimaced and leaned against the wall, knocking her head back on the plaster with a sigh. "I'm going to end up killing myself before I get used to this."

Seeing the ragged, shaken look on her face, Baron let go of the door handle and cupped her face in his hands. "You'll do just fine, baby," he assured her. "You're not alone in this." He stepped in close, crowding her. Her breathing caught nicely as she met his gaze, and he lowered his mouth. This time their kiss was softer, deeper, but no less urgent. When she raised her arms to clutch him closer, Baron groaned and angled his hips into the vee of her thighs, pressing her body hard against the wall.

Things were quickly getting out of hand, especially considering where they were and that anyone could wander by. With a sigh, he pressed one last kiss to Max's mouth before stepping away. He noted the passion clouding her eyes with satisfaction. Good, he thought. Maybe she hadn't yet written him off completely. "Stay here while I go in and draw the drapes, okay?"

She nodded. "Where would I go?"

Baron went inside, closing the door behind him. Sure enough, bright morning sunshine was streaming into the apartment through a long bank of windows that spanned an entire wall. He took a quick look around, noting the neat clean lines of her modern styled furniture. She'd used soft pastel colors to give the room depth, splashed here and there by way of those frilly pillows women always had to have. There were several nice watercolors hanging on the plain painters' white walls, and not a dirty dish or dust bunny in sight.

Aware that he'd left her standing in the hall, Baron made quick work of the curtains in the living room and kitchen and then went to the bedroom. He avoided looking at the bed, but couldn't help noticing the slinky black negligee Max had left draped across a chair. He closed his eyes and forced himself to leave the room without touching it, returning to the front door to let her know it was safe to come inside.

Chapter Twenty-nine

"Thanks," Max said to Baron as he opened the door and let her in. She'd just had a fairly awkward encounter with her neighbor old Mr. Dawson. He'd come out of the elevator and asked why she was just standing out here in the hall. Max told him she thought she'd seen a rat in the kitchen and refused to go inside until her friend came back to tell her it had been taken care of. She hated giving anyone the impression she was that much of a wuss, but it was better than saying she couldn't go into her own place because the sun would reduce her to ash all over the nice white carpets her landlord had installed last spring.

Looking around and feeling as if she had returned from a long vacation, Max took a few moments just to breathe.

"It feels different...almost as if this stuff isn't mine anymore." She glanced over at Baron.

"I know." He wrapped her up in his arms, and only then did she feel like she'd really come home. She let herself indulge in the warm strength of his embrace for a few moments, burrowing as close to him as she could get. With a sigh, she lay her head against the broad width of his chest. She breathed in his spicy vanilla scent, overlaid with a sweaty musk from their exertions in the woods. He was running his hands soothingly up and down her back, but his attempt at comfort was belied by the erection that prodded her belly.

More than anything Max wanted to lose herself in him, in the pleasure he would give her, but she couldn't let go of the fear that still lingered. Even knowing that Devon was gone for good, Max worried that Justice might have been right about her—what if she couldn't control the beast? Even now, the sound of Baron's heart pounding with those strong, measured beats was enough to make her teeth ache.

Lifting her head from his chest, she saw something flicker there. He held her to him with one arm wrapped around her waist.

"Let me go," she said.

"Hell no." He kissed her. Hard. She fought to remain impassive in his arms, fearing that if she gave in to the passion building steadily inside her, she would be helpless against the bloodlust—and she couldn't bear it if she hurt him again.

She pushed against him, her hands on his chest, until he lifted his head. "What's the matter?" he asked.

"Nothing," she replied shortly. "I just...don't want this."

"Bullshit." His eyes blazed down at her, reflecting his desire and calling her out for the liar she was. "You want this." He rubbed his thumb over the inside of her wrist and pulled her back to him. "I can feel your pulse racing," he murmured. His breathe teased the side of her neck as he moved in closer. "I can scent the sweet musk of your need. Oh yeah, you want this. Why are you still fighting it? Fighting us?"

"*Us?*" Max shook her head and leaned back from him, refusing to look him in the eye. "Since when did this turn into an us?"

"This has been all about *us* for years, and you know it," he said. "I'm done running from you, Max." With a hand under her chin, he tilted her head up until she was forced to see the sincerity shining in those silvery eyes. "I love you."

She twisted in his hold, desperate to get away before she violated his words with her bloodlust. "Stop," she whispered. "Don't say that. Get away from me."

"Why do you have such a big problem with me telling you that I care?"

She snorted and redoubled her efforts to be free of him. Her head was starting to pound and she could feel the beast rising. "Go tell it to someone else, Baron. I've had enough of your bullshit."

"*Bullshit*? God, you know I'm getting tired of this wicked rollercoaster the two of us always seem to be riding. You think my feelings for you are bullshit? That's great. Just fucking wonderful. Woman, if saying I love you is bullshit, if saving your life is bullshit, then what the hell more do you want from me?"

He finally let her go, and Max stumbled back. She pressed the back of her hand to her mouth, trying to push down the hunger. Glaring at him she said, "Nothing. Don't you get it yet? I don't want anything from you. Not ever again."

Eyeing her carefully, Baron laughed bitterly. "Now who's talking bullshit, eh, Max?"

Baron took a step forward, and Max took another step back, but he just kept coming and she soon found herself against the wall. She knew he could see in her eyes that she was very near the edge. "Baron, please," she begged.

"Please what?" he demanded, his voice hard. "Please get the fuck away from me? Please never darken my door again? Is that really what you want?" He braced both arms on either side of her head and leaned in close. "Say it," he urged.

She opened her mouth to say the words. She should tell him to leave. It would be so much easier, safer, simpler if he left.

If he left then she could convince herself she'd been right all along about him—that he was irresponsible and unreliable, that he was just like her father and not worth taking a chance on. If Baron left, she could try to go back to her safe life, where there was no one who could hurt her, and she relied only on herself. She wouldn't have to be so terrified that he would see just how close her monster was to the surface, just how afraid she was that it would get out of control.

If he left, he was going to take her heart right along with him.

"What is it going to be, Max?"

She opened her eyes and met his gaze. Her heart was beating quickly, pounding hard inside her chest. "Please," she whispered. "Please...stay. Stay and love me...like I love you."

"Thank God." He stood close, pressed a kiss to her eyelids, her cheeks, lightly on her lips. He touched his forehcad to hers and sighed. "You had me worried for a minute."

She felt tears burning hot in her eyes, and she wanted to turn away, to hide them from him so he couldn't see how much she hurt. Instead, with a deep breath, she raised a hand and cupped his cheek, drawing his gaze to hers. "I'm afraid, Baron."

Dropping his arms, he drew her close. "I know, baby. I know. But I promise," he murmured, touching his lips to hers in gentle reassurance. "I promise I'll be here for you. I won't leave you ever again."

"I believe you," she smiled sadly. "What I don't understand is why? I'm still the trailer trash daughter of a drunken whore whose father couldn't even love her enough to stick around. I'm still your brother's best friend, and the woman you found it so easy to run out on two years ago. And if that wasn't enough, there's an evil inside me, Baron. What if Justice was right? What if I can't control this?"

"You really don't see what I see in you, do you?" He smoothed a hand over her hair, tucking a few loose strands behind her ear. His expression was reflective. "You may look at yourself and still see that unwanted little girl. But when I look at you, I see a woman. A woman of strength and determination. I see a woman of so much character, capable of so much love. Someone who rose above, and who has never let circumstance or misfortune bring her down."

He paused and gazed deeply into her eyes. "That woman could handle anything. *You* can handle anything. You will deal with this. I wasn't lying when I told that Enforcer you were the strongest woman I've ever known. And even though I know you can do this all on your own, I want you to know that you don't have to. You'll never have to be alone again."

Their lips met in a tender fusion of body and soul. Max gladly gave herself up to it, his confidence in her giving her the strength she needed, his trust freeing her. She reached for him, sliding her hands beneath his shirt to lift it from him. He was happy to oblige, raising his arms and letting her peel the snug cotton from his body. In turn, he dragged the bulky sweater off her, lifting her in his arms and carrying her to the bedroom.

They undressed each other with slow attention, each inch of skin revealed receiving glorious, dizzying attention from mouth and hands. Baron trailed hot kisses over her breasts, flicked her tight, aching nipples with his tongue. She clutched him closer, wanting him inside her already, needing his hard, thick length to fill her. He chuckled huskily at her eagerness, but showed no sign of hurrying things along.

Max decided to take matters into her own hands, pushing him to his back. Baron settled his head on her pillow as she straddled him. He radiated heat, his eyes revealing just how much he desired her, for once hiding nothing, making her feel more love than she had ever known.

Lowering herself, she braced her hands on his chest

and took him inside her in one long, smooth glide, her tissues wet and ready for him. He groaned and lifted his hips, thrusting deeper. She opened herself to every sensation that Baron stirred in her. They were joined—not only at the throbbing juncture of her slippery thighs—but body, mind, and soul. He was a part of her, sharing every sense, every feeling.

They made love with eyes wide open, each drinking in the soft sighs and gasps and moans of pleasure from the other. Touching and tasting, bodies sliding up and down, in and out in a drugging rhythm.

Baron took Max's breasts in his hands, cupping and squeezing them as she moved languidly atop him. She was so beautiful. Her shining blond hair swaying with her movements, grazing the tops of her shoulders and framing her face, which glowed with love and her pleasure. He felt so proud of her, and so lucky to have been given a second chance. He just hoped he didn't screw it up.

His balls tensed at the slide of his cock in her tight passage as she lifted herself along his length. With a groan, he grasped her hips and held her still.

"What is it?" she asked, her voice husky with her mounting need. "What's the matter?"

"Nothing, baby," he assured her, pulling her down to him for a deep, wet kiss. "Everything's perfect...except that I know you need to feed."

Her body froze, and her eyes dropped. She moved to pull back, but he held her still on top of him. "Hey, look at me," he urged. "I don't want any more uncertainty between us. From now and for forever you need to know that I am here for you. I want to be what you need in every way."

"But, that's so..."

"So what? It's nothing. You need blood, and I can give it to you. It's as simple as that."

"Are you sure?"

He laughed. "Are you kidding me? Having you squirming around naked on top of me with those sexy teeth buried in my neck is just the first of many dirty little fantasies I'm going to force you to live out with me over the next hundred years or so."

Her body finally relaxed, and her return smile was flirty and seductive. She did squirm for him then, rotating her hips to take him in deeper, and he groaned. "Come on, baby, show me what you've got," he teased.

She kissed him lightly, flicking her tongue over his lips, darting in and out of his mouth before moving to his chin and teasing him with a little nip. When her teeth sank deep into his neck in one sure strike, he closed his eyes and thrust his hips hard between her thighs, his cock pounding her pussy with long deep strokes that quickly took them both over the edge.

When it was over, they lay curled in each other's arms. He stroked her hair and waited for his heart to return to a normal rhythm.

Trouble was, with Max around his heart was constantly pounding, his breathing constantly irregular. She tortured him with a simple smile, and sent him to the moon with a soft touch—And he'd come to realize that these were things he didn't want to live without.

"Are you okay?" she murmured her question into his neck, touching her tongue lightly to the punctures she'd made with her teeth as if to soothe him. Her husky voice sounded satisfied and sleepy.

Tucking her beneath him, he kissed her deeply, noting with satisfaction that her drowsiness melted away and was quickly replaced with more of her eager, passionate responses.

Gazing into her eyes, he grinned. "I don't know, babe. I'm feeling a little woozy."

She gasped. "Oh no, I'm so sorry, Baron. Did I...take too much blood?"

"No, but you took my heart, and now it's yours forever."

"Well, that's good then," she said with a smile. "Because forever has been looking better and better lately."

Epilogue

Max couldn't believe the news when Jackson told them. And from the look on his face, he was having a hard time believing it himself.

"Really?" she said...again. "It's working?"

"Well, we won't know anything for certain until the allogeneic stem cell transplant thing takes. If it does work, then it will help my body grow a new supply of red cells, white cells, and platelets—and I might actually live a few more years."

"Oh my God." She had to sit down.

The damn chair was all the way on the other side of the damn room.

"Oh my God." She was babbling and tears were streaming down her face, but she couldn't seem to stop them.

Baron laughed and put an arm around her waist to hold her steady. "I told you she was going to cry," he said to his brother. "You owe me fifty bucks."

"Hah. You can take it off my hospital bill," Jackson replied with a grin. "Since it has mysteriously been paid in full."

She couldn't describe how good it felt seeing the two brothers together like this—even if they were making fun at her expense. "Stop it, you two. I'm trying to have a moment here," she chided good naturedly.

"Will you be able to leave the hospital..." She wanted to say "soon", but she knew that just yesterday the question she would have been asking was "at all", and the words got stuck in her throat. She didn't want to get Jackson's hopes too high in case his treatment didn't take, but even so, she couldn't help feeling as if the sun were shining down on them all after a long, long period of rain. Ironic for someone who would never again see real sunshine, but if Jackson was really going to be okay even that didn't seem so horrible any more.

"I don't know; it will probably be a while yet before my doctor lets me out of here."

Max glanced at Baron.

"We're staying." He assured her, with a reassuring squeeze of her hand. Turning his grin on Jackson, he said, "You're going to regret sending Max after me, bro."

Jackson smiled as he looked from his brother to his best friend. "Oh, I don't know about that. It'll be diverting to watch Max wipe the floor with you on a daily basis." They chuckled. Max could tear her eyes from the two men who seemed so different at first glance.

"Baron, are...are you sure?" she asked. Just because he put his responsibilities on hold when Max dropped back into his life, didn't mean that he could continue doing so indefinitely. She knew he had obligations to his fellow Immortals. She understood the kind of war he was fighting.

Baron looked at Jackson when he answered. "I'm sure there are just as many evil demons for me to slay here and in Chicago as there are in Chandler." They'd already told Jackson everything. About Max and the vampire, about Baron being an Immortal and exactly what that meant. He had taken it all rather well, but he'd still been skeptical until Max had done a little show and tell with her claws and her teeth. "I'll talk to Rhys about it as soon as I can, but don't expect to be seeing the back of me...not ever again."

Max looked at the smiling faces of her two men. The two people she loved most in the world. Her family.

The End

Turn the page for a look at

Dark Immortal

Book Three of
The Immortal Series
By J.K. Coi

Coming in January 2009
Brought to you by Linden Bay Romance

Chapter One

Diana Latimer looked up from her site plans and down at her watch. She had been working in this tunnel, hunched over these drawings with little light for...three more hours than she'd originally intended.

With a groan she straightened, rolling her shoulders and stretching out the crick in her neck. She was almost ready to pack it up and head back to the surface. But it didn't mean she was finished. Tugging on her simple ponytail to tighten the sliding elastic band that held her long hair out of her face, she closed her tired eyes. Just for a moment. There was still a lot of work to do before she could sink into her soft bed and sleep. This job was proving to be the death of her.

But Diana had known what she was in for before applying for the position. This subway tunnel excavation was her first big project as lead site supervisor for the construction company she worked for—a position she had fought dearly to get. Harder than any of the men who made supervisor ahead of her on previous contracts, that was for damn sure.

She knew going in that the job would mean a lot of extra hours double and triple checking every drawing, every test, every architectural and environmental report.

Because nothing was going to go wrong on her project.

Rolling her blueprints and packing up her tools, Diana moved to the last tunnel and brought out her map. In her mind she was already running down the extensive list of things that still had to be completed tonight. Once she was done here, she would go back to the office and input the soil and rock samples, and the air quality levels into the computer system, then run another set of calculations before preparing her final report to the general foreman. He wanted everyone ready to go first thing in the morning, so she had to be able to give him the green light.

Then there were calls to make. She sighed, already feeling exhaustion creeping up on her. It would be late, but her instructions were to inform the subcontracts when they had the go ahead, no matter what time of day. So she was going to have to contact the demo guys and the electrical team, and...

She hesitated. What was that noise?

It was faint, soft, but sounded close by. Where was it coming from? Everywhere and nowhere. She looked back over her shoulder. Unable to stifle the nerves she swung her head to the left and to the right. There was no one there. Just darkness. Nothing except darkness and quiet behind her. All around her.

"Must be rats," she murmured, but somehow she didn't think so. "Big rats." She cringed. Her whisper echoed off of the damp walls of the underground tunnels. For the first time, Diana thought her present situation could actually be thought of as creepy. She had been too busy to care before, but now it seemed that the shadows were thicker, every sound louder. Closer. The dripping water from long-neglected pipes running over her head, the muted, motorized roar of subway cars zooming through the adjacent tunnels, and maybe the scurrying of little feet beside her in the darkness.

No, this sound was different, something else.

Something almost sinister...

There it was again, a kind of fluttering. Like a panicked sparrow frantically flapping its wings inside a steel cage. Goosebumps rose on the surface of her arms. She shook herself, trying to ignore the uneasy feeling settling in her blood. She turned her focus back to the map—this was the last section she had to inspect. All of a sudden Diana wanted it done, sooner rather than later.

That's when she noticed the inconsistency in the drawings. Looking up, she saw the problem. Ahead of her was a rocky barrier of fallen rubble. It was old, definitely not a recent slide. She could tell by the settled placement of the lower rock.

But it wasn't supposed to be there. It wasn't on her plans.

She approached the wall, conscious of the nattering, which seemed to be only in her head. It was getting more pronounced with each step she took.

The debris was tightly packed. This obstruction had definitely been in place for a long while. Curious, Diana poked and prodded, searching until she ferreted out a weak spot. Using the back end of her flashlight, she dug out a pocket of dirt and realized that the barrier wasn't as deep as it had seemed on first glance. She managed to poke through to the other side within a few minutes.

Ignoring the dirt that was getting packed underneath her fingernails, Diana made a hole big enough to see through. She aimed her flashlight and squinted into the darkness. Her head was killing her, a constant thrumming that pounded away inside of her brain.

The noise. What was that noise? It wasn't here in the tunnel, she realized. It was in her mind. Like a shadow.

Diana needed to find the source, get it to stop. She had come to the realization that somehow whatever lay or lurked behind this wall was responsible. The noise she was hearing constantly now had to be coming from the other side. She didn't know how she knew that, but she felt it as a certainty.

She swung the light in a slow, horizontal slash, but the beam didn't travel very deep before being sucked down to nothing by the impenetrable shadows.

Wait. Right...there. What was that?

As Diana focused the stream of light on the object that had caught her attention, Hollywood images of skeletal remains and buried treasure rose in her mind. She forced a laugh. It came out sounding more like a frightened squeak.

Wait.

Holy hell, was that movement? Something moved. She would swear it.

"Just a rat. That's all it is. Probably just a rat." She'd seen enough of them in these tunnels since starting the job three weeks ago. Still, warning bells were shooting off in her head like fireworks in Time Square on New Year's Eve.

Diana decided to try to get inside for a better look, knowing that it was a bad idea even as she started to pull away more of the rock. She made short work of the loose rubble and discovered that she was standing at the entrance to what looked like an underground cavern, or at least what had been an underground cavern at one time. But not recently. A long time ago. A very long time.

Diana continued until she had made an opening large enough to crawl through, and when she looked inside, she thought she had a pretty good idea of why this place had been sealed up all nice and tight.

There was a *body* in there. Propped upright and spread-eagled against the inner rock wall of the cavern. No, not propped, but *hung*. The body was chained to the wall.

Shit. Shit. Shit. Why me?

She let her flashlight droop, trying to keep from seeing any more, although the image was already sandblasted upon her mind's eye forevermore. *Definitely a body. Where the hell is Indiana Jones when you need him?*

Wait a minute, this has got to be another one of the crew's practical jokes. As the only woman on the team, and as the site supervisor for this project, there had been quite a few bruised male egos when Diana got the job and she'd put up with a lot of anonymously expressed grief. Granted, this particular prank was sicker than plastic wrap on her toilet seat or a tool box stuffed with tampons that fell open in front of the whole crew when she picked it up. Still, Diana wouldn't put it past them to have gone to the trouble of creating this scene, especially since everyone knew she was going to be here alone since the rest of the crew was finishing up another job across town.

It looked damn real though. If she didn't know it was impossible, she would have sworn that no one had been in this cavern for several decades.

She squinted through the hole again, training her flashlight on the mannequin against the back wall. It had to be a mannequin or a Halloween dummy or something. But the longer she stood there, the less she believed that. Diana had been in the presence of death before, and this place reeked of it.

She groaned, closing her eyes and massaging her forehead. Her headache was raging, the fluttering sound in her mind no longer reminding her of a bird flapping at the walls of its cage, but a thousand bat wings beating over her head, all around her, right in this tunnel with her. She started to think that the environmental test results she'd gotten back were inaccurate. There must be a leak somewhere. Gas. Maybe too much methane and carbon dioxide was leaching into the tunnel from the other lines.

Because of the possibility that this wasn't a sick joke that would necessitate the firing of her entire staff, Diana examined the scene more closely—at least as best she could from her current position.

The body was indeed chained to the wall, the beam of her flashlight glinted off the steel chain links as it passed over. The clothing covering the body was tattered, but not completely decomposed. The rags prevented her from having to see any whitened bones. *Thank God for that at least.* The corpse's head hung down, long, stringy hair covering its face.

Damn. What was she going to do? This was looking more and more like a crime scene by the minute.

Do I really want to go in there?

No, she really did not.

What she wanted to do was go back up to the surface and find someone else to dump this disaster on. *This is my job, my responsibility.*

She gazed into the cavern and shuddered. *Too bad, I don't want it.*

Diana turned to leave, but out of the corner of her eye something moved. That movement, combined with a distinct scuffling sound and something else that sounded unmistakably like a low groan, made her heart jump into her throat and tore a small shriek from her lips.

It had come from inside the cavern.

Oh no, it couldn't be.

Alive?

Her headache spiked to an unbearable level, forcing Diana to her knees. She dropped her flashlight to the ground and pressed the heels of both hands hard against her temples. "Ah. Stop. Stop. Stop...*Please*," she moaned. The body inside that darkness. She knew it. The call in her mind was insistent, unrelenting, demanding.

Diana fought her way back to her feet and stumbled over her fallen flashlight. Bending over to pick it up, she shone the beam through the tunnel's opening once more. Her hand was shaking, and her visibility was so blurred from the pain that it was even more difficult to see through the shadows.

Had it really moved? Was it her imagination, or

was the head now raised and pointing right at her? She couldn't see them, but she could feel eyes burning into her with an angry, hungry stare. *Alive.*

Release me.

No. This could not be happening. The body in that cavern could *not* be alive. There were only two possibilities she was willing to consider for this situation: Halloween freakshow or ancient mausoleum. Living skeletons in the darkness just wasn't going to happen. Diana had pulled away the barrier of dirt herself—nothing alive had been in here for many years. Something else was going on. Perhaps she was being accosted by a ghost. Diana didn't necessary believe in ghosts, but she had never written off the idea that such things could be possible and right now that sounded safer than the alternative.

This feeling would go away if she just went back up to the surf—

RELEASE ME!

"Oh God...I can't...stand any more. You have to stop." Falling back to the ground, Diana clutched her stomach and heaved up what was left of the chicken sandwich and green salad she had scarfed down as an early dinner a few hours ago when she'd been eager to get to work.

On all fours, Diana crawled through the tunnel entrance to the other side. Sharp pieces of stone dug deep into her hands and knees and dust fell into her hair and clogged the air, but it didn't matter. Nothing mattered except getting that sound out of her head. Even if it meant going inside for an up-close-and-personal look to convince her psyche that all of this was nothing more than a methane-induced delirium caused by fumes filtering into the air from the active subway lines.

With her flashlight clutched tightly in one hand, Diana used her other to brace against the stone walls of the cavern as she forced her legs beneath her again. She stood, but her thighs quivered like jelly and she remained unmoving for several minutes just breathing. One breath, then another...and another. Finally, she stepped forward and tried to force her eyes to focus beyond the pain that continued to batter away at the insides of her temples, to see clearly what was going on in this little tract of hell.

Her beam of light waned. The batteries were fading fast. But there was still enough of a glow for her to see the next step ahead of her, enough light to cast larger shadows behind and beside her, to convince her she stumbled deeper into a place that would be impossible to escape from. Yet she couldn't turn back.

Diana found her way to the bundle of rags that was indeed...a body.

But is it alive?

From here, by the light of her dying flashlight, she could see more than had been possible from the entrance to the cavern. More than she wanted to. Ever. She could see the chain links made of heavy black metal, tunneling out from the rock, the thick steel manacles wrapped around bony wrists attached to gnarled, claw-like hands. She could see through the veil of grimy hair to the protruding cheekbones of the face beneath.

He opened his eyes.

Diana shrieked, but she couldn't move. She was caught by his eyes. Caught by those deep pockets of crystallized pain. Pain that she felt all the way to her soul.

Release me.

Had he spoken out loud? She shivered and tried to tear herself away from those eyes, focusing instead on the chains that bound him to the wall.

Oh lord. Who would do such a thing? How long had he been trapped here?

Long enough that he probably should be dead.

Most of his face was covered in a scraggly beard, and his matted, dirty hair fell well past his shoulders, though it couldn't disguise the harsh angles of his face or the thin, white skin that stretched taut across his cheekbones. The sight reminded her of a statue she had seen once of the Emaciated Buddha during her one and only vacation—a trip to Japan to visit her sister. Looking on that Buddha, Diana had understood the significance of the image and tried to feel the kind of awe and reverence that she was sure it deserved, but hadn't been able to. She kept thinking Buddha must be insane. Such acute starvation, combined with the isolation of extreme meditation—or in this case, imprisonment—could very easily cause a person to go mad.

Mad. It was there in the eyes that were focused with such intensity on her. Eyes that shone with more than madness. They pleaded with her for help–no, they demanded it from her.

Diana knew such sorrow at the signs of his suffering—she understood now that the pain in her head was his, that she was somehow sharing it with him. The pain in her head increased, acting on her with swift efficiency, causing her heart to pound and instilling a sense of desperate urgency. But even without the added impetus of his mental influence, Diana would have been just as anxious to find a way to free him. She couldn't stand to see him like this. Had to get him out of here. Now.

He flinched and hissed at her when she reached to examine the cuffs around his wrist. She forced herself to go slow. No sudden movements. No loud noises.

"Shh," she whispered, keeping her voice as even as she could manage. She reluctantly met his eyes once more. They tracked her relentlessly, fathomless pits that sent ice cold daggers shooting through her body. His growl was a constant rumble of mistrust.

"I won't hurt you, I promise." She tried to look on him like she would a wild animal in pain—a wolf with its foot caught in a trap—knowing that he was dangerous, that he could turn on her in an instant. *Take it easy, take it slow.*

Almost instinctively, Diana used her mind to send soothing reassurance. She forced herself to pretend at being calm, to transmit thoughts of patience, needing him to know that she only wanted to help him. Maybe then he wouldn't try to take her arm off.

They faced off for long moments until he blinked. He didn't lower his eyes, but he stopped growling at her, and Diana was relieved to find that his psychic barrage against her wasn't so insistent. She could actually breathe again.

When she brought her hand to his wrist once more, he didn't move, but his eyes watched her with a guarded wariness. She got the distinct impression that even though he was the one confined, one false move and it would be *her* life at his mercy.

She kept up her mental mantra of reassurance as she tested the chains that bound him. They were secure. Tight on his wrists and wedged firmly into the rock.

"Damn," she muttered. She would have to go up top to find some help. Diana tried to keep the fear and fatigue out of her voice. He wasn't going to like this.

"I have to go for help—"

The attack on her mind ratcheted up again, igniting an inferno that was even worse than before. She was on her knees again, retching up foul green bile, and still the pain intensified. "Stop," she whispered. Her nose was bleeding. She could feel the thick blood trickling down her face.

"Stop. STOP!" She raised her head and glared up at him, though the pain had rendered her vision to a filmy red haze. "If you...kill...me, then I really won't be able to...help you."

He seemed not to hear, or not to care because the horrible pain continued.

I'm going to die.

Suddenly, she felt the pressure ease up slightly. Not

much. Just enough for her to take in a deep breath. She was shaking all over, chills shuddering through her body as she knelt on the ground at his feet.

Release me.

"I will get you out of here." She swiped at her mouth and nose with her sleeve, and groaned when it came away stained with her blood. "You have to trust me."

It wasn't going to work. He was too far gone to understand her. But if he didn't let her go, then he would kill her here in this dark place that already stank of death, and then surely die soon after as well. There had to be another way to do this. Diana tried to think what tools were in her box out in the tunnel. What she really wanted was a heavy-duty set of bolt cutters, but knew she didn't have anything like that with her. "We need help," she said again.

His eyes pierced her with their intensity. Silver shards of glass glittering in the darkness. "What if I promise to get what I need from my truck and come right back." She hesitated. "Alone. I'll come alone. I promise."

Silence.

Utter silence. No demands, no more pressure inside her poor hemorrhaging brain. He was going to let her go.

Diana let out a sigh of relief, and carefully pushed herself to her feet.

"I'll come back. I promise."

About the Author:

J.K. Coi lives in Ontario with her amazingly supportive husband and son. She graduated university with a degree in history and in law, and has worked for many years in the legal field, with a current focus in intellectual property law.

Writing has always been an important part of her life, and when she leaves the office, she leaves it all behind to immerse herself in a world of fantasy—of demons and magic, fascinating warriors, and the women strong enough to love them.

Also by J.K. Coi:

My Immortal (Immortal Series Book One)

Evil lurks in the darkest of shadows, but a band of warriors stands ready to defend humanity against hell's own monsters—Immortal men hand-picked by destiny and taken out of time hold the fate of the world in their hands.

One of the oldest of his kind, Immortal warrior Rhys Morgan spends his nights on the streets of Chandler protecting the city's innocents from the demons that hunt them. Unyielding in purpose and uncompromising in battle, Rhys thought he'd never meet his match, until he met Amy Bennett

Rash and impetuous, Amy dashes into a fight, taking Rhys by surprise. He can't decide whether she's incredibly brave or incredibly stupid. But when the fight is over and Rhys is unable to get the beautiful human out of his head or his dreams, he knows his life is about to get complicated.

The barriers between the unlikely pair may be as thick and strong as the evil that threatens them, but some things can't be denied…and dark, mysterious, sexy Rhys Morgan is one of them.

This is a publication of
Linden Bay Romance
WWW.LINDENBAYROMANCE.COM

Recommended Read:

Forbidden: The Revolution
by Samantha Sommersby

Experience the magic…

Twenty-five years ago Dell Renfield's father started a revolution. Dell plans to finish it. Sorcerer, sexy vampire, secret weapon, he's spent his entire life training for what he believes to be his fate. The one deterrent he isn't equipped for? Special Agent Alexandria Sanchez.

Alex is quick-witted, hot-tempered, and strikingly beautiful. Normally focused on getting the job done, she's completely unprepared for her new partner, Dell, and his mysterious ability to drive her to distraction.

Posing as lovers, Alex and Dell infiltrate a dangerous culture where the macabre seems mundane and passion is power. Unable to deny their attraction or resist temptation they begin a journey, entering into a torrid affair that will forever change their destiny.

An age-old secret, a consort held hostage, a curse demanding to be broken, and an unforgettable battle with a mercenary master mage will have you holding your breath. Let Samantha Sommersby lead you into a world like no other, a world where vampires are real, where magic is possible, and where love still conquers all.

Indulge in the *Forbidden*, because sometimes giving in to temptation can be a good thing.